Adornments of the Storm

PAUL MELOY

First published 2019 by Solaris
an imprint of Rebellion Publishing Ltd,
Riverside House, Osney Mead,
Oxford, OX2 0ES, UK

www.solarisbooks.com

ISBN: 978 1 78108 595 0

10 9 8 7 6 5 4 3 2 1

A CIP catalogue record for this book is available from the British Library.

Designed & typeset by Rebellion Publishing

Printed in the UK

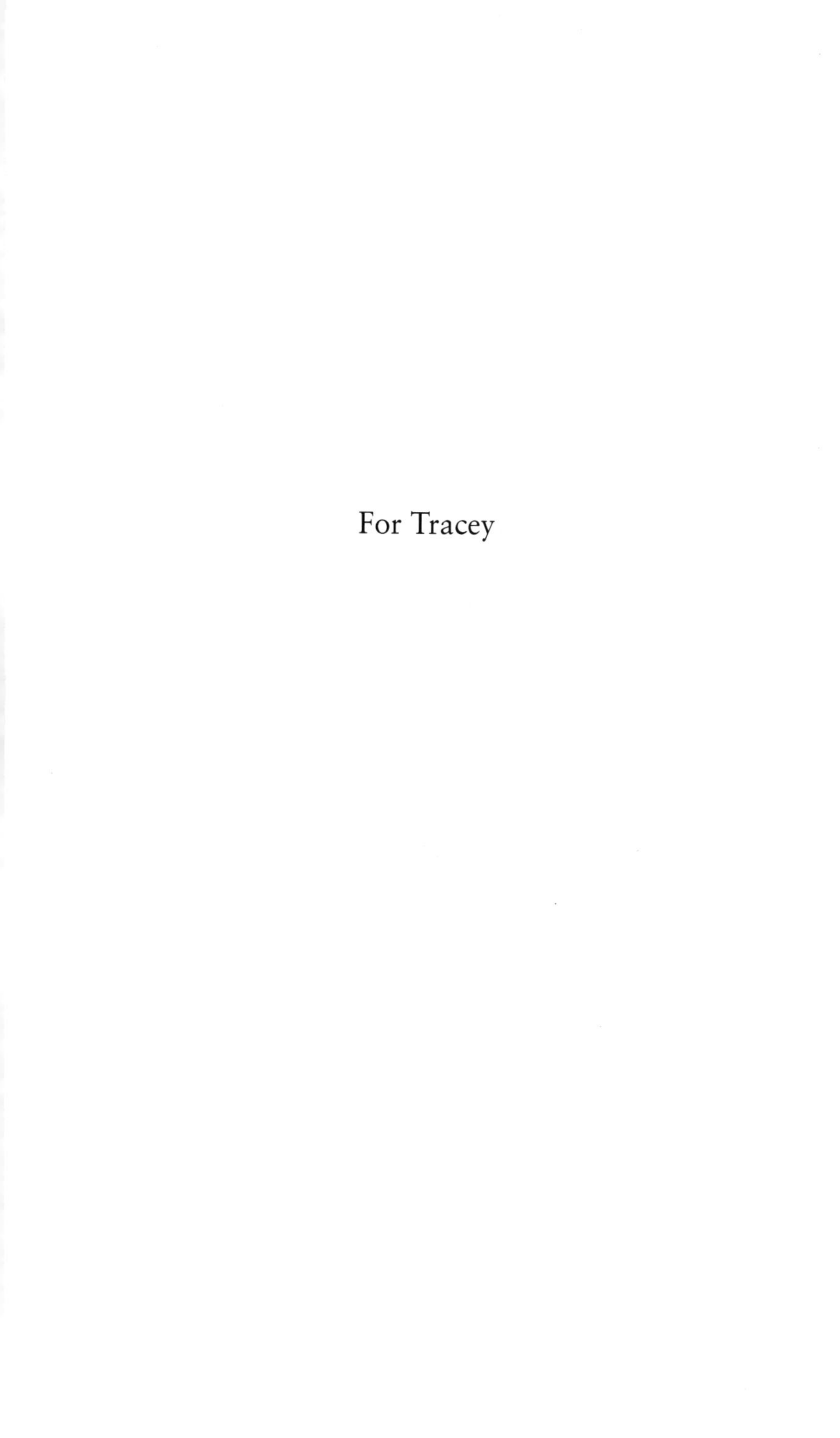

For Tracey

Part One

Flying Ant Weather

ROB LITCHIN WAS drunk for the first time in seven years.

Pissed on the sofa in his mum's lounge at ten o'clock in the morning. How easy it had been to sink back into the cushions and unplug that two-litre bottle; the plastic suppleness and the liquid weight of it, the slosh, the flex in his fist as agreeable as squeezing high up on a young girl's thigh.

And the lively flood of sour factory cider. Cheap and pale, rinsing the fuzzy brush of his tongue, sluicing down his neck, hitting his empty stomach and leaching into his blood like herbicide up the stems of mortified plants.

Rob closed his eyes. His long hair, very grey now in streaks and roots, hung over his face. A sigh shuddered through him and he reached out for the bottle on his mum's coffee table. His thin, trembling fingers prodded it, and it rocked on the moulded crown of its base and toppled over with a hollow, playful sound: *boink-bok bok bok bokbokbokbok*.

Empty, or as good as, with less than a mouthful swilling about along the flank of the bottle, streaked through with plankton-like flukes of dribble. Backwash, you called that. Never share a bottle with someone who's eating biscuits. Rob lifted his head and looked at it, lying there on its side on the dainty little table. You could put a ship in that, he thought. A shit one. A ship of fools. A shit little ship of fools.

But, Rob not being a hobbyist, the bottle would never be anything more than recyclable. He reached down between his heavy black biker boots and pulled another two-litre bottle from a carrier bag. SHOP AT BALV'S it said on the side of the bag, which Rob had been happy to do. Beanie the dwarf had been surprised but not dissuasive when Rob had pitched up at half seven that morning and gone straight to the drinks aisle. No concern for Rob's wellbeing, just a small mittened fist to snatch the notes and push across some negligible change. "Bin a while, chap," Beanie had said. "Back on the jink, is it?" He had withheld thirty-seven pence in coppers, payment for the plastic bag. Overheads. Rob had declined to reply, demurring to mutter about the ramped-up price of the packaging. His mouth was too dry. He wasn't even gratified to notice Beanie was sporting a black eye and a fat lip.

Rob unscrewed the cap of the new bottle and shot a cupful against his tonsils with a precise squeeze. He swallowed, eyes watering, and put the bottle between his knees. He slumped back against the floral bolsters and let the first real tears come.

Doctor Mocking was dying.

His girls were there: Lesley, in her late teens, beautiful, her blonde curly hair tied up in a pony tail; Anna, younger, dark, quiet, as mysterious as Lesley was open and frank. Gifted girls, marvellous girls.

Doctor Mocking smiled. He looked up as the door to his bedroom opened and a man walked in. The man ducked beneath the lintel and stood immobile, looking down at the bed. He was huge, beard and hair wild and tangled as briars, long coat to his calves; his eyes held all the sorrow of an endless Gethsemane night.

"You came," the Doctor said in his gentle voice. "Bismuth."

"Of course," the giant said. "Old friend."

Doctor Mocking lifted a hand and the other man took it in his huge fist. He swept his coat away from the backs of his legs and sat on the edge of the bed. He peered down at the Doctor.

Lesley and Anna both kissed the man, once on each bearded cheek. Bismuth looked at them with tired eyes. They fell against him and he held them, staring over their heads at the far wall while they cried, and when eventually they calmed and released him, he spoke softly to them and sent them away.

"What is it?" Bismuth asked. "Your heart?"

"Yes. It's weak now." Doctor Mocking sighed and patted the back of Bismuth's hand. The hand was huge, calloused, tanned.

Doctor Mocking closed his eyes and rested, his breathing shallow, while Bismuth told him what he had found.

THE AUTOSCOPE SQUIRMED beneath Bismuth's boot. Bismuth trod hard on its throat and drove his Egress Lever into its face. The brass Lever punched through the black skin between its verminous eyes, driving through its brain and the back of its skull to puncture the filthy, sodden ground beneath it. Bismuth gripped the handle at the top of the Lever and a Gantry opened in the middle of its head and it was sucked away like slurry, infolding and tearing, screaming, ravelling into the slot Bismuth had summoned inside it.

Bismuth lifted his boot and glared at the sky. He roared, and yanked the Lever out of the earth. He turned as another Autoscope roiled across the silted and stinking surface of the dump. It cast a spray of wet filth before it and a cloud of gulls rose screeching from the colossal piles of refuse through which it thundered. They hung on the disturbed currents of night air like cinders blown from a dead fire.

Bismuth stepped forward and swung the Lever but the Autoscope hit him and they fell back against a heap of junk. Bismuth felt the edges of cold metal dig into his back. He twisted, pushing at the same time, sending the Autoscope stumbling away to his side. He moved, backing into the gap through which the Autoscope had just passed, his Lever back in his belt, his fists raised.

The Autoscope spun around, six eyes blazing beneath a diadem of splintered horns, the diamond-shaped wings that hung from its flanks rippling black kites. It advanced on Bismuth slowly, claws digging in the muck.

Bismuth felt the air move and threw himself towards the advancing Autoscope just as an Incursion Gantry opened a foot away from where he had been standing. His heavy boots pounded the dirt and he leaped to the side at the moment the Autoscope darted its head at him. Long, curving tusks slid from slits beside its mouth and it swung its face, goring the fetid air. It shook its head and ropes of purple saliva spooled from its mouth, fuming in the dirt where they spattered.

Bismuth landed against a stack of tyres and shouldered himself off, colliding with the side of the Autoscope. He grasped a bony wing and twisted it, wringing it like a sheet. The Autoscope howled, twisting its body and biting the air in front of Bismuth's face. The bone snapped and the creature slumped to the side, its legs buckling in agony. Bismuth kicked it beneath the abdomen, the tip of his boot finding a soft spot between two overlapping chitinous plates and sinking into something meaty that felt like it was wrapped in polythene. The Autoscope collapsed, its howl strident and enraged. Bismuth twisted the wing again and leaped onto its back, driving his knees into its shoulder blades. The Autoscope bucked, trying to throw him off, but he hung on, reaching forward to grasp the hilts of the tusks that jutted from the sides of its mouth.

Bismuth looked up, staring through the ring of horns protruding from the monster's brow, and watched as a woman stepped from the Incursion Gantry.

She ducked through the livid crimson slot as if emerging from a limitless space built to house a dying sun. The enormity of what lay behind her made Bismuth shudder. He glimpsed things moving at her back that he knew were the size of cathedrals, made paltry by their distance, shuttling to and fro, engulfed by that terrible light.

The woman was naked but for a decomposing strip of flesh wound around her chest covering her breasts and another strip fashioned into a garment between her legs and over her narrow hips. Dark hair fell to her shoulders, and her white face, with its pointed chin and full, dark lips, was framed beneath a heavy fringe. Beautiful but for the eyes, which opened to display corneas the colour of infected piss, each eye containing a set of six pupils like holes bored into the white of a putrid egg.

Bismuth held fast to the tusks, pulling the Autoscope's head down into its neck, the muscles of his shoulders and arms taut and burning with the effort.

The Autoscope that had emerged from the Gantry reached behind her back and drew a bone saw from the belt of flesh. Its serrated teeth were rusty with blood. She tossed her head and glared at Bismuth with those alien, pitiless eyes, the bone saw held loosely in her slender, manicured hand.

"*Long Man*," she hissed. "*Come down and fight.*"

Bismuth released the tusk he was gripping in his right hand. The downward force of his left hand and the sudden freedom of movement given to the straining muscles in the Autoscope's neck caused it to wrench its head sideways, and Bismuth pulled the Lever from his belt and plunged it into the creature's temple. He depressed the handle and the Autoscope's head began to collapse. It slumped to its knees and Bismuth slid from its back and crouched over it, the tusk still clenched in his fist, as he monitored the dissolution.

The female stepped forward, bone saw swinging.

The Autoscope twitched in the dirt, its torso sucking away into the slot. Bismuth waited until it was almost consumed and wrenched the Lever from its withered skull. He rose with it clamped beneath his arm, the tusk held in his fist, and charged the female as she came at him, the saw raised and coming around in a fast arc.

Bismuth blocked the swing and felt the teeth of the saw snag on the thick material of his coat sleeve. He drove forward and rammed the tusk into her belly.

The Autoscope gasped and Bismuth propelled her backwards. Her long-nailed feet scrabbled in the dirt and her dark, dead blood welled around the tusk in her gut in a thick, oily collar. Bismuth felt the tip of the tusk strike bone and he wrenched upwards, fastening it between her vertebrae and lifting her from her feet.

The Autoscope had dropped the saw. Her arms hung loose at her sides. Her hair covered her face, but he could see her eyes between strands of fringe, blazing like pots of disease in her face. She wasn't dead, nor would she die from this. Bismuth carried her towards the dwindling red light issuing from her Gantry. It shone a pinkish glow across the floor of the dump, a blood-and-water colour, sluice from abattoir tiles.

Don't close, he thought. *I want you to have these back!*

He reached the Gantry as it was closing. Bismuth could feel the air clench and he shoved the conjoined Autoscopes through the gap before it sealed itself. They were snatched away by the currents within the Gantry and hurtled into the red blaze.

The Gantry closed and Bismuth stood alone in the trench between the mountains of junk. He slid his Lever back into his belt and pulled his coat together. He turned and headed towards the back wall of the dump and what leaned there.

As he walked he thought about the female Autoscope. It was the first time he had encountered the bitch, but he knew of her.

The Despatrix.

She was a high-level Autoscope, ancient and unique. A primordial predator so successful at what she did that she had never lost her original form; unlike the others Bismuth had killed, this one was almost as beautiful as when she had been created. Before she had fallen. And if *she* was being sent out to face him then something was either very wrong, or he was doing something very right.

Bismuth had been coming to this place for seven years, and every night he came he killed more of them. They had always outnumbered Bismuth and his kind but now, just maybe, they were running low on numbers. Unleashing the Higher Ones must be significant.

Bismuth reached the crumbling wall at the back of the dump and stood looking at the old refrigerator leaning against it. It had been placed upon a low pile of rotten and flattened cardboard boxes. The words *English Electric* were stamped on the door with raised chrome letters. He reached out and grasped the handle. It looked like the handle on an old car door. It had an ivory-coloured button, which he pressed hard with his thumb, knowing it would stick, and pulled the handle. He opened the door; it came away with a dry sucking sound, its rubber seal parched and powdery, and he stepped back, ready for what might come out but expecting it to be empty, as it was every night.

But this time it was full.

Bismuth moved forward and swung the door shut on it. But not before he had seen something move within, come floating up to engage him, to mock his wasted years and efforts. Bismuth closed his eyes and leaned his back against the refrigerator door. He was trembling.

After a while he opened his eyes and straightened up. The gulls had drifted back to the piles of rubbish and the dump was silent but for the irregular ticks and groans of junk settling throughout the yard.

Bismuth set off back the way he had come, through the trench of refuse, heading for the gate that led out onto a bombsite, a terrain of rubble he would cross to reach another door. A door set in a wall that opened into a shop at the end of a long arcade.

The arcade is empty now; all the little units are shut. He is the only one who comes here but he can still smell the perfume from the flower stall as he passes, and the air is resonant with memories of life. It has been a long time since Bismuth has brought anyone out through here from the bombsite. He had hoped for so long to bring just one more. Pigeons used to roost in the iron struts that ran beneath the long corrugated roof, but they are gone too. It is dark in the arcade.

The blackouts are down.

"A BLOCK OF living darkness," Bismuth said. "As if the refrigerator was a mould full of its substance. And there were eyes in there. They floated up through the darkness and hung at the surface looking out at me. They were the boy's eyes. He's gone. I couldn't save him."

Doctor Mocking was sitting up against his headboard supported by his pillows. He was pale but alert. He reached out and put his hand on Bismuth's. Bismuth stared at the floor.

"Is the Despatrix dead?" Doctor Mocking asked.

"No," said Bismuth. "Not *this* time."

"And you think the boy is gone?"

"Yes."

"You did everything you could. You've destroyed more Autoscopes than the rest of us put together."

"It wasn't enough. I kept getting close but every time something pulled him away. The Night Clock is running down."

Doctor Mocking shook his head. "No. But I think it's weakening, because of my frailty. That thing you saw, somehow the devil-in-dreams is reaching out again. I hoped this was over."

"It will never be over."

"The devil-in-dreams has found a way to reach its Autoscopes. There's a crack in the containment somewhere. It's giving them power. We have to close it up."

Bismuth nodded and stood, his shadow enormous against the walls and ceiling. He took Doctor Mocking's hand.

"You know what to do."

"Yes," said Bismuth. "I'll find Daniel."

"Find him and tell him what you've seen. If the Despatrix is emerging then so might the remaining Higher Ones. They're using a stream of Dark Time somewhere, I can feel it. You've got to seal it up."

Bismuth walked to the door.

"Send Anna up," Doctor Mocking said. "And please warn Lesley before you go."

Bismuth nodded, and went out.

DANIEL AWOKE TO find Dr Natus sitting on his chest.

"Come with me," Dr Natus said.

Daniel stared up at the tiny bleached creature. It wasn't the weight that had woken him—Dr Natus was as light as an empty paper bag—it was the smell. The vinegary stink of formaldehyde. And beneath that he could determine another smell, something of sugar and sloes, of viscid homemade gin. Not on Dr Natus' breath. Dr Natus couldn't breathe. Had never drawn breath, dead in all ways but one from his mother's extraordinary womb. It was what Daniel had pickled him in, back then. Back then when he was insane. Back when he had thought he'd needed Dr Natus.

Daniel turned his head on the pillow and glanced at Elizabeth asleep beside him. She was on her side, facing him, her breathing slow and regular.

"Why?" Daniel whispered to Dr Natus.

Dr Natus stared at Daniel through huge, sealed-shut eyes. The black pinpricks of his pupils were visible behind the fragile, translucent bulges of his eyelids, through the superfine network of veins underlying them. His tiny hands plucked at the hem of the sheets at Daniel's throat, a ripple of strengthless white, damp cilia.

"I was dreaming," Daniel said.

"I know," said Dr Natus. "You were amongst the cans."

"I was."

Daniel closed his eyes. He had been in a forest, walking a path. Ahead was a dense stand of trees. Elms, elegant and tall, downlit by the pale autumn sun, a knot of hushed archangels. As he drew near he saw that the lower branches were hung with thousands of old tin cans. They were rusty and pitted, with holes punched into their sides near the rims and strung through with fine silver chains. They hung still and heavy. Daniel walked amongst them and looked inside them and saw they were all brim-full with rainwater and that all the surfaces of the waters flickered with the anxious movement of a billion mosquito larvae. Daniel was repulsed by so much movement, so many basic units of parasitism; all that carbon, all that potassium, all that nitrogen, knitted into cans full of bloodsuckers and hung from the branches of such beautiful trees.

Shaking with fury, the emotional pitch of the dream degrading into nightmare, Daniel reached down to the forest floor and took up a branch that had broken from the trunk of one of the elms. It was mossy and felt cool and damp. Daniel swung the branch at the nearest crop of cans. He beat at them, a man loose amongst an array of terrible, industrial *piñatas,* the clangs and waterlogged chimes echoing around the forest. They clattered against each other, a dull, dismaying campanology, spilling gouts of infested water across the forest floor. Daniel strode amongst the trees and smashed the cans from the branches and trod them flat. The mulch beneath his feet wormed with black, dying germs.

"Wake up, Daniel," said Dr Natus.

Daniel opened his eyes.

"I was dreaming," he said again.

Dr Natus slid from Daniel's chest and onto the floor. He stood at the side of Daniel's bed. He was the size of a doll. Daniel had once held him cradled in the palms of his hands. Dr Natus walked across to the bedroom door. Daniel watched. He had never seen Dr Natus walk before. He took tiny, unsteady steps, like hops from one foot to another, his little frail back bent beneath the disproportionate head, spine like a stack of coins defined against the fabric of a silk pocket, arms limp and useless as a frog's.

Daniel got out of bed and followed Dr Natus from the bedroom. He took a dressing gown from a hook on the back of the door and slipped it on over his pyjamas. Dr Natus stood on the small landing at the top of the stairs.

"Help me," he said.

Daniel picked him up and carried him downstairs to the front door of Elizabeth's house. Daniel thought of the last time he had held Dr Natus, lifting him from the broken shards of a jar on a street in a dream-place some seven years ago, holding him and weeping.

"Why are you back?" Daniel asked.

Dr Natus pointed to the front door. Daniel held him in the crook of his left arm and reached out to open it. He noticed that the door was different. The chintzy voiles that framed the glass above the letterbox were gone. The door was bigger than he remembered, and the paint was dirty and flaking and discoloured by rainwater. He knew this door well.

He turned the handle, an old steel lever, and the door opened. Daniel stood at the foot of a steep flight of uncarpeted wooden stairs. He could smell dust. The walls were scraped and scuffed, narrow and rising to a high sloping ceiling illuminated by a single low-wattage bulb that hung from a dusty cord.

There was an empty matwell full of aged and yellowing circulars and junk mail. Untidy piles of unread free local newspapers were stacked against the first stair riser.

Daniel stepped over the junk and started up the stairs. He reached the landing and stood facing another door. This one was open. He put Dr Natus down between his feet and stood. He experienced a moment of anxiety and felt light-headed. He blinked and took a deep breath, and the feeling passed.

He pushed open the door and followed Dr Natus inside. He reached for the light switch but nothing happened when he flicked it on. Daniel stood at the threshold and waited for his eyes to accustom to the gloom.

He watched the indistinct figure of Dr Natus shuffling across the linoleum floor of the bare living room. Dr Natus swivelled his heavy head and beckoned with a limp flick of his wrist for Daniel to follow him.

Daniel stepped across the threshold of the flat he had lived in during his most desolate days, nearly a decade ago. Here he had spun his delusions, a frightened and lost man, trying to find his purpose again in fantasy and terrible dreams. Here he had brought Dr Natus to life, in a Kilner jar at the back of a cupboard in a room at the top of this building. Dr Natus; totem, guide, phantasm. Floating in a preservative of sloe gin and purple sediment.

Daniel felt himself begin to tremble. He closed his eyes for a moment and willed himself to settle. The smell of the place, its age and unlit, sealed darkness, brought with it memories of the despair he had felt living here, and it shook him that they could arise so quickly, with such harsh and harrowing novelty.

He opened his eyes and bared his teeth at the room. He had been at his lowest here, trapped and treated with a barbarism that denied him his true calling and subdued his abilities to nothing more than a dull memory. Here he had been able to do nothing more than force everything he had been, was capable of, into bringing this strange, pale, dead creature into a jar at the back of a closet and projecting his true self into it, a symbol of furious preservation. And it was here he had eventually decided to end it all.

Dr Natus had crossed the room and stood at the entrance to a small space at the back of the flat. Two steps led up into Daniel's old bedroom, an eight-foot-square box beneath the sloping eaves at the top of the building. Daniel stepped into the room.

The room was uncarpeted and Daniel could feel the gaps between the narrow wooden planks plucking at the soles of his bare feet. It was empty but for an old wooden wardrobe against the back wall. The wardrobe leaned to the left, awry on perishing joints. The doors were held closed by a piece of string tied through the handles but they were also askew on their hinges allowing a narrow tapering gap between them.

Daniel could see fire flickering through the gap. It throbbed and fluttered, orange-yellow, filling the interior of the wardrobe. There was no smoke, no sound. He walked towards the silent blaze and reached out a hand. His fingers flinched away from the handles as he touched them, expecting them to burn, but they were cold and tacky with the mildew that coated them. The string snapped like hay when he pulled the door open.

He stumbled backwards, away from the thing inside that burned.

Daniel looked down at the jar that was full of fire. It was a Kilner jar but bigger than any he had seen. And what it held, what burned unendingly inside it without heat and without being consumed, had not been put there by Daniel. He went down on one knee and watched the fire rage inside the glass.

The head was blackened, a charred skull papered with crisps of skin and running with fat. The features had been burned away, leaving a hole where the nose and mouth had been and from within which flames pulsed and flickered. The tongue was gone, and the throat. The teeth were charcoal nubs. But the eyes were open, and they were a clear, demented blue.

And as Daniel sat heavily on the floorboards, his legs giving way, the rest of its eyes opened, too.

DANIEL JERKED AWAKE with a shout. He sat up, staring around the bedroom, his heart pounding.

Elizabeth touched his arm. Daniel turned to look at her, his eyes wide. She patted the bed between them. He sank down onto the mattress and lay next to her as she stroked his arm. He was breathing as if he'd just run up a flight of stairs.

"You were dreaming," she said.

Daniel stared at the ceiling.

"That wasn't a dream," he said.

4

"TELL ME YOUR history," said Trevena.

Chapel sat forward in his chair. His posture was attentive but his intelligent eyes were unfocused, looking inward to the past. His fingers were loosely clasped between his knees. "It's fragmented," he said. "I will try."

Trevena listened to Chapel's story.

I WAS BORN in the 'sixties, but I was raised in the 'fifties.

By which I mean the attitudes and sensibilities of my parents, which had been formed by poverty, war and few expectations beyond their historical working-class roots, were embodied throughout our household and kept in rigid opposition to the chances and opportunities my decade was providing. The 'sixties were being gradually shaded in pastels, a deliberate attempt to drive out the deprivations and armament-gray of the first half of the century by a generation my parents might have felt a part of but didn't. For them the world was changing too fast. They were disoriented by it, and deeply threatened.

My mother went to the shops along the high street every day

and bought just enough to make an evening meal. There were no impulse buys. I went with her. I liked the bustle of the supermarket with its tills clacking like old typewriters. Mum shopped like we were still on rations. I understood this. The war hadn't been over long enough. We *were* on rations. I have always been on rations. Once a week on payday, dad would come home from the factory with a paper bag of sweets. They were what I thought of as adult sweets: Toblerone, Fry's chocolate, Revels, Ripple, a Walnut Whip. I wasn't allowed any of these. It was a time when even spontaneity was planned; a treat meant something. It was an event.

There was a cheap shop run by a spiv called Dave. He had a large, longhaired Alsatian called Flash. Dave flirted with the women and seemed very fashionable. He was probably only in his twenties but those ages and beyond were, to me, staring up, staring around, mythical. There were men who worked in shops along the high street with their wives. They had been there forever, starting their businesses in a post-war time before my birth. It was a time when workingmen could see a future unchanging, and drew their modest plans accordingly. One of these, a man called Eric, died one day of a heart attack. He was of the stocky build and age where men drop prematurely dead. He was full of good humour and worked in the fruit and vegetable shop at the top of our road. I liked him. Mum told me he had died but there was to be no discussion. I was just aware that something I had assumed was fixed in the world, that had perhaps always been there, had gone, a nail head banged too far into the wood. Eric had been banged too far into the wood. In my young head a brain was developing, a personality shaping out of the events of the life I witnessed and perceived and their action on the temperament I was born with. A forming of neural pathways as inimitable as the trajectories of asteroids colliding through the spiral of a galaxy.

I know now that there is no reason to be sad about anything. Happiness, too, is a thin gas, a puff of vapour between axons, a neurotransmitter's peculiar waste.

There can be no extremes now, just reactions to reactions.

Pressures remain, and the tension that arises. But when they are no more than the trembling of moving air against the hairs on your arms, or the grit in your eye, or the sudden blood that sheets across your brain bringing with it the end of you, or the partial erasure, then what of them?

"Tell me," said Trevena.

Chapel sat back in his chair and stared at the ceiling. He reached for a glass of water and took a sip.

Our house had been built in the 'thirties. A mid-terrace house in a side road off the high street. The interior of our house was as it had always been. Windows were single-glazed in aluminium frames; they wept with condensation and made puddles on the sills. The gas-fire had a tiny tiled hearth. The tiles were pinkish like a feverish cuticle. Thin carpets with newspaper underlay, and paraffin heaters to carry from room to room. A picture above the fire, the kind that was framed but without glass. It was of a woodland with a path and beyond a field and a distant church spire. It was a pleasant picture. I would sit on the worn red sofa opposite, with the gas fire fluttering and the early dark of four o'clock outside, and walk that path away from winter.

Our TV was black and white, and rented. The world it showed was moving on. There was colour out there, thwarted deliberately by monochrome, and change. Sudden, ill-conceived change it seemed. I think my parents were actually soothed by the introduction of the three-day week and power cuts. It put them in mind of the war, and happier times. Their youth was gone and mine was beginning and they wanted for me the life they had had. When the lights went out and the candles came out from under the sink, the atmosphere in the house was one of stoic good cheer. I think they dreamed of the sound of bombs dropping. They were happiest in the gloom.

I played outside in all weather. I played alone for much of the time; the population of children my age was small, a sequestered demographic. They played indoors, or with siblings. I was an only child. I roamed the alleyways and allotments, tips and back roads on foot or on an old bike I had made with my dad from parts donated by the men he worked with. For months I waited for a Raleigh racing frame that was promised but never delivered. There was a smell of cinders and oil on me. The turn-ups on my jeans were friable with streaks of black grease from the chain of my bike.

I watched the autumn spiders grow fat in their webs in the blackberry bushes that lined the alleys. I scooped crane flies from the air, hating their ineptitude, their indecent size, and threw them onto the webs where they stuck and flailed, and watched them succumb like balsa in the jaws of the spiders.

In winter I played, lost in mist and hoar frost, the trees silvery white, disappearing into the vapour like cables tethering something above, vast and unknowable. Sounds were muffled, blunted; even time seemed muffled by the mist, stretching, diminishing, stretching and diminishing. I had been out for hours. I had been out for days.

At night I dreamed of polygons in the sky.

Black polygons tethered one to another, all around the world.

ONE SUMMER I spent some time playing with a girl called Louise. Her mother and mine had become friends and so therefore it had been expected that we should, too. She was quiet, gentle, almost spectral, with a pretty oval face and very blonde hair cut short and boyish. I remember nothing else about her. Her personality, her voice, her laugh are gone from my memory. I can just see her face, and her expression when I hit her.

Louise was an only child too, and perhaps like me, had lacked the formative stimulus of fighting and competing for love, belongings, attention, or whatever it is that toughens us up and prepares us for life. I didn't fight for things. What I had, I had. My parents didn't argue in front of me, or raise their voices. I didn't learn the language of confrontation from them and despite applying certain strategies later on in life I've never felt comfortable raising my voice.

I think her vulnerability enraged me. Her soft deference generated aversion and untapped a well of spite I didn't know I harboured. When we were alone, playing together in the gardens of our mothers' houses, I thrilled to touch her, pinch her, hold her limbs too tightly.

One day, beneath the apple tree at the bottom of my garden, I punched her in the stomach.

Her shock and surprise registered on her face before the pain did. And then her pretty face crumpled and she hobbled away from me, and she was made even more insubstantial by the watery dapples of sunlight that passed over her head and shoulders through the apple tree leaves.

Her mother was of course furious and took Louise away, her face tight-lipped and white. Nothing was said, no voices raised, no cries for retribution. I cried then, but only for myself, and the sudden astonishment that the world sees what you do and when the screen rolls back all that was hidden is projected onto it. The effect on all the other players. The unexpected and abrupt change to their roles.

My father was told on his return from work and I stood before him as he paced the floor. He was ashamed, humiliated by my behaviour. As punishment he took one of my toys, a wooden model aeroplane I loved, and tore the wings from it in front of me. By then I was wailing and my mother held me. She held me with love, I believe, but still she held me to the kiln of my father's rage. I watched him snap the wings off the plane and I thought of the crane flies thrashing in the spiders' webs.

There was a difference to the way my parents watched me after the incident with Louise. I imagine they forgave me. I imagine also that the protective process of denial played a large part in their forgiveness. I had wailed my innocence despite knowing I was lying; I had said we were playing and I had hit her by accident. I had wanted to believe it myself. The enormity of it went way beyond the act itself, I perceived. And even then I knew I must shore up the terrible fissure I had clubbed through the gauzy fabric of my world, through which it seemed a nail head could be hammered and disappear, even if it was with lies.

CHAPEL STOPPED TALKING. *He glanced out of the window, his eyes flicking upwards, searching the clouds.*

"I've always been sensitive to changes in the air," he said. "To what drives us, affects our behaviours. I think it was oppressive that afternoon, when I hit Louise. Humid."

"What else do you remember about growing up?"

I ALWAYS KNEW when the flying ants were ready to swarm.

I would feel the readiness in the air, the combination of humidity and pressure that heralded their flight. It was primal, pure physics, a force that I felt in my lungs, and against my skin, which brought me out of the house as it brought them out of their nests.

They had nests made in the soft earth at the sides of lawns and around the edges of drains. The earth looked sandy, granulated, and fine. And in the tension of the evening, the air thickening with pheromones and apprehension, the queens would emerge, dragging their larval bodies and their transitory, tear-drop wings, and rise up on the slow, oppressive currents of air.

And they were pursued by the males, which came in greater profusion, specks of panic in the air, unaccomplished flyers too, but better proportioned, diminutive in comparison, their wings minuscule, a donning of genetic information to enable dispersion and a one-time act of insemination.

Once they have mated, the sexual organs of the male explode and they crawl off to die. I wonder, as our population increases, will this process evolve in us, too? Will the junk in our DNA tumble over like dice and provide the new information necessary for this kind of change? Or perhaps women will develop teeth sharp enough, and the poison sufficient in glands in the roofs of their mouths, to eat us after we fuck. Some may say this is already happening.

Will we be glad to go? With our seed implanted at long last, blown in a brutal spray against the necks of their wombs? No longer a tiny death, but an actual death. I could go on with this, but there really is no point. Speculation will ultimately lead to overstatement, and there is little point to absurdity now because the graveyard we whistled past once is now gaping wide, and there is nothing to pry out the nail head, not even a little, or even dignify it with a decorative brass cap.

Chapel paused. Took another sip of water. Until now his speech had been fluent, eloquent, his tone modulating as he described the past, his repressed and confounding childhood. He had seemed comfortable despite the intensity of his recollections and their impact on him. Now he looked at Trevena, his eyes focused on him, and his face was pale and his voice resumed flat and halting.

Now polygons fill the entire sky.

Yesterday there was low cloud, and a warm mist that surged across the rooftops, and they were concealed. I knew they were everywhere, packed behind the wood we are being hammered into. They appear and disappear with a pure randomness impossible to forecast. They are not matter.

They are nothing.

"Where were you?"

I was in the park, below the mist. It was as if the air we breathe, the dimension we inhabit, had been pressed down into a low yet broad rhombus of dull light.

My child played on the swing. He had his back to me and kicked his legs out to make himself go higher. His coat was brown, his hood was up, and as his legs kicked out in front, and his back arched into the ascent, he appeared larval, protean. I wondered, if I took him down from the swing and unzipped his coat, would he emerge with wet wings unfolding like polythene, and look at me with dumb thousand-lensed eyes?

I watched two boys run across the tarmac. They had been tearing around all the time we had been there, faces red and ferocious. Their fun looked awful. I thought back to my own childhood and the long, timeless days. Their play appears more urgent now, as if imaginary worlds are to be sacked and burned before their vanity depletes them.

Childhood is no longer quietly left behind, but ravaged and then set ablaze.

I have always dreamed of these things, black polygons throughout the sky. I always knew they were there. And then: they were there.

They meant everything, and then they meant nothing. And nothing is now everything. I communicated with them but they did not communicate back. They do not exist, yet they are all that exists. How many are there? How high do they go? Where do they come from?

Satellites cannot see them. There are no images from space. I see them only when I look up. Telescopes cannot see them. There are no observatories studying these shapes and calculating their extent. They cannot be touched, or detected by anything other than my eyes. They emit *nothing*.

I wanted truth.

But I got Truth.

"You got a different truth to the one you would have liked?"

We all invent our own truths. The Truth? The Truth is the end of everything. Once it's unavoidable how can you go back to anything else? Denial can only take you so far. But you know you're lying.

I knew I was lying to my parents as a child and it was enough to get me through the self-abhorrence, the shame. But it was only repressed. I've got no one to lie to, only myself, and there's no point to that, not now. The dissonance is unbearable. It swills like dark matter alongside every thought, rocking them, shaking them, like some beast crouched over a cot. From waking to trying to sleep, and the awakening in the night.

"You believe you know the Truth?"

Chapel threw his arms wide. He turned his head and looked out of the window. He laughed without any humour.

"You don't see them?"

"I don't see them, Andrew," said Trevena. "But I believe you do."

Chapel slumped in the chair. Not with relief, thought Trevena, but with resignation. People want gods, interventions, life on other planets, multi-universes, even panspermia or protein carrying comets. Just something to hang their denial on, even the atheists. They might not want a god, but they still want something. But Chapel had experienced a revelation that had removed all possibility of meaning. Trevena knew different, but how to break down this man's complex and obstinate delusion? With time, he thought, and patience.

"What happened this morning?"

Chapel lifted his chin and looked at Trevena. He went on.

As the mist receded, a million black polygons appeared. It was still humid.

My head was aching and I could feel the tension in the air. The hairs on my arms and the back of my neck were alert to the pressure.

In the grass at the side of the playground the earth was granulated and fine. I saw heaps pushed up all along the edge, and things beginning to emerge.

I pushed the toe of my boot into a narrow heap of earth. It

disgusted me, this frothing from below, this unseemly lathering of the dirt from which hideous, blind and groping fecundity was breaking out. I stamped them flat—fat, egg-laden things, encasing them in pats of soil, wriggling and straining.

I heard my child call out in surprise. He had stumbled and fallen dismounting from the swing. I watched the black lozenge of the seat coil and twist on its chains above his head. He had hurt his leg and grazed his face.

The air around us was full of ants. They pattered and ticked against the fabric of my coat.

My child was crying. There were ants fucking in his hair.

I walked away.

"And they found you half a mile away," Trevena said. "Trying to hang yourself in the woods."

Chapel sighed, put the fingers of his right hand to his throat.

"Do you still want to die?" Trevena asked.

Chapel looked out of the window. "More than anything," he said.

5

"I *GOOGLED* HIM," said Peter Foreman.

"Good thinking," said Trevena. "I hope you did it on your phone."

Peter looked up from his desk, his eyes narrowed with contempt behind his glasses. "What do you think, Phil? There's eyes everywhere now. There're little fuckers in Human Resources going through our search histories just trying to catch us out. Won't risk it." He sneered, his teeth showing in a derisive gleam behind his beard.

"Anyway, what do you think?" said Trevena. "From a Social Worker's perspective, of course."

"Bit of a twat," said Peter.

"Okay," said Trevena. "What else?"

"Appears to be reclusive. Can't tell whether he's minted or not but he must be worth a bit. He's won awards for his sculptures. Studied at London College of Art in the 'eighties. Pretentious associates. He's not really that well known outside of certain circles. No history of doing anything particularly mad, other than creating bad art. Genuine psychosis, d'you think?"

"I don't know. There was something not quite right. He mentioned lying and the mechanisms of denial. That's insightful. His history seemed a bit scripted, too, rehearsed. There's definitely personality stuff going on, and over-valued ideas. But the psychotic stuff? Still not sure. If it is though, it's full-blown."

"I wouldn't mind having a look at him myself," said Peter.

Trevena smiled and put a hand on Peter's shoulder.

"I would, Peter."

OVER HIS LUNCH in the hospital canteen, Trevena had another look at Andrew Chapel's Wikipedia page on his phone. His finger scrolled the screen through *early life, career, work, exhibitions, awards, references* and *links*, although the links were only to a few short interviews he had done over the years. Chapel didn't appear to have a website, which Trevena thought unusual but not particularly remarkable. Not everyone felt the need to parade themselves throughout the ether. There were a couple of photos beneath the *exhibitions* heading showing an installation he had won an award for at the Tate Modern seven years ago. It was called, Trevena was unsurprised to observe, *Polygon Storm*. Large sharp-edged blocks of gleaming black stone (Trevena *assumed* it was stone—Chapel's medium of choice) braced against the vaulted ceiling of a gallery with an intricate framework of scaffolding. The whole effect was oppressive and perilous. According to a description beneath the photograph, people were encouraged to enter the room and walk through it resisting the urge to look up. Art without spectator. One was encouraged to experience the installation through repressed senses, knowing it was there but not acknowledging it. No wonder it won an award, thought Trevena.

Trevena put the phone flat on the table and ruminatively sipped a spoonful of tomato soup. Something was bothering him.

He put the spoon down and picked up his phone again. He scrolled through the Wikipedia page again, this time more slowly. He sat back and looked out across the canteen, thinking. Perhaps it wasn't that important.

There was no mention of Chapel's son anywhere on the page.

Part Two

Rainscissor and Morgoder's Autoscopic Calavalcade

1985

Mr Chard was in his shoemender's hut. He had his charges, small, broken men in gray overalls that he bullied and tortured, as was his habit. The men had bowed backs and shuffled along the narrow space of the workshop wearing dirty clothes beneath their overalls that were often many sizes too small because when they awoke on their cold, vaulted wards, they would put on each other's clothes, whatever first came to hand.

Old Lenny explored the inside of an ancient boot with long, white fingers. He located bare nail heads and a thin ruck of stinking insole. Lenny's file, held in a thick blue NHS cardboard binder at the back of a cupboard in the Charge Nurse's office on Kestrel ward, labelled him an *imbecile*. He turned to Mr Chard, who sat on a wooden stool at the bench on which they worked. He grinned; but then Lenny always grinned, and Mr Chard stared at him through his wire-framed spectacles with pale and emotionless eyes. He continued to stir his boiling hot tea, the spoon rattling against the thick municipal china, which was decades old, stained and chipped—not unlike Mr Chard's teeth, which were bared within a lipless sneer, as if the man himself was a product of the system he characterized, an organic extrusion formed from the very clay upon which the asylum stood.

Lenny held out the boot and nodded his small hairless head. His eyes, like the eyelets in the boots he repaired and laced, were dull and black; he was given draughts of psychotropic medication, brown as swill, three times a day in crude measures. Mr Chard reached out and encircled Lenny's wrist with his fingers and pulled him a step closer. Lenny grinned. Mr Chard took the spoon from his steaming tea and pressed it hard against the sagging web of flesh between Lenny's thumb and forefinger, and held it there. Lenny twitched and his hips cocked backwards but he didn't pull away. He grinned. If he didn't grin, or should he pull away, he knew what would be next. Mr Chard had pockets in his long white coat that were full of bradawls, and it wasn't just shoe leather he liked to gouge strips from.

LATER, WITH THE day's work behind him again, another day like all the others spent against the bench in that timeless place that smelt of feet and old leather, supervising the menial work of idiots, Mr Chard sat at the bar in the staff social club and drank his bottle of Mann's brown ale from his half-pint pewter tankard. He smoked cigarettes, knocking the ash off in quick, impatient taps after each pull, before it could build up and hang from the end like a wilting bore of his sick and dirty right lung.

He still wore his white coat, having come to the single-storey, one-room prefabricated building immediately after work. Some of the porters were still rumbling about on their electric floats, carrying mattresses and stacks of timber from the collapsed ward, delivering sheets and stacks of towels, office equipment and files. None of them waved or acknowledged Mr Chard as he crossed the roads that wound through the grounds and struck out across the football field towards the club. Mr Chard didn't care; they were all fools.

The air had been cold and he had felt it like a charge in his chest.

It had been dark, and the crescent moon was low. Mr Chard had regarded it with enmity, thinking it looked like something sent by God to hook him and reel him away.

Mr Chard lit another cigarette. The stool next to him was pulled out and a man sat down.

"Evening, Chardy," the man said.

"Good evening, Griff," Mr Chard said without looking up.

"Pint, Malcolm, please," Griff said to the barman.

Malcolm poured Griff a pint of subsidised lager from one of only two pumps fixed to the bar. He coughed, a damp, vicious rattle, and he expelled something from his mouth that stippled the frothing muffin-like head on Griff's pint. He glanced up but Griff was talking to Mr Chard.

Griff was the head porter and his long face seemed, to Mr Chard, to lengthen further with each year of service the man put in. It nodded towards Mr Chard from the neck of the porter's blue overall like something gouged out from a huge, elongated bean.

Mr Chard sipped his ale and stared at the back of the bar as Griff spoke.

"Busy day tomorrow, Chardy. Don't know why they bother year in year out. As if the boys don't have enough to do without working a fucking Saturday for that crap."

The overtime Griff was referring to was preparation for Fun Day, a desultory fete the staff were obliged to put on twice a year, in summer and before Christmas, for the patients and their families. Families never came, and the patients were corralled around the green at the front of the hospital by therapists and nurses for a couple of hours. The cricket pavilion was full of junk for the stalls: stocks and boxes of diseased sponges to be thrown by weak arms in the direction of a volunteer target, usually a student nurse still dedicated enough to get involved, a test-your-strength machine made from old boxes and a cricket ball, folding tables for the tombola and bric-a-brac, reams of tangled and antique fairy lights that would be looped around the green like a jolly sparking, sputtering electric fence, and a stack of other heartbreaking tat that had to be transported, assembled, disassembled and transported back within the six hour window allotted for it by the nursing officers.

Mr Chard didn't care. He would spend Saturday lying in his bed in his room in the staff accommodation watching *Grandstand* as he always did, filling the ashtray on his bedside table with dog-ends until it was time to go to the club and drink. Shoemenders had nothing to offer Fun Day and he didn't need the overtime.

Griff drained his pint and asked for another. Malcolm poured the lager into Griff's dirty glass. He looked up as the door opened and a couple of student nurses came in. They were pink-faced from the cold and laughing. Thick Steve, one of Griff's boys, followed them in and made for the bar.

"Pay day," he announced. He had a big white face capped with a thinning mat of greasy blond hair. Mr Chard wanted to hurt him.

Griff had almost necked his second pint, and tipped the glass towards Thick Steve, his eyebrows raised.

"Paid Friday," Steve muttered. "Skint Saturday." He ordered two lagers, which Malcolm duly provided, vectoring a generous film of phlegm onto both sloshing inch-deep heads.

"Cover your mouf, you dirty old cunt," Steve said as Malcolm set the glasses before them on the bar.

"Drink somewhere else then, you daft flid," Malcolm replied.

"Gonna," Steve said. He swallowed his pint in a single open-throated gulp and smacked his lips. "Goin' into town. On the piss."

"Another one?" asked Malcolm.

"Go on then."

Mr Chard stopped listening. He was watching the two student nurses from the corner of his eye. A pretty girl with short dark hair and a tall fair-haired boy, both aged about nineteen. Mr Chard had seen them about, on their placements, looking keen and happy. Here they were, eking out their paltry grants. Well, the boy would be; the girl probably wouldn't pay for anything. She'd be repaying him later the way girls do, with an obliging, tight little quimful.

Mr Chard drank his ale and thought about the last time he had fucked anything. Mr Dugdale, the night nurse on Pegasus ward, used to be able to provide female patients for little get-togethers but he had retired two years ago and since then Mr Chard's satiation had been thwarted. He pictured the girl, pictured thrusting into her hairy hole, her face pressed into a plastic pillow, his knees chiming off the metal bed frame like bony clappers against a thin iron bell, trousers round his ankles and white coat open and flapping like a shroud. Dugdale had given her a bath and she smelt of laundry and corridors. Her anus was still greasy with whatever he had scrubbed her with. She might have been pretty if her face hadn't been slackened by brainlessness and he was glad he didn't have to look at it, with its cracked lips and walleye.

Mr Chard turned and glanced at the couple. They were sitting at a small round table, chatting away. The girl kept touching the boy's hand. Had they been together yet, he wondered? Was tonight the night? A Friday two weeks before Christmas? Money in the pocket? That sweet relaxation of early evening alcohol in a warm place and a hot promise for later? Mr Chard turned back to the bar and ordered another drink, using the bottle opener on his heavy key ring to prise off the cap before pouring it into his tilted tankard.

He was aware of movement behind him as someone walked over to Griff and punched him in the face.

Mr Chard swung around on his stool to watch. The girl squealed and the boy rose from his seat to stand in front of her.

"Don't, Phil," Mr Chard heard her say.

Mr Chard looked down. Griff was on the floor. His eyes were closed but his fists were raised in a defensive and instinctive catalepsy. The man who had clumped him stepped in and shoed Griff in the exposed throat. The girl squealed again and the boy moved towards the ruck.

The assailant was a big man, wadded into a tight leather jacket with a suede collar. His face was dark and broad and his whole head fluttered with fury like interference on a screen breaking up the picture his features would normally make; he was so livid he had lost his cerebral hold.

Griff was stirring. He tired to sit up. His jaw was dislocated and it hung, revealing what remained of his bottom set of teeth, like that of a ruminating horse.

"*Djase*," Griff said. His tongue did all the work, belling in his palate, because his lips wouldn't go together. "*Sowwy, mwate. Don' urt mwe.*"

"Jase!"

It was the boy. Mr Chard swallowed a mouthful of ale and leaned an elbow against the bar. This was interesting.

The boy walked across the room and stood between Griff and his attacker. He held his hands up, open, palms towards the bigger man.

"What you doing, Jase?" the boy asked.

The man pointed a trembling finger at Griff, who was sitting propped against the bar as if thrown down there like an old coat. Griff tried to use a hand to close his mouth but his jaw moved with a horrible unfastened sagginess and he let go with a dismayed choke.

"What about him?" the boy asked. "What's he done?"

The big man said, "He tried to fuck my wife."

Griff was shaking his head. He tried to shake just the top of it. He groaned. "*I nwever.*"

Now Mr Chard recognised the man. He was one of the Mauritian nurses the hospital had recently shipped over to make up the staffing levels. They came over every year in planefulls, recruited by the managers because they were cheap and worked like dogs. They were also, unfortunately, as honest as the day was long.

The boy was guiding the man away, talking softly to him. He opened the door and walked the man out, patting him the shoulder. Mr Chard heard the boy say, "I'll see you tomorrow." This confirmed what Mr Chard had surmised, that they were working on the same ward. Maybe the Mauritian was the boy's mentor, or at least responsible for acting like one, which explained the boy's confidence in deference to him and the man's reaction. Shame. Mr Chard had fancied watching the boy get smacked.

The boy closed the door against the bitter evening and came back over to where the girl was standing. She had put her coat on and was holding out the boy's jacket. She had a look in her eye, noticed Mr Chard. He finished his ale, watching them over the rim of the tankard.

The boy slipped on his jacket and drained his pint, then brought their glasses over to the bar and put them down in front of Malcolm.

"You might want to get him to a hospital," the boy said.

Malcolm shrugged and took the glasses. The boy turned and looked at Thick Steve, who had shuffled away from the action and was standing at the corner of the bar eating peanuts. The boy raised his eyebrows.

"Oh for fuck *sake*," Steve muttered, "I'll take him. In a minute."

"Good for you," the boy said.

The girl had come over and her body language was all, *let's get out of here*. Mr Chard put his tankard in the right-hand pocket of his white coat.

The boy smiled and took her arm and they walked towards the door. She snuggled in to the boy's side and he put an arm around her slender waist.

They walked out. Mr Chard stood up, stepped over Griff, and followed them.

Steve watched him go, chewing a cud of peanuts. "Nuvver one, Malcolm," he said, holding out his glass.

Keeping the couple in sight, Mr Chard trailed them across the football field. The moon was covered now with dark winter cloud. Missed me, thought Mr Chard, pulling the collar of his coat tight against the back of his neck just in case it re-emerged and made a last attempt to snag him with its ascending barb and carry him off. He imagined himself the grotesque monster in a childrens' fairy tale, the shoemender on the moon's hook, maybe. Something sent out to dangle over the houses of slothful boys and girls, undead in airless space, arms and legs stiff as a scarecrow, tatty white coat rattling and full of awful tools, to nail heavy iron boots to their sleeping feet with rusty tacks. Mr Chard grinned a fierce, chipped grin. Not tonight, you slit, he thought, and watched as the young couple made their way up the steps into the nurse's accommodation block.

He hurried to the entrance and slipped inside. This nursing block was little more than a corridor providing access to eight single rooms, four on each side, with a small kitchen at the end and a communal bathroom facing the kitchen. Mr Chard ducked his head and peered through the glass set in the door leading off the entrance hall. His breathing was coming fast, and he felt the loathsome pinch in his right lung. He concentrated on slowing his respiration and watched the couple stop outside the room third on the right. They were kissing. Not just a peck goodnight, this. Their mouths were pressed against each other and his hands were in her hair. She broke the kiss and turned to put her key in the door. The boy was stroking the back of her neck. The door opened and they fell inside, laughing. The door shut, and Mr Chard crept down the corridor and stood outside the room. He looked at his watch. It was half past six in the evening. A strange time for nurses. He calculated that the law of averages dictated that at least half the occupants of the rooms were on late shifts, which finished around nine, and that the remaining few would be either asleep or getting ready to go out later. The girl and boy were occupied, so he just hoped no one fancied a snack and made a trip to the kitchen. In his experience, student nurses rarely cooked and almost never had customary meal times, so he reckoned the odds were working in his favour since it was regular teatime for most folks.

Over the past years, Mr Chard had been along this corridor many times. The doors were thin and damaged by decades of careless use. Their paint was chipped and faded and some of the panels were split or loose. Into each door, three feet above ground level, Mr Chard had bored small holes with a bradawl.

He waited for the timer to switch off the two fluorescent lights in the ceiling along the corridor, and in darkness, teeth wet with saliva, Mr Chard knelt and peered into the girl's room. He had used the master key on his key ring to have a look in all the rooms and knew where the beds were, which was the prime factor in the location of his peepholes. This girl had her bed up against the right hand wall, headboard beneath the window, which was good of her; perfect for all positions. The peephole was only about five millimetres in diameter—the widest he dared risk—but as he put his eye to the opening he was afforded a decent perspective, enough to get the details.

She was lying on her back on the bed and the boy was sitting sidesaddle, facing her, his backside resting against her hip, feet on the floor. The bedside lamp was on and backlit them perfectly. The boy lowered his head and kissed her. She shifted against him and her legs swayed opened with an instinctual languor. Her short skirt rode up a little revealing the taut gusset of her black winter tights. The boy ran a hand across her belly and gently squeezed her thigh. Her legs moved with that slow distraction while he stroked higher. They broke their kiss and she sat up and dragged her tights down her legs, flicking them from her toes with a giggle.

Mr Chard closed his eyes for a second and put his forehead against the wood. He breathed deeply and recommenced his witness.

The boy had taken off his shirt. Still sitting on the side of the bed, he caressed her thighs. The girl lifted her bum and he pushed her skirt up, bunching it around her waist. He pressed his palm against the fabric of her panties, sliding his fingers so that the tips rubbed and stroked the goblet of shadow that lay between the tendon at the top of her thigh and the soft flesh beneath it. She moaned and pushed him away.

Shit, thought Mr Chard.

The boy stood up. The girl reached out and undid his jeans and they fell to the floor. He kicked them off as she was pulling at his pants, getting them halfway down his thighs, and she lay back against her pillows, gazing with uncontained anticipation at what she had revealed. Without taking her eyes off his craning cock, she pulled off her knickers, affording Mr Chard the briefest of glimpses of what pouted there, gleaming and rosy between her scissoring legs, and then she swivelled her hips and sat on the side of the bed.

The boy stood there, mesmerised, and reached out both hands to cup her pretty upturned face. She tilted her chin and looked up at him and undid the buttons of her blouse. It slid from her shoulders and Mr Chard could see her little tits, pushed up in a lacy black bra.

The girl smiled and Mr Chard could see the boy go tense. The cheeks of his buttocks hardened and the fingers that held the girl's face tightened their grip. They dug into her hair as she opened her mouth and Mr Chard could see her tongue gleam in the lamplight as it moistened her bottom lip.

She put her hands on the backs of the boy's thighs just beneath the curve of his bottom, pulled him gently towards her face and put her mouth...

The door at the end of the corridor opened.

Mr Chard threw himself sideways, away from the peephole and sprawled across the linoleum floor. He rolled and came up in one move and was already walking towards the exit, hands in his coat pockets, head down and gaze averted before anyone had stepped into the corridor and turned on the lights. He maintained a reasonable walking pace, aware that someone had now come through the door and was treading slowly towards him. Whoever it was smelled like he had trodden in something. With both feet. Mr Chard wrinkled his nose. Why hadn't they put the lights on? Well, all the better for him if they didn't.

He was furious. He felt as if he had just been woken from the best dream of his life, at the precise moment of penetration, frustrated as usual by his own repressed subconscious. *Why was it always like this?*

Despite his intention to remain inconspicuous, he looked up, raging inside, to see who had entered the corridor. To see who had brought that stink in with him and ruined his night. He wanted to remember this person. There was self-preservation in it, too. He might have to make excuses if he was recognised.

And then the lights did come on as a large fist smacked against the timer button. He blinked as the fluorescents flickered and burst into life with a low hum.

The presence was large, seeming to push the shitty smell ahead of it, and as Mr Chard looked up, he saw why.

It wasn't a *person* at all.

PHIL THOUGHT HE heard a stifled scream from the corridor. It was probably someone's television on too loud in one of the other rooms. The walls were like loo paper. His ears were buzzing a bit, too, from the increase in his heart rate. Anyway, what was he going to do about it right now?

"Did you hear that, Carol?"

Carol shook her head.

"Um-um."

Phil's knees buckled slightly. *Wow.*

THE NEXT MORNING Phil dressed and let himself out of Carol's room without waking her. She was on a late shift and after last night he wished he were too. His eyes felt grainy with exhaustion. Everything below his belly felt hollow, including his legs. He grinned. This morning's shift was going to be a long one.

He shrugged on his jacket as he walked down the corridor and as he was peering down to fasten the zip he noticed fresh scuffmarks on the pale blue linoleum floor. They were shaped like black chevrons and went all the way down the corridor to the door at the end, alternating left and right like footprints. To Phil it looked like someone had been dragged kicking the entire length of the corridor, the scuffs rubber from lashing heels.

He noticed something else. It was lying against the skirting board beneath a Perspex covered sign screwed to the wall advising *What To Do In The Event Of A Fire.* Someone had written on the Perspex in red felt-tip: *MELT*

Phil bent down and retrieved the item. It looked like a screwdriver but it had a sharp point. The handle was wood and the ferrule was rusty. Phil pursed his lips and stood, putting the bradawl in his jacket pocket.

If someone had been in a fight or dragged from the place, surely there would have been more noise. Phil continued walking up the corridor considering other scenarios. Maybe they weren't boot prints. Maybe someone had walked a piece of furniture out of their room leaving leg or castor marks on the lino. Why would they do that in the middle of the night? Because they were student nurses. The strangest, most non-conformist lot on the planet. He had come home to his own digs one night after a party to find two of his cohort attempting to coax one of the horses from the meadow at the back of the cricket field along the corridor. One of them was riding on its back; the other was shuffling backwards holding out a fistful of Murray Mints. Phil had watched for a moment and then stepped over a fresh pile of manure to let himself into his room. He had passed out fully clothed on his bed and never did find out what had happened to that horse.

He stepped outside. It was bitter cold, still dark, and misty. He shoved his hands into the pockets of his jeans and headed off across the hospital grounds towards the wards. As he reached the drive that led from the hospital gates up to the main building he stopped, squinting through the mist, and stared at what had come silently in the night and set itself up on the green.

The drive encircled the green, looping in front of the old Victorian building, and was bordered on both sides with dense and untended juniper bushes. The frosted globe lamp was lit above the arched entrance to the hospital, giving the mist an eerie, diffuse radiance, and Phil could see the coloured lights on the Christmas tree in the lobby twinkling through the long window beside the porch. Phil walked slowly up the drive, all thoughts of the mystery of the scuffmarks fading from his head as he took in what had pitched up in front of the hospital.

It looked like the dirtiest, most disreputable fair ever to be convened. Shabby stalls overhung with tatty awnings dotted the churned earth. Fresh, glistening ruts criss-crossed what was left of the grass where caravans and trailers had been driven and hauled up off the drive. In the centre of the green was a circus tent made from a nasty-looking glossy material that made Phil think of human skin. There were black and grey pennants draped around its conical roof, their points dripping moisture. At the far side of the green, covered in an oily tarpaulin stood a cage on the back of a trailer.

As he circled the green he glanced at a trio of old caravans wedged together between a couple of hastily erected stalls. They were in darkness with frayed curtains pulled across their small, grimy windows. Next to these was what he first took to be a pile of rusty machine parts but on closer inspection proved to be some kind of mangled bicycle. It must be part of some ride, he thought, because it appeared to have wooden frames like wing-struts folded into its side which were covered with ragged fabric and it had a small engine beneath the saddle that looked powerful enough to run a petrol mower. It was tilted to the side and its front wheel was buried in a deep ruck of mud. It looked like it had flown in and executed a rough landing.

Phil continued around the path until he reached the cage on the trailer. He stood with his back to the hospital and approached the cage. He could smell festering straw and something higher, more acidic. Thatches of straw stuck out between the bars beneath the tarp, dripping condensation.

He stopped, his fingers an inch from the bottom of the tarpaulin, and pulled his hand back.

Something had moved inside the cage, something heavy enough to rock the trailer on its axles. It grunted, a single, deep, phlegm-filled snort, and the tarpaulin rippled where Phil had been about to put his hand.

Phil backed away from the cage. Who in their right mind had organised for this lot to come here? He thought back to the summer, and to the previous Christmas when he was only three months into his training, and the previous Fun Days the staff had put on for the patients. They had been nothing like this. No invited performers, just knackered old stalls and a bit of *Now That's What I Call Music* played on a record player connected to tinny speakers.

They'd come piling out of the wards, lurching and stumbling to get their groove on to *Walking On Sunshine*, and the hideous irony of it all was heart-rending. This was a terrible place, and its days were numbered, and all Phil had to do was go through another year and a half to qualify and he could get a job in the community in preparation for the influx of work that would come when the old asylums were shut down.

Perhaps some charity had donated this? Who knew what went on behind the scenes? The management was old school, as institutionalised as the patients. Their decisions were often arbitrary and counter-productive, or self-serving and brutal. Phil was young and modern enough in his outlook to be staggered that this hospital still used a *Punishment* Ward, a flagging, cruel and inhuman extension from the first half of the century, where patients that didn't toe the line were sent for months of reprimand and reconditioning.

He was about to go inside when he noticed something lying in the mud at the edge of the green. A piece of paper had been pressed into a rut by the wheels of one of the trailers. It looked like a chip wrapper but when he bent to retrieve it, flicking wet grass and mud from it, Phil could see that it was a fly-poster. He shook it out and read:

RAINSCISSOR AND MORGODER
PRESENT
A CONGRESS OF SPECTACULAR
ENTERTAINMENT AND A COLOSSAL
COMBINATION OF ALL THAT IS
BREATH TAKING AND IMPLAUSIBLE

Beneath this was a drawing of a glum little clown holding a hoop, and within the circle of the hoop was the outline of a dark and savage-looking beast. Phil pursed his lips. It looked a bit like a bear. He tilted his head, and it looked more like a wolf. It had a slovenly ursine slouch to its shoulders but the snout was long and narrow. Phil didn't like the look of it, whatever it was, and dropped the flyer back into the mud. He took another look at the cage with the tarp over it.

Nothing could persuade him to lift the tarp again, not after hearing that nasal rattle, and he was starting to feel exposed out there in the glazed, damp pre-dawn darkness. Phil shuddered, pushing away any further curiosity, and walked off towards the entrance to the hospital.

He went through the door into the foyer. It was deserted; nobody manned reception anymore. Layoffs in preparation for closure were evident everywhere. An entire ward had been demolished recently, consigned to history in a single afternoon. The workmen, facemasked against asbestos, had left nothing but a remnant of claw-footed baths, miles of lead plumbing and cast iron Victorian column radiators. It had looked like a vandalised reclamation yard, tossed into a pile and left to tarnish, rust and rot, its traces of atrocity, madness and affliction ghosting off it like fumes.

Phil looked along the corridor that stretched away to his right. It was dark and could have been a mile long as it disappeared into the distance. He could hear a muted flapping sound. The opening at the far end of the corridor gave onto a slope that led off into the baroque hinterland of the asylum and was protected from the elements by heavy strips of opaque and durable plastic that always made Phil feel oddly phobic as he pushed through them. They allowed the trundling passage of the porters' trucks without the inconvenience of doors but to Phil they looked like a heavyweight fly blind hung up against the onslaught of a great and meaty species of insect he had no wish to encounter battering itself mindlessly against them.

He squinted and peered into the gloom. The lights on the Christmas tree flickered through a timed cycle, and then there was a pop as a tiny bulb blew somewhere amongst the untidy coils and the tree went dark. Phil jumped, unnerved. As the lights had died he had seen something emerging from the darkness at the end of the corridor. A figure in a white coat, groping along the wall, its face a pale thumbnail and its mouth open black and wide.

Phil recoiled from the sight and turned and headed in a fast walk away to the left, out of the foyer and through a short corridor leading to the admin offices and staff canteen. He hoped to find someone, perhaps a domestic, or a kitchen porter, but the corridors and offices were deserted. He stopped in a small atrium that housed the patients' shop. The shutter was down. He looked about, listened for movement or a sign of human activity anywhere. He heard nothing to comfort him, but was able to make out the shuffling sound of something coming towards the atrium, something that made use of the walls to guide it.

Phil swallowed, his mouth dry, and turned and headed off again. He took a right at the end of the atrium and hurried along another long, darkened corridor, one parallel to the corridor that led off the foyer. He passed the doors that opened onto a large hall where occasional discos were held. The doors had been propped open with fire extinguishers and he glanced left and could see the low stage at the back of the hall, and on it, prancing, the shadows of things moving, enacting something that looked obscene. He didn't stop, but looked back over his shoulder as he hurried past.

The groping figure had negotiated the atrium and was coming towards him, picking up speed as its hands fingered the wall, its mouth hanging open and its eyes glittering. Phil began to run, all meaning gone from the day now but for an awareness of terrible menace. Thoughts of Carol dissipated like a dream; their first, precious lovemaking a fantasy. He was aware only that there was a thin light coming now, through the skylights set in the high, flaking ceiling of the corridor, and it was daybreak, but all it was bringing was an illness of clarity he would rather not have.

And now he could see something else, and it was craning against the low ceiling of the corridor ahead of him, its long blue face dipping, reaching thin arms with tiny fists that were the skulls of birds, empty-socketed, beaks opening and closing with horrid dry clicks.

How, he could not fathom, but somewhere in his mind a word formed as if whispered and Phil knew this thing that strutted towards him, knew what it called itself. Knew this was

Rainscissor

and he slid to a stop on the buckled linoleum, his mind spooling into white panic. There was a sign hanging from the ceiling above him. It read:

ARMAGH
TIZARD
KESTREL

and Phil threw himself left and along the corridor that led to the wards as the thing jolted forwards, a terrible, clattering insect racing up a pipe to seize him. He reached the door to Kestrel ward and fumbled for the handle. Rainscissor had reached the entrance to the corridor and was clambering towards him as if rising up through a well. Phil looked down at his hands, raking at the handle and willed himself to grasp it, to turn it. He leaned against the door and shoved inwards, wrenching the handle, and as he did so, a door further along the corridor opened and he heard a calm voice say:

"Phil. Don't open that door. Come here."

Phil threw a glance towards the voice, his eyes wild, and the skin crawling over every inch of his body. The dreadful, speckled shadow of Rainscissor cast itself across the scuffed lino, reaching for him as its arms unhinged and the birdskull fists clicked like dice, pecking the air.

A man was standing in the doorway. He was wearing a long coat and worn-looking desert boots. He had a trimmed gray beard and clear, intense blue eyes. He pointed through the door from which he had stepped, indicating that they should make haste.

Phil dropped his hands from the door to Kestrel ward and stepped towards the man.

"Don't look," the man said. "Run."

But Phil did look, was unable not to as the door swung open. The smell snagged him and he glanced through, and could see all the carnage wrought there. And just glimpsed enough to know what it was that had done the killing, because she was hunched over the body of Jase, her hacking stilled for a moment as she turned her mad, grinning, heavily jowled face towards the door, her long, tangled red hair swinging like a mat of bloodied Hessian.

Phil ran. The man stepped aside and swept him into the room, guiding his blind panic with a firm grip on Phil's arm. Phil stumbled against an old wooden desk and the man closed the door behind them.

Phil swung around, hands held before him in a wild gesture of defence.

The man stepped towards him and Phil cowered back against the edge of the desk. They were in an abandoned office and there was grainy light coming in from a single window that looked out across the cricket field.

The man held his own hands up.

"Try and relax, son," he said.

Phil pulled a face, a grimace. It was all he could muster in way of response.

The man took another step towards him.

"My name is Daniel," he said. "I am the Hypnopomp. You're dreaming, Phil."

Phil dropped his arms and his eyelids fluttered. There was a serene expression on his face. He sighed. "Yes," he said with a tone of relieved comprehension.

"Close your eyes," Daniel said.

Phil closed his eyes.

Daniel opened a Gantry and led them through.

WHEN PHIL OPENED his eyes he was sitting on a stool at a bar in a busy pub.

He blinked and looked around. He felt content. The pub had low, beamed ceilings and a wooden floor, and there was a fireplace in the far wall that was swept and full of dried flowers. He smiled as he looked around. The place was packed and noisy and smoky. The sounds of children playing outside threaded through the low murmurs and sudden roars of laughter from the adults like bright, colourful fish darting through deep, silted water. He could smell beer and cigarettes and the hospitable aroma of a barbecue working away outside.

He looked at the bar and saw that he had a pint ready.

Somebody said, "Crusader, Phil. Best beer in the world. On the house."

Phil looked up, the sweet nature of the dream infusing him.

A man stood next to him. He was in his late fifties, tall and rangy. He was wearing a red pullover. His face was kind and his eyes were shining with a joy usually only ever seen in those of a delighted child.

"How quickly we lose that," Phil found himself saying.

The man smiled. "We get it back," he said and both he and Phil laughed, the sound loud even above the conversation and merriment around them. People turned and looked in their direction, all smiles and approval. Some nodded and raised glasses. Phil stared at the man who was talking to him, his eyes wide, and still laughing.

"Have a drink, Phil, and I'll tell you more," the man said.

Phil took his pint and sipped it. It was cool and golden and unbearably lovely. Despite the lucidity and good humour of the dream he felt a sudden, palpable sorrow for a moment, that he would never taste anything like it again. He put the glass down, his face a picture of wonder reflected back at him from the mirror behind the bar.

"So," said Phil.

"Let's go outside for a little while," the man said. "It's noisy and we need to talk."

Phil obliged. He stood and followed the man to the door. Before they went outside, Phil took hold of the man's elbow.

The man turned, his hand on the door handle.

"Who are you?" Phil said.

"I'm Les," he said. "Come on."

They went outside. Phil blinked and squinted against the sudden brightness of the day. They were standing at the edge of a road that ran through a village. The pub was called The Dog With Its Eyes Shut, and it stood on a bend in the road, and across the road he could see what looked like a building site. There was a high chain-link fence ringing a large pit and there were piles of masonry scattered across a wide vacant slab of land. Beyond this he could see hills climbing off into the distance. He looked up. The sky was blue and clear and full of planets.

"Wow," he said.

There were hundreds. They speckled the blue like filmy, exotic baubles. They were misty with reflected light from the sun the way a hint of summer moon looks ethereal and oddly astray in a morning sky. Some were small, no bigger than the moon, but others hung immense, their rims pale arcs visible beyond the hills.

Les said, "The Firmament Surgeons are working on the exoplanets. They've drawn them here to the Quay to adjust their orbits and monitor the retrograde paths."

Phil nodded, understanding nothing, still peering up. As he watched a number of planets disappeared, popping out of existence it, seemed, like soap bubbles.

Phil laughed; it all seemed very jolly.

Les leaned forward, just a little, so that for a second Phil thought he was going to whisper in his ear, but instead, Les tried to bite him.

Phil stumbled away, horrified. He stood, arms raised, halfway across the narrow street.

Les had changed. He had claws.

There was silence now. Above, the planets had evaporated and the sky was an uninterrupted blue. There was no sound coming from the pub although Phil could see movement behind the windows; a muffling pressure had descended over the village and it was humid. Phil turned and ran towards the vacant lot and the fenced-in pit.

Les dropped to the ground and scrabbled towards him, his thorax bulging and tearing the fabric of the red jumper. Les had an insect's head now, and sepia coloured wings like nicotine-stained net curtains unfolding from his back, sliding from between the rents in the jumper. Serrated bolt-cutter jaws slid from beneath his bugging compound eyes.

Phil reached the ring of chain-link and span around, hearing the clatter of the Les-bug as it raced towards him. Despite his terror

Phil was aware that details of his surroundings were snagging his vision, drawing his attention. He could see that the earth around the lip of the pit was granulated and fine, no longer a spill of tumbled masonry. And something was coming, rising up from the depths. Phil could hear their legs rattling, and their wings pulsing.

He had nowhere to go. He turned.

The Les-bug was almost upon him. Its jaws pincered and its claws were reaching for him.

Phil prepared himself to fight, bunching his fists and stepping forward to kick the thing in the head, but he knew he had no chance. This was a dream, he thought, I can make something happen.

And as he stepped forward to plant his boot beneath the thing's throat, something did happen.

The door to the pub opened and a tiger sauntered out. A man so tall he had to duck a full foot to get beneath the lintel followed it. He was carrying levers.

Phil lowered his foot and pressed himself back against the chain link fence. He could feel the air move behind him, pushing up moist and warm. It smelt of minerals and earth mined by beasts and churned to paste, of depths turned to chemicals with things set in it to rot. He watched as the tiger and the tall man (*long man*, he heard in the back of his mind; again, he *knew*, the dream told him) crossed the road. The man was wearing a coat that swung to his ankles and heavy boots dusty and worn with age and momentous journeys. He held a lever in each huge fist, brass pipes with handles that looked like shoehorns, or the gear levers of old cars. The Les-bug sensed their approach and swung around, its shadow hard-edged beneath it. All human form was gone; it raised its shining head and its abdomen twitched, and something that looked like a funnel slid from beneath a fleshy hood at the base of it.

The tiger kept coming, padding across the road. It was huge, and dramatic in the sunlight, and Phil thought it might be better suited *there*, amongst the hydrogen jungles (*the relentless hydrogen jungles of the sun,* Phil thought, astonished by its implication) and coronal plains.

The insect reared up on its back legs and lifted its abdomen, pointing the funnel at the tiger. It sprayed a jet of electric-blue fluid with a grotesque, rippling contraction of its body. The arc hit the dry earth of the road and hissed with a sound like fatty meat frying, but it had missed the tiger, because the tiger was already in the air.

It leaped as the insect reared up, anticipating the move, and vaulted the jet of acid. The tiger hit the insect's midsection and threw it to the ground. Its front paws came down, pinning the crumpled wings to the road and the tiger opened its jaws and bit into the monster's throat. There was a splintering sound and the tiger tore off the insect's head with a single twist of its neck. It fell back onto the road like a Halloween mask, its calliper jaws closing slowly over each other as its muscles relaxed. The tiger shook the rest of it out of its mouth, bits that looked like shattered razor shells, and stepped from the deflating body.

As the tiger finished off the insect, the tall man walked to the fence at the edge of the pit. He didn't look at Phil, hadn't once glanced in any direction other than the fence and the piece of land it penned. He went down on one knee and raised the lever he held in his right hand. He narrowed his eyes and plunged the lever into the rocky dirt near the bottom of the fence. He compressed the handle.

He looked up at Phil then, seemed to notice him for the first time pressed frozen against the fence, his fingers entwined in the links by his waist in an instinctive grip of fear.

"Go back into the pub, son."

Phil let go of the fence. The links had made livid red marks in his palm and between his fingers. He stepped away from the pit on unsteady legs. The tiger had come over and it stood next to the kneeling man. Phil gaped at it, not because of its size or proximity, but because it had been the tiger that had spoken.

The tiger held his gaze, and seemed to grin.

Phil circled away, his mind reeling. As he backed across the road he saw light bloom in air above the middle of the pit. It glowed like a fuel rod and expanded, broadening into a searing cylinder. Phil shielded his eyes, lingering in the doorway of the pub. The tiger was still watching him and it lowered it head in a restrained assent. Its lips were curling and Phil hoped it wouldn't roar at him, because that sound, from those disquieting and implacable jaws might blow him apart like a bundle of sticks.

He felt a hand on his arm and turned into the cool shadow of the pub.

A man stood there, a kindly man with bright eyes full of delight. He was in his fifties. He was wearing a blue jumper the colour of the sky outside.

"I'm Les," he said. "Come in, Phil. Have a pint and we'll all talk."

PHIL, LES AND the tall man—his name was Bismuth, Les had informed Phil—sat at a table at the back of the pub. Phil and Les each had a pint of Crusader, but Bismuth wasn't drinking. The tiger—Bronze John—was curled up by the fireplace, watching them with his head resting on his front paws. There was a yellow plastic washing-up bowl full of water by his side from which he took an occasional languid lap and a scattering of crisps and peanuts on the floor, snacks people in the pub had delighted in putting down for him. They didn't seem at all worried that they were sharing their pub with a massive tiger, and Bronze John seemed quite happy to let them stroke the fur beneath his throat and tickle behind his ears. He had sat with enormous patience while a little girl aged about six had climbed onto his back and ridden him like a pony.

Phil had been warned about going outside. "You were tricked. We all were." Les had explained. He had pointed to his jumper. "Blue," he had said. "I wear blue. They can't seem to manufacture the colour. Always comes out a muddy red. Watch out for it, Phil, it's a clue, a giveaway. A *tell*, if you like, like a liar's tic."

Phil had asked who 'they' were. Were 'they' the same as the thing he had seen in the corridors of the asylum?

"Rainscissor? No. *That* is an Autoscope, a terrible, ancient thing. The Les you met before was a dupe, a Toyceiver. They serve the

Autoscopes. They can mimic people like me, but they can't mimic a Firmament Surgeon. Like your man Bismuth here."

"They don't have the balls," Bismuth said. It was the first time he had spoken.

Phil grinned. He liked these men. They felt like old friends. The dream was as vivid a one as he'd ever had. He pondered the words they had spoken, the strange neologisms and descriptors, savouring them like the nectar of his pint. Was his subconscious making all this up? He had no idea he could be so creative. Perhaps making love to Carol had loosened something up. The words seemed familiar to him, though, like hazy memories of the names of exotic places visited as a child.

He came out of his reverie, a drift within a dream, as Les continued to speak.

"What bothers us is how it managed to get in here. How it reached you before I did. You're safe now Bismuth and Bronze John are here, but don't leave the pub. Daniel brought you here because it's a safe place. None safer in all the Quays."

"What went on out there?" Phil was looking out of the window, past the bulk of Bismuth's shoulder. He could see a portion of the fence glittering in the sunlight like chain mail. The sides of the pit were steeper now, and the hole wider, where Bismuth had shut down the invasion.

"It's an Incursion Gantry," Les said. "We closed it off once but now it's opening again. We're trying to find out why and we have some ideas."

Bismuth shifted in his seat. He sighed. Phil looked at him.

"One of us is dying," Bismuth said.

"And we think that because of this the Autoscopes are gaining power. And if they gain enough power they might be able to breach the containment we've set up to imprison their Lord, the devil-in-dreams," said Les.

"I'm dreaming, right?" said Phil. He lifted his glass and tipped it towards the two men. He wasn't losing the moment exactly, but he was aware of a feeling of caution threading its way through his contentment; he could feel it there at his heart, like a fine thread of dark silk being pulled through the muscles of his chest. He took another sip of Crusader, which reinforced his sense of unreality with its heavenly flavour. He closed his eyes as it went down. "That's what Daniel told me."

"Not strictly," Les said.

Phil's glass wavered at the top of its salute.

"You are and you aren't."

"I am and I'm not?"

"The reason you're accepting what we tell you is because of Daniel. You're in a hypnopompic state. He's maintaining it so we can protect you. Also, you know all this already."

Phil put his glass down. He leaned forward.

"I do?"

"Yes. But it's in your future. Because the Autoscopes know how important you are to us they tried to take you out using a narrow flux of Dark Time. They hunted for you and went back to while you were training to be a nurse in order to stop you becoming one. A good one. A hope-giver. They hate hope, Phil. It thwarts them."

"What do I do?"

Les smiled and made an expansive gesture taking in the pub and the gardens beyond. "Stay here. Make friends. Drink! Have a hotdog."

Phil looked around. A couple of people acknowledged him with a nod and a motion towards the bar.

Phil pursed his lips.

"Okay," he said.

In 1985 a man and his dog step into a corridor from the room into which Daniel had moments earlier taken a young and terrified Phil Trevena. A young woman follows him. She is strikingly beautiful, with curling shoulder-length golden hair and green eyes. She carries herself with authority and precision of purpose. She has a crossbow in her left hand, cocked and loaded. She indicates that they should proceed along the corridor with great care. The man nods, and smiles at her, his fearless and wonderful Lesley, and together they head up the corridor beneath its low and mottled corrugated roof. There are large Perspex windows set into the frame of the prefabricated passage and the sun is up now and it shines down on the vicinity of buildings and sheds, chimneys, water towers and alleyways at the back of the asylum with a flat, oppressive light.

There is a door to their right and they stop outside it. The sign above the door reads KESTREL WARD. The door is ajar. The man, tall, fair-haired and rather tired-looking—it's not *fatigue* his features impart, though, more an expression of relaxed contentment one carries after a good night's sleep. His name is John Stainwright, and he used to be an apprehensive chap, rather isolative, but the last seven years have been good to him and he's never felt so happy. He watches Lesley as she approaches the door, and he is still smiling as she pushes it open with the palm of her hand.

The three of them, Lesley, John and his dog go through the door and look around. It is a huge ward, with scuffed and peeling columns holding up the high, arching ceiling. The floor is blue lino and the walls are tiled and chipped. There are chairs and some low tables scattered about. There is a long room off to their left and they can see rows of iron beds and piles of clothes and dirty sheets on and beneath them. To their right is a door leading to an office.

On the floor right in front of them is a dead man. He is lying on his back, arms and legs splayed, a deep gash in his throat and another in his belly that looks pulled apart and rifled. His guts glisten like a trough full of offal beneath a butcher's block. The vitiated air of the ward is leaden with the stink of blood and meat. The flies that at all times circle the ceilings of the ward and crawl the filth of the huge sash windows—too heavy to open, or painted shut, their ropes and pulleys greasy with dust —have found something fresh to alight on. As Lesley and John approach, they rise from the body in a clot.

"Where are the patients?" John asks, mostly to himself. He steps past the body and heads into the dormitory. There is a large double door in the wall at the end of the ward and it is wide open. Curious, John walks the length of the dormitory, past the beds with their attendant sad, empty cabinets that display no photographs of families, no trinkets, just overflowing ashtrays and some blue china hospital property teacups, and takes a look outside.

Milling about in a wide concrete enclosure are about twenty old men. They are huddled in corners or wandering about clutching precious possessions: comics, annuals, and transistor radios. They are all in various states of dress. Some have managed to pull on trousers and shirts; some have shoes. One is in underpants and by the size of them they might not be his. Some are sharing the remains of cigarettes they have found scattered around the square, a habit that has, over time, caramelised their fingers and top lips as they smoke the butts down to a washer.

John pulls the doors shut, leaving them out in the relative safety of the yard, and goes back to Lesley and the dog. The dog has trotted over to the closed office door and is sitting there, ears flat against the side of his head. He isn't growling, but John can see that the dog is keyed up.

"Coming over, Bix," John says and he and Lesley go to the door.

It must be the nursing office, because they can see what look like ranks of filing cabinets against the back wall through the frosted glass. There is a desk, too, and movement behind it.

John looks at Lesley. Lesley nods. "Stay here, Bix," John says.

He tries the handle and the door opens.

THERE IS A young man sitting behind the desk. He is wide-eyed with terror. He is about twenty years old. As John and Lesley step into the room he opens his mouth but he is too late to shout any warning.

But John catches a warning in the slight glance the young man gives to his left, towards the filing cabinets lining the wall of the office. Except they are not lining the wall; some are askew as though something has squeezed behind them.

John puts an arm across Lesley's chest to prevent her going

further into the room. He is just in time, because something shoves the filing cabinets from behind and three of them crash to the floor a few feet away from where John and Lesley are standing.

The man behind the desk flinches but doesn't move from his chair, and he cries out as the thing that was hiding behind the cabinets is revealed.

It clambers over the fallen cabinets, buckled shoes denting the steel and making it groan. It sees Lesley in the doorway and hoots, its bulk tottering astride two of the cabinets, and waves the bloodied blade it is carrying in front of its slack, mad, terrible face.

It's Nurse Melt, and she and Lesley have history.

Lesley's turns to protect John. She grabs him by the arm and pulls him out of the office. At the same time she raises the crossbow and points it at Nurse Melt.

She fires, and the bolt hits Melt in the shoulder, throwing her against the wall. Melt's hand spasms and she drops the knife. It hits the back of a cabinet with a clang and bounces beneath the desk. Melt slumps against the wall, her torn mouth hanging open revealing black pegs of teeth. She looks down at the bolt protruding from her shoulder, a bloodless wound. Her coarse and knotted red hair swings across her face as she shakes her head. It is impossible to tell whether she is in pain or merely stunned. It gives Lesley enough time to reload, though, and she pulls back the bolt and lifts the crossbow. This time she tries to take better aim but Melt is moving again.

Melt leaps sideways, towards the desk, with a ghastly, nimble grace. The dented steel pops back into shape with a hollow clang as she launches off the backs of the cabinets. She lands on the desktop, scattering a pile of green folders, and perches there, unbalanced, her flabby arms wheeling. The man in the chair could shove her backwards off the desk, but still he doesn't move, just presses himself further into the chair as Melt looms over him. Her hair covers the lumpy obesity of her back like a shawl. Lesley swings the crossbow and fires, cursing her lack of aim, and the bolt flies wide. It hits the discoloured wall and punches out a chunk of plaster.

Lesley reaches to take another bolt from her belt and as she does so, Melt swivels her head and glares at her. She has regained some balance and squats there on the edge of the desk and looks like she is about to take a dump off the edge of it. Her broad backside beneath the stretched and filthy fabric of her uniform dress wiggles and clenches, but she isn't about to eliminate; her muscles are bunching. Her calves bulge and as Lesley reloads, she leaps from the desk and crashes through the sash window in the wall behind the desk. Thick chunks of glass blow outwards and splinter against the sill. Melt hits the pane with her outstretched hands and her weight carries her most of the way out. She has misjudged the trajectory and as her body tumbles through, her knees smash down onto the sill and are sliced to ribbons by the shards still sticking up from the wooden frame. She howls as she falls forward and thuds onto the concrete below.

Lesley and John run to the man in the chair. He is crying now, an open expression of childlike distress on his bloodied face. As they come around the desk they see why he cannot move. Melt has tied his arms and legs to the chair with thick hanks of her own hair, pulled from her bloodless scalp in astonishing fistfuls. John comforts the man as he takes a penknife from his pocket. He pulls out the blade and eases the flat of it beneath the hair cinching the flesh of the man's wrist. The man is still weeping but he is gaining coherence. John says *shush* and slices through the hair. The man lifts his hand and shakes the copper strands from his wrist, his face a grimace of disgust. John works at the other wrist.

Lesley has gone over to the window. There is no blood—Melt is *congealed* inside—but plenty of flesh hanging in grey strips from the frame. Lesley brushes fragments of glass from the sill and leans out. She can see Nurse Melt crawling along a path leading around to the front of the asylum, the flesh at the backs of her thighs blotchy and hanging like dough.

"We have to be quick, John," she says.

"Got 'em," John replies as he releases the last of the bonds around the man's left ankle. He places a restraining hand on the man's chest because it looks like he wants to bolt. The man sits back, chest heaving with panic.

"Be calm," John says, and the man relaxes beneath the gentle pressure of his hand. His eyes roll and then re-focus. Lesley comes around and squats in front of him and despite his shock, the horror of his ordeal, the man cannot help but be aware of her beauty—his pupils dilate and his face softens—and is soothed by it.

"What's your name?" She asks.

"Charlie," the man says in almost a whisper.

"You're safe now, Charlie. What happened?"

Charlie looks away, towards the open office door and the ward beyond. John feels him resist the pressure of his hand. "Look at Lesley," he says.

Charlie looks back at the girl, gazes into her wide green eyes.

"We were just getting the boys up," he whispers. Lesley lifts her chin slightly and cocks her head, a gesture for him to speak up. Charlie coughs, then goes on, "We were getting the boys up for breakfast. The main door opened and that *thing* walked in. Just walked in. It jumped on Jase and... and stabbed him in the guts. There was only Jase and me on this morning and all I could think of was to get the old boys out into the back yard. I was shutting the doors, but that thing came running up the dorm behind me and grabbed me and dragged me in here. I thought she was going to... *torture* me."

"You were brave," Lesley says. "You did a good thing for those men. She would have killed them all."

"What is she?"

"It doesn't matter, Charlie. You're going to sleep for a while now. John and I are going to go and make it like none of this happened, but we have to move fast."

Charlie strains against John's hand again but his resolve is weak. Lesley holds his gaze. She smiles, leans forward and kisses him on the lips.

Charlie slumps in his chair and sighs. His eyes close.

Lesley and John leave the office and go to Bix, who is standing guard in the corridor outside the ward.

"Anything, Bix?" John asks.

Bix growls low in his throat and starts off up the corridor.

John turns to Lesley. "He can smell them," he says.

Lesley wrinkles her nose.

"Can't you?"

John laughs. He takes a quick look back into the ward. He can see Charlie asleep in the chair behind the desk in the office. His head is resting against the back of the chair, but even at that angle John can see that he is smiling.

John shakes his head and follows Lesley and Bix up the corridor.

THEY REACH THE main corridor that runs perpendicular to the prefabricated passage that leads back to Kestrel ward and stand under a sign (KESTREL TIZARD ARMAGH) to think.

"Split up?" Lesley suggests.

John isn't sure. It's a huge place and it makes sense, but there's unknown dangers here, unknown numbers.

"If you take Bix with you," he says.

Bix looks up at him, then at Lesley. He wags his tail.

"It's ok," she says. "I'll be fine."

John is adamant. "It's dangerous, Lesley."

Lesley smiles. "You think?" she says and looks past John, back along the corridor they have just passed through. A door has opened.

Something is coming.

SOMEONE HANDS PHIL a hotdog. It's wrapped in a yellow serviette and smothered with onions and tomato relish. He looks up to say thank you and sees that it's Les.

"Thanks, Les."

"Having fun?" Les asks.

Phil nods, his mouth full of hotdog. He is on his third pint and has been playing pool with a couple of the lads. He feels safe and happy. There's a free jukebox on the wall over by the gents and he's unsurprised to see that many of his favourite albums are on the play list.

Les has been outside in the garden all afternoon. His family are there. Phil watched them for a while, through a window. He hasn't wanted to interrupt them; their time together looks precious. Les has a pretty wife and two young boys, and they are laughing and playing and scoffing burgers and chips at a table towards the rear of the garden in the shade of a willow tree. If Les wants to introduce them, Phil will wait until he's ready.

Phil looks around the pub. Bismuth and Bronze John are gone.

"Where...?" he begins, but Les points outside.

Phil looks through the window and sees them standing on the path outside. Bismuth is looking down at the tiger and consulting with him. Bronze John strolls across the road and Bismuth walks with him.

They reach the far side of the road and Bismuth locates a patch of earth to the left of the fence ringing the pit. He pushes a lever into the dirt and compresses the handle. A Gantry opens, a line of white light.

Bronze John tenses, and leaps through.

"AH," SAYS JOHN Stainwright. Bix barks and his tail becomes a blur.

Bronze John sways up the corridor. Lesley kneels and embraces his neck, caresses the soft flames of his cheek with her own.

John and Bix strike off left, heading towards the rear of the hospital. Lesley and her tiger go right, back towards the foyer at the entrance. They intend making a circular sweep of the hospital and grounds before meeting up again on the green at the front.

They don't get far.

PHIL WATCHES AS Bismuth returns to the pub. He feels relief as the giant ducks beneath the lintel and comes across, retaking his seat at the table. His sense of well-being notches up again and he asks his companion if he would like a drink now.

Bismuth leans back against the wall and glances at the bar and the pumps and optics displayed there. All those ales and malts. He frowns and scratches his chin, his huge fingers deep in the thick fronds of his wild beard.

"I'll have a Martini," he says. "Thank you."

BRONZE JOHN SEES it first as they round the bend at the top of the corridor.

There is a dark atrium ahead, and something clawing the walls.

There are no lights on anywhere in the asylum; the corridors of the main building are more like tunnels, or shafts, the ancient brick of their walls cold and impregnable. Small windows let in narrow, dusty stanchions of grey light. Bronze John's eyes have adjusted and he sees clearly. Lesley squints but can see movement.

The thing in the atrium blunders its hands across the metal shutter covering the counter of the patients' shop and its fingers rattle with a sound like rats teeming over a tin roof. As the sound echoes, Lesley and Bronze John approach and enter the atrium.

The thing stops. It stands with its shoulders slumped beneath its soiled white coat. It turns its head.

Lesley has seen much horror, but this Toyceiver is foul.

It has a mouth, which is open like a hole, and a nose, which is clogged with blood, but it has no eyes. But it sees them. Somehow, through the two narrow cylindrical brass peepholes that have been pushed into its jellied sockets, the puckered skin of its eyelids sewn around them with shoelaces in tight, brutal loops, it sees them.

What sickening, hall-of-mirrors distortions must it glimpse come lurching towards it? A stilted tiger billowing against the roof of the atrium like some paper Chinese carnival puppet and a waddling girl beneath it, rippling, concave-faced, convex-throated, carrying something blunt in her swollen fists.

It juts its face towards Lesley and Bronze John, its entire head a crucible of molten agony, and waves its arms before it, trying to judge their distance. It is looking down twin red tunnels of buckled glass.

Lesley fires a bolt into what remains of its left eye and kills it.

It collapses to the floor and Lesley and Bronze John go past it. Lesley reloads.

JOHN STAINWRIGHT AND Bix head towards the back of the asylum. The corridor is empty, cold. An intermittent draught moves the air around them. High double doors to their right give onto a large staff canteen. They comb the room with caution, through ranks of tables cluttered with the remains of the previous evening's meal and check behind the counter. They search the kitchen and establish it's clear. It stinks of unwashed pans, plates and dishes. They return to the corridor.

John tries every door they come to but they are all locked. He wonders what is behind them. Wards, offices, storage rooms probably. Nothing comes to investigate his attempts to open the doors.

Bix trots at his side alert as ever, even though he's an old boy now. His muzzle is mostly gray and his eyesight isn't what it once was. Bix is a saluki, a sight-hound, and he's still an elegant dog. His coat is lush and the feathering of hair at the backs of his legs, and his lively brush of a tail, are as fine as they ever were.

They reach the end of the corridor and push through thick, heavy strips of plastic to get out into the open.

They stand at the top of a wide slope. It leads down to a road that winds off through ranks of single-storey buildings. There is a small car park fenced with iron railings, its surface pot-holed and gritty. Directly ahead is a laundry. John can see huge stainless steel washing machines and oblong flumes bolted to the walls and ceiling. It looks like a ship's turbine room.

Behind this is a long L-shaped building. They walk down the slope and go past the laundry. The L-shaped building is an industrial therapy unit. Daniel has told John about these places. Daniel used to work in one similar to this, when he was a patient. It was menial work to occupy them. Making paper hats and stuffing cocktail sticks in tubes. Never eat anything off a cocktail stick, Daniel had warned John. You never knew who'd been masturbating while they packed them.

They go on, past the industrial therapy unit with its rows of long, rickety Formica topped benches piled with folded cardboard boxes and packing tape. John can see cockroaches squeezed into the gaps between the flattened boxes. Daniel had told John that they infested the hospitals; when he took a flattened box and popped it open hundreds would clatter to the floor around his feet and scuttle into corners and up the walls. They left behind a miserable greasy stink and the insides of the boxes were smeared with oils from their glands. In went the cocktail sticks.

There is a row of huts with blinds drawn down over the windows. Workshops of some kind. As they walk past John notices movement in his periphery and turns to see one of the blinds being rolled up. In the darkness of the hut someone has appeared at the window. A lean face peers out at them, dark-eyed and hollow-cheeked. He has a bald head with tufts of white hair sprouting above each ear. He is grinning.

John and Bix stop. The bald man gestures, pointing to the door. John looks at Bix. Bix wags his tail.

John goes up to the door and tries the handle. It opens and he sticks his head in. There is an all-pervading stench of hoof glue and leather that reminds John of a key-cutting kiosk. He looks around. There are shoes and boots scattered across a narrow workbench and stacked beneath it in boxes.

The bald man emerges from the shadows at the back of the workshop. He shuffles across the floorboards, his shoulders narrow and hunched. He is wearing a grey overall. He holds out a hand that is bruised, scratched and covered in strange oval blisters.

"Lenny," he says, still grinning. John takes his hand and looks into the man's fear-filled eyes.

"I'm John."

"Lenny!" the man says brightly.

Bix peers into the shack and Lenny points and grins more widely.

"Lenny?" he says with less assurance.

John nods. "That's Bix. He's my friend."

Lenny appears satisfied and steps up to the bench. He pulls out a stool and begins sorting through a pile of old worn boots.

John is about to leave him to it but Lenny turns to him and says, *"Get the fuck out. Get out before I hunt you down and kill you both and that bitch and her toy tiger."*

John freezes. His mouth dries. Bix lowers his head and whines.

Lenny is no longer grinning. He turns the boot he is holding over and over in his bony hands, the laces flopping and the black leather tongue lolling as if in derision. Lenny's eyes are blank in their dark, baggy sockets.

Bix stands at John's side.

John says, "You think we fear you?"

"I think you do."

John shakes his head and laughs. "You even lie to yourself."

Lenny's lips are pressed together in a tight, furious line. They gleam with spit. A cloud passes over the sun and the flat mean morning light turns grey and cavernous. A horde of dark, extraordinary shadows invade the asylum. John hears things racing around outside, things thundering through the lanes and passageways, fumbling against the buildings and flexing in the lines between the doors.

John kneels and puts an arm around Bix's neck.

"Shut your eyes, Bix," he says.

Bix nuzzles John's arm and closes his eyes.

JOHN AND BIX connect. They see the same things now, through one set of eyes. John has the benefit of Bix's heightened perceptions and at once feels alert and powerful and incredibly vigilant. He stands and turns to Lenny. Lenny has dropped the boot and is sitting slumped against the bench. His face is sagging with terror. Surrounding him is an aura. It is black and soulless. It is full of eyes and they swirl, planets in hellish orbits without a sun to bind them. The darkness is at once fathomless and bound by an indissoluble force. It rages against that force. John can feel it, sense it invading his mind with tendrils against the smallest of cracks. John can see where the containment is failing.

Outside, the shadows crash about. There is desperation and fury about their passes, but they are unseeing, unable to locate the man and his dog now they have connected and can see their enemy on better terms. John sees this place though a watery green light. The shadows weaken in this uncanny light, fade and disband. It is silent outside. John approaches the darkness encompassing the man at the bench. He peers into it and feels the entity recoil. The eyes that float in its mass draw back, gathering in a clump. It is like looking at the compound eye of some rank and incensed pest damned to the Pit.

"You burned," said John. "Forever."

The dark beast says something that John cannot fully understand.

The devil-in-dreams says, "Not all of him."

Lesley and Bronze John are standing outside the entrance to the asylum concealed by the recess of the porch. The monstrous fair is spread before them across the green. There is movement now, some activity of preparation. There's no joy to this, no animation that comes with the setting up of a grand entertainment. White fleshed creatures move as broken slaves across the churned mud of the green. They are carrying large pieces of machinery but they are not the parts of rides or stalls. They appear to be scavenged components of fierce machines, corroded, serrated, heavy. They are lugged to the middle of the green and thrown onto a growing pile in front of the circus tent where other Toyceivers are constructing contraptions and modifying apparatus from the heap. The black and grey pennants dangling from the tent look like rotten fangs. Most of the caravans and trailers that circle the green have their doors open and Lesley can see that they are damp, empty shells containing nothing more than filthy mattresses.

Lesley rests a hand lightly on Bronze John's neck.

"Shall we?" she says.

Bronze John flexes his shoulders, rolls the muscles beneath his pelt.

They leave the shelter of the alcove and race towards the green.

JOHN STAINWRIGHT AND Bix open their eyes. John is shaken. Bix whines. The asylum is silent, all the shadows are gone and the sun is shining again, dousing them with its jaded light.

Lenny is on the floor. He has collapsed from his stool and lies curled up beneath the bench. John goes to him.

"Lenny?" he says and tries to sit the man up.

Lenny moans and blinks. He jolts at John's touch and cringes against a pile of boxes stacked beneath the bench.

"It's all right," Johns says. "It's gone."

He helps Lenny stand. The man is trembling. He has wet himself.

John looks around. On a hook on the back of the door is a long white coat. He takes it down and encourages Lenny to put it on, buttoning it for him and covering the dark patch that has spread across the front of his overalls.

Lenny looks at John and grins.

"You'd better come with us," John says, and is unabashed when the man gently takes his hand. They leave the workshop and make their way along the path away from the back of the hospital. The path curves around, past a redbrick wing that is probably a ward and they follow it, heading towards the front of the hospital.

They can hear something now, an intermittent clang and jangle. It reminds John of the sound of metal dropping into a skip from a magnet in a scrap yard. And above that, coming closer, the sound of an electric motor labouring to propel something overloaded along the uneven ground of the path.

Lenny grips John's hand. "*Lenny*!" he says.

A porter's float rumbles around the bend. It has been modified, as has the driver.

It rides low on its small narrow wheels. Its electric motor wheezes beneath the weight of the modifications, the blades and spinning toothed wheels that have been welded and wired into it. The canopy that covered the flat bed at the rear is gone, torn from its struts, to make room for the craning arm that swings out over the cab and slashes at John and Lenny with a rusty sickle.

John pulls Lenny out of the path of the sweeping blade. Bix barks and ducks beneath it and approaches the cab. The driver glares at the dog and stamps on the accelerator. The float lurches forward and the blades fitted beneath the chassis scissor from between the axles and almost hack Bix in half.

Bix leaps as the blades chop together and they close an inch shy of his back legs. Bix hits the driver and knocks its foot from the pedal. The float drifts to a stop.

The driver flails at the dog. It is wearing a dark blue porter's overall and its lower jaw has been wired shut, the thick copper strands threaded through the flesh beneath its chin and soldered in a molten knot at the top of its long, nodding head.

It kicks out and sends Bix sprawling from the cab.

Lenny grabs John's hand again and presses something into his palm. John looks down. It is a stubby bradawl. Lenny pulls open the deep pockets on either side of the white coat and John sees they are filled with the things.

John turns just as the float lunges forward again with a straining electric whine and watches, horrified, as a slender cone made from a rolled sheet of steel lances from a box fitted to the side of the cab and plunges through Lenny's chest.

John steps back and Lenny falls to the ground. The lance slides free and retracts back into the compartment bolted to the flank of the float. John can hear a heavy spring winding and the sound of a ratchet clacking.

He has to leave Lenny. Bix is up and preparing to leap. He has caught the driver's attention and it floors the accelerator to prevent Bix leaping into the cab again. John dodges around the side of the float as it rumbles towards him and swings up onto the footplate to the left of the driver. The steering wheel is in the centre of the cab and the driver is unable to decide from which side the most danger is coming. It bends over the wheel and presses the accelerator into the floor.

John leans into the cab and plunges the bradawl into the long, sloping nape at the base of the driver's neck. The driver spasms and its hands fly off the wheel. It scrabbles behind its head but John twists the wooden handle of the bradawl and drives it in deeper, right up to the ferrule. The driver mewls and hisses a thin fan of blood and saliva through the wires clamping its jaw. Its back goes ramrod straight and its fingers rattle against the sloping fibreglass rear of the cab. John shoves forward and the driver collapses over the steering wheel. The float jars to a halt.

John breathes deeply. He steps down from the cab and goes over to where Lenny is lying in a pool of blood.

He kneels and takes Lenny's hand. Lenny opens his eyes and grins. His teeth are red with blood. His breath bubbles in the back of his throat. The hole in his chest is dark and deep with an exit wound that has torn through the fabric at the back of the white coat.

"Sorry, Lenny," John says. Lenny squeezes his hand.

Bix comes over. He cocks his head and John nods.

Bix licks John's face and is gone, running off around the bulk of the float to find Lesley and Bronze John.

John Stainwright sits beside Lenny and holds his head in his lap. He whispers something and Lenny's grin softens. It becomes a smile.

John opens a Gantry and discharges Lenny from the asylum.

As they storm the green, Lesley realises they are outnumbered.

Not only by the white-fleshed Toyceivers, who are feeble and drained of vitality, but by what they have let out of a cage at the edge of the green.

And then by what emerges from the tent in front of them, its long blue head ducking through the fleshy pleats that conceal the opening, to stand clicking its fists and working its gash of a mouth as it switches a dreadful ancient face around to locate them.

Bronze John doesn't pause; he continues his arcing trajectory and tears apart four of the Toyceivers even before the monster has a chance to pull its heavy, lobed abdomen from the darkness of the tent. The tiger skids to a halt on the churned earth and darts across Lesley's path as she charges the Autoscope.

He faces the thing slouching down from the cage.

It is a huge black bear. It is old, with a vast sagging belly and rolling gait. It lumbers towards the tiger and shakes its head spooling great caramel-coloured loops of saliva either side of its muzzle. Its eyes are gluey, almost closed with muck but they gleam, hazardous and savage, from the slits it can muster. It bellows and its jaw unhinges, webbed with mottled flesh and reveals the well of its throat and its blunted, tusk-like incisors.

Bronze John roars and they meet, head-on, and roll in the dirt tearing at each other. Lesley doesn't spare them a look. She continues on her way towards the Autoscope, her crossbow taking out two Toyceivers who are caught in her path dragging something made of chains. They look startled, but only for a second.

Lesley vaults their bodies and lands six feet away from Rainscissor.

She tries to reload but the Autoscope is fast now that it is free of the tent, and it shuttles towards her and flings out one of its long, bony arms. It catches her in the chest with a bird-skull fist and Lesley is thrown backwards. She loses the crossbow and lands amongst the chains and dead Toyceivers. She kicks her heels, her chest throbbing, and untangles herself. She slides her backside in the dirt, pushing herself away from the advancing monster. Rainscissor drops its head and opens its mouth to reveal three rows of square, ridged teeth in black gums. It makes an awful whistling sound in the back of its throat and clicks the sharp beaks of its fists together like blades.

Bronze John has rolled on top of the bear and has the bear's jaws clenched shut between his own. He bites down and feels the sinuses collapse and the fangs break and tear free of decaying gums. The bear blows twin pipes of grey snot from its nostrils and tries to twist its head but the tiger has him fast. It flails a paw at Bronze John's flank and its talons tear open an old wound, a long curving scar beneath the tiger's ribs. The tiger jumps to the side, twisting with its mouth, and the bear's muzzle comes away with a brutal, *carnivorous* sound, pelt being ripped straight from the muscle. Bronze John takes a few paces backwards, the bear's face in its mouth and spits it onto the ground.

Somehow the bear manages to roll onto its belly. It pushes with its front legs and lifts its head. It looks at the tiger with eyes that are now lidless and wide in their exposed sockets. It has a hole that is splinters of bone and strands of red meat in its head beneath them. Its brown tongue lolls and dangles almost to the ground. It is so badly maimed that it can express nothing, just expel clouds of rank air from the hole where its jaws had been as its chest heaves, but it drops its head and lays back its grizzled ears and that is enough.

Bronze John approaches it, lashes a paw and breaks its neck in mercy.

LESLEY STANDS. SHE thinks she might have a fractured sternum. She bends and tries to pull a length of chain out of the mud to use as a weapon, but pain lances though her chest and she gasps for air, unable to complete the move. She backs away.

Rainscissor steps towards her, over the chains, and raises its arms.

Bronze John is too far away. Lesley glances to her right and he looks like a toy over there at the edge of the green. He is running now, getting bigger, but still too small. She looks up at the Autoscope and stands as tall as her injury will allow. Her breath is catching, stitches of fire between her breasts. She brushes a curl of golden hair behind her ear and winces at the pain this causes. She will fight, though she will be beaten this time. She just hopes her tiger will get away.

Lesley is thinking of her father as Rainscissor comes for her.

DOCTOR MOCKING OPENS his eyes.

He has a visitor.

"How long have you been here?" he asks, smiling.

The man is sitting in an armchair by a window that looks out over an apple orchard. He closes his book and rests it on the arm of his chair. He is a large man, well muscled, blond. He looks to be in his late thirties or early forties. He is wearing a blue pullover. When he speaks, Doctor Mocking can see the silver piercing in his tongue. It is, he knows, a tiny silver strawberry.

"About an hour," Jon Index says. He is the oldest of them all. He has never been reborn, never beaten, never died. He has led them all this far. He reassembled the Night Clock and holds them all together.

Doctor Mocking is about to speak but then his eyes widen and he cries out. His eyes close tight with pain. He presses a hand to his chest.

The man comes off his chair and is by the bed in an instant.

Doctor Mocking shakes his head. Tears run from the corners of his eyes. He is struggling for breath.

"Not... me," he manages to say. He looks up at Jon Index, his expression imploring.

"The girls?"

"*Lesley.*"

Index touches Doctor Mocking on the shoulder.

"I'll take care of it," he says.

DARK TIME, THAT flux above the linear.

Jon Index feels it move around him, the interconnectedness between which he drives his Gantry.

He calculates quantum equations, reckons the paradoxes; allows the Night Clock to chime. He calls his Firmament Surgeons to combat.

AND THEY STEP from their Gantries, on the green where the carnival rots, and go to battle for Lesley.

* * *

PHIL HEARS SOMETHING shatter and looks up from the pool table. He is about to take on a tricky black.

There is a broken Martini glass on the floor over by his table.

Bismuth has gone again.

Phil misses his black by a country mile and the white goes in.

"Bollocks," he says and laughs.

"Rack 'em up again, Phil," says his new mate, Lenny.

RAINSCISSOR SNIPS AT the air in front of Lesley's face with his birdskull fists. Its face looms long and blue, the smoky lenses of its huge unblinking eyes peer down at her. Lesley can see her face reflected in the pearly film that coats them. She draws back her arm, wanting to get in a shot, a blow to one of those gawping dead-squid-eyes.

And something holds her, is pulling her backwards. Her chest explodes with pain and she screams but the pressure is unyielding and she almost greys out. She bites down on her bottom lip and twists against the pressure encompassing her chest but she can do nothing. She looks up. Rainscissor is not advancing. Its head switches about. It appears double-minded. It steps forward. Stops. Steps back. It raises its arms and clicks its fists. It whistles.

Lesley is placed on the ground. She looks up.

"Index!" she says.

The man has grown, glorified. He stands blazing by her side. He is angelic, a form of pressure and temperature contained in a field. He has tusks of blinding white glass. He drops his head and charges the monster.

Index hits Rainscissor beneath the throat and tosses it back against the tent. The frame gives beneath it and bows inwards, wrapping it in folds of greasy material. Index continues his charge and stands over the thrashing beast. He gores at it, tearing chunks from it, rips it apart. Its arms fall by its sides and the bird skulls open and do not close.

Bronze John trots over and Lesley embraces him. She examines the wound in his side, but it is superficial. The tough flesh of the scar has borne the brunt of it.

Lesley leans against the tiger's flank, her vision blurring.

Bronze John supports her until the light-headedness passes.

She looks across the green. There is Bismuth, stomping on the remains of a couple of Toyceivers over by the bear's cage. And John is back. Bix comes running around the corner of the hospital, sees him and barks. He races over, tail thrashing and leaps onto the back of the Toyceiver John is wrestling with. It is a big thing, more grey than white, and swings huge clubbed fists around John's head. He ducks out of the way and as Bix hits the thing low in the back, he steps in and kicks its stumpy legs away from under it. It flops to the ground and John drives something small and sharp into the back of its head.

Lesley can see the others moving through the wreckage. Eliot looks up and waves. He and Alex are in their late teens now and are both fine young men. She can't see Chloe or Anna, but her sister is probably tending to their father, and Chloe is different to them all. She doesn't fight like they do. She is only seven, but what she can do is far more powerful.

Alex and Eliot come over.

"You ok?" Eliot asks. He strokes Bronze John under the chin.

Lesley nods. "I think that bastard just broke my breast bone. Feels like a horse has kicked me. I'll live. What you got there?"

The lads hold up rectangular petrol cans.

"Found them in the cricket pavilion," Alex says.

"Nice work," says Lesley.

The boys laugh and head off to the edge of the green where they begin dousing everything with fuel. They slop it over the sides and in through the doors of the trailers and spew it over the filthy straw matting inside the bear's cage.

Jon Index comes over. He is just a man again. Lesley thinks he is incredibly handsome. He smiles and his blue eyes sparkle. Lesley reddens and smiles back. She doesn't see Jon Index very often. None of them do. But he is there with them nonetheless, in the background, running the Night Clock. Always.

"How you doing, Lesley?" He asks. He touches her arm and Lesley thrills. She wants to hug him but the pain in her chest won't let her. Shame.

"Thanks, Jon," she says. "I thought I'd had it there."

Jon reaches out and ruffles her hair. A curl drops over her eyes and she flicks it out of the way. The feel of his strong fingers in her hair and across the top of her head makes her knees feel weak but it makes her feel childlike, too, and oddly conflicted. She isn't much older than Alex and Eliot after all.

They gather in the middle of the green in preparation to go back. Daniel has remained at the pub with Phil. They have decided one of them should always be with him while things are as they are. The rest of them will go and be with Doctor Mocking. They need to make plans with him and ascertain his wishes. Before gathering they had scouted the entire carnival to ensure they had killed everything. Rainscissor is dead and already starting to rot in its shroud of tent fabric but there is no sign of the other Autoscope it travels with. Morgoder is gone, if it had been here at all.

"I don't sense it," Index says as he gazes up at the front of the asylum.

"It's not here," Bismuth states. "You'd smell it."

Index pulls out a silver Zippo lighter and flips open the lid. They can all smell the petrol as it soaks into the remains of the carnival. He thumbs the wheel and a wide yellow flame flutters in the breeze.

He tosses the lighter beneath the bear's cage and they watch as the flames spread, igniting the caravans and trailers and half-constructed Uproar Contraptions. A thick runnel of fire races across the green and engulfs the remains of the tent and the monster tangled up in it. It stinks.

Index nods at Bismuth. The bearded giant takes a lever from his belt and spears it into the earth. He compresses the handle.

A Gantry opens in the middle of the ring of fire and they all go through.

* * *

NURSE MELT WATCHES the carnival burn.

She waits in the shelter of a juniper bush, her shredded knees planted in the earth beneath her bulk. She watches the Firmament Surgeons leave and waits for the Gantry to close. When she is certain they have gone she crawls out from beneath the bush and pulls herself across the road to the edge of the green. The tendons in her knees are gashed to ribbons and her lower legs drag and flop, insensible as bags of sand. One of her buckled shoes is gone.

Nurse Melt grits what remain of her rotten teeth and pulls herself up onto the green. Fire bakes at her and she feels her matted fringe crisp and burn off in acrid wisps. She reaches a fat, trembling hand into the blaze and pulls at something sheltered from the worst of it between two trailers. She yanks at it and it slides towards her through the mud.

Melt pulls herself up by the handles and throws a thigh over the crossbar. She fumbles with a cord beneath the seat and tugs it in her fist. The engine coughs, fires, and dies. Melt pulls the cord again and it chops into life. The casing is hot and Melt wonders, in a deep recess where a nub of reason still remains, whether the small fuel tank will blow up beneath her, blasting shards of blazing metal up her fish-white mouldering arsehole. She wrenches the accelerator. The cloudbike shoots forward, the wooden frames of its wings catching against the sides of the trailers. Melt looks round. The wood and scabrous fabric covering the frames are starting to turn brown. If they catch fire that's the end of her dear old bike.

Melt twists the throttle again and leans forward. The bike judders and lifts off the ground. Melt hoots.

Screaming, trailing smoke like a missile, Nurse Melt spirals up into the sky.

"I HAVEN'T WON a game since you came in," Phil says.

Lenny smiles and salutes with the tip of his cue.

Daniel comes over. He has been outside, sitting with Les and his family in the sun. "Time to go, Phil," he says.

Phil puts his cue on the table.

"Okay," he says equably. He is starting to feel drowsy and fancies a lie down. Daniel takes his elbow and guides him around the pool table and out through the back of the pub. They go into the garden and cross the tidy square of lawn, past the still smoking barbecue, and stand at Les's table. Les looks up.

"You off?" he says.

"Yes," says Daniel. "It's finished there."

"Everyone okay?"

"Fine."

"Great! Phil, you haven't met my family. This is Charlotte, my lady."

Phil smiles and holds out his hand. Charlotte shakes it. She is pretty, with long red hair and shrewd green eyes.

"Thank you for everything you do for Les," she says.

Phil shrugs. He has no idea what she is talking about. He is starting to feel very tired. Charlotte laughs.

Two boys run up. "Our two," Les says. He puts an arm around Charlotte's waist and she puts her head on his shoulder. The boys have been back to the barbecue. Their mouths are salty and their fingers are sticky and their shirts bear the evidence of all manner of relishes. Phil thinks they are adorable. He would like to have sons like them one day.

"Hi, fellas," he says. The boys hug him, a quick squeeze each, and run off to play.

"Great kids, Les," Phil says.

Les stands up and comes around the bench. He takes both of Phil's hands in his.

"I lost them all once," he says in a quiet voice so that no one else will hear. "My illness. The voices. You helped give them back to me, Phil. I will always love you for that." He surprises Phil by kissing him on the cheek, dry and fatherly, a take- care-on-your-journey kind of peck. Phil sees that Les has tears in his eyes.

"No problem," he says. He turns to Daniel, eyebrows raised.

Daniel says, "Close your eyes, Phil."

Les lets go of his hands and Phil closes his eyes.

He hears Daniel say, "You'll always remember some of this, Phil. It'll be like a dream you had as a boy. It'll help when we need you. When the time comes. It'll help you survive."

Phil feels himself drifting and he puts his arms out to stop himself falling over.

THE ASYLUM WAS quiet. No one was about much before an early shift. The office workers and medical staff didn't get in until around nine.

Phil strolled past the green and up to the main door. He could see the Christmas tree winking away in the foyer. It had been hard leaving Carol in bed this morning, curled up warm and naked beneath the duvet, but it had been wonderful waking up next to her and he was hopeful of more of the same later tonight. He had no idea where the relationship was heading but why worry about that now? Early days. He entered the foyer and headed down towards the wards, past the patients' shop, which was locked up with its steel shutter. He turned right, walked past the dance hall and then went left beneath the sign for Kestrel ward.

This was going to be a long shift he thought, and yawned. He took hold of the heavy brass handle that let onto the ward and stopped. He felt light-headed. He closed his eyes and experienced a brief flashback to the dream he had had that night. He took his hand from the handle and glanced further along the corridor. It was still dark and the corrugated roof was a low, rippling slope into shadows. He remembered a door opening down there. There had been a man, calling him. And a pub, with heavenly ale. Phil licked his lips. *Crusader.*

He blinked and shook his head. He took the handle again, opened the door and walked onto Kestrel ward.

"Phil!" shouted Jase. Get your arse in here. Have you heard the news?"

Phil saw Jase standing in the nursing office. He was putting down the phone. He looked overjoyed, with the kind of prurient excitement only scandalous institutionalised gossip could induce.

"What?" said Phil as he crossed the day room and went into the office. A couple of the old boys were up already, smoking and drinking cups of tea. He shrugged off his jacket and put it on the top of a filing cabinet.

"One of the cleaners just found Mr Chard dead. Someone did him in last night. Bashed his head in with a tankard. And one of his boys, Lenny, is missing off Chase ward. What a fucking drama. Police'll be all over this place in a minute."

Phil was stunned. Hadn't he seen the old shoe mender sitting at the bar in the social club last night? "What about you and Griff?" Phil asked. "You caught him good and proper."

Jase shrugged. "Haven't seen him," he said. "And he don't want to see me." He flexed his hand, made a huge fist. Phil could see where the knuckles were raw.

"Anyway, go help Charlie with meds. We need to get these boys up. It's Fun Day! Whoo-hoo."

Phil laughed and went off to find Charlie.

Part Three

Roasting the Stymphalian Bird

"HOW'S THAT MATE of yours?" asked Dean Brazil.

Mickey Mitre stopped shovelling shit and leaned on his spade.

"Who, Barwise?" he said.

"Yeah. That Barwise."

Mickey shook his head. "Terrible," he said. He shook a Richmond from a battered pack and offered one to Dean.

"Cheers." They lit their cigarettes from Mickey's non-refillable *Bic* and stood puffing by the low stone wall of the pigsty.

"Terrible?"

"Yeah. Fuckin' awful."

Dean gazed down at the shit around his boots. It was garnished with half a pack's worth of cigarette butts. He really couldn't be arsed with this job Mickey had got for him. He wanted to get back to delivery work, but wouldn't get his licence back for another year. He missed the fry-ups, the shop birds, the lunchtime pints.

"What's wrong with the bloke?" Dean asked. "Ain't he pleased to be out?"

"When I see him last night," Mickey said, "he's just sitting in his flat sayin' he wishes he was dead. I mean, I know he's done his time but they shouldn't've just let him out like that. He's a liability."

"Seven years for doing his bird and that bloke in," Dean reflected. "Should've got life. Don't know how lucky he is. Couldn't get him on it though, could they? Beak give him diminished whatsisname."

"Responsibilities," supplied Mickey.

"Yeah. That diminished responsibilities."

"Reckoned he'd had some sort of breakdown. He's never copped for it though. Denies it. *He* says it was a suicide pack. Trish just couldn't live without him."

"She left *'im.*"

Mickey nodded, flicking his fag into the mud.

"And why would her bloke top 'imself? It's not like *he* couldn't live without Barwise, is it?"

"You should've been a lawyer, Dean."

"I know," said Dean, and resumed ploughing pigshit about until it was time to stop.

TREVENA SPENT THE afternoon writing up Chapel's assessment. There was still a lot to go over with the man, mostly more recent history, but he wanted to get the gist of it down while it was still fresh in his mind.

It wasn't Trevena's job to diagnose, but he was experienced enough to take a stab anyway, for his own amusement. Chapel had schizoid personality traits and co- morbid depression and anxiety. It was possible he was on the brink of something worse but it had a pseudo-psychotic feel, a personality-driven cover for his failures. There was a grandiosity about it that was less to do with illness and more to do with subconscious awareness of his frailty as a human being. His description of his childhood had been cold, aloof, and there had been no mention of significant relationships, apart from the almost dispassionate mention of a child. Still, Trevena wasn't going to put that in his assessment. The shrinks got paid the big money to label people. It would help him dig in the right direction, though, when he spoke to Chapel again.

His phone rang.

"Phil Trevena."

"Hi Phil. It's Miles from Occupational Therapy."

"Miles."

"Just letting you know, that fella Andrew Chapel. He's absconded."

"What?"

"We were doing the Art Group and he just excused himself and walked off."

"You didn't try and stop him? There weren't any nurses there?"

"He's not on a Section, Phil. He came in voluntarily. He asked to attend the group and the ward let him. He's an *artist.*" Miles was getting shirty.

"Yeah, but, what about a five four? One of the nurses could have detained him. He's a *massive* risk."

There was silence for a moment and then Miles said. "We were outside, Phil. Off the premises. Can't detain someone if they're off the ward."

This time it was Trevena who paused. He leaned forward on his desk and squeezed the bridge of his nose with his thumb and forefinger.

"What was he doing outside, Miles?"

Miles drew a breath. Trevena could hear it whistle through his lips.

"He wanted to look at the sculptures in the Relaxation Area. I thought it—"

"A toadstool from the Garden Centre and a fucking dog-licking-its-arse water feature? Are you serious?"

"Phil—"

"Have you called the police? Have you told the *ward*?"

"The ward is aware," Miles said, his tone flat. "They will contact the police."

Trevena hung up.

"Fucking basket-weavers," he said, staring at his computer screen.

His phone rang again.

"'lo."

"Hi, Phil, it's Emily on reception. There's someone here asking to see you. Rob Litchin. Says it's urgent."

Trevena sat back in his chair and closed his eyes. A headache was forming over his right eye.

"Thanks, Em. Tell him I'll be down in a bit."

"Will do," she said brightly.

Trevena sighed and saved his document. He logged off, got up and went out of his office to see what ailed Rob.

ROB WAS SITTING in a large rattan chair by the glassed-in reception desk. He was wearing army fatigues and heavy, buckled biker boots. His long grey hair was tied back in a ponytail and his beard was substantial but in terrible condition. It stuck out in greasy spikes and sprouted tendrils down his throat; it looked like he had scooped out all the plugholes in a cheap hotel and plastered the contents on his cheeks and under his chin. His eyes were inadequately focused over the required distance, and when Phil walked into the foyer at the front of the Mental Health Unit, Rob blinked and half-closed them, trying to induce the correct resolution, but with minimal success.

"Phil?" he said, half rising from the chair.

Trevena came over and put a hand on Rob's shoulder. Rob sat back in the chair and closed his eyes. "Thank God," he breathed.

Trevena squatted down so that he was at eye-level with Rob.

"What's up, mate?"

Rob shook his head. "I'm so pissed, Phil."

Trevena glanced up at Emily sitting at her desk in the reception booth. She shrugged and resumed typing on her computer keyboard. The sliding doors at the entrance swished open behind them and Rob flinched and stared over Trevena's shoulder.

"It's alright, Rob. Doesn't matter. You want to come through to the side room and have a chat?"

Rob nodded. He leaned forward and put his head in his hands. "I'm wankered, mate."

Trevena helped Rob to his feet and guided him around reception and into the corridor that led up to the wards. There was a small room to the left where nurses saw clients for reviews and assessments. There were two low blue metal-framed chairs and a coffee table beneath a locked window. It was the same room he'd seen Andrew Chapel in earlier that morning. Trevena planted Rob in one of the chairs and took the other. He put a notebook and biro on the coffee table, sat back and crossed his legs.

"What's happened, Rob?"

Rob looked up and stared at Trevena with watery eyes. His complexion was sallow and his breath smelt fusty with evaporating cider. He paused, his mouth open, a look of great distaste on his face, and moved his pallid tongue around behind his teeth as if prospecting for words that might be stuck between them like old food.

Eventually he said, "He's back, Phil."

Trevena picked up his pad and pen. A filament of unease was running up his spine. He had an idea what was coming. He said, "Who, Rob?"

Trevena was writing the name on his pad even as Rob was saying it, his voice breaking and tears welling in his eyes.

"It's Neil, Phil. Neil Gollick's back."

"NEIL'S DEAD, ROB," Trevena said. "They found his body on the concrete beneath your flat. Do you remember?" He had worked with Rob for years on this and Trevena had thought that he had finally got Rob to believe that what he had experienced all those years ago outside his flat had been hallucinations and delusions. But Rob's denial persisted, and not surprisingly, really. Because, Trevena knew, it had all been real.

Rob shook his head. "I was out of it. I didn't see anything. I woke up on my sofa with an ambulance man standing there."

"But they told you. We've talked about this. Neil died in the fall. He was trying to terrorise you but something happened and he fell over the balcony. You weren't to blame."

"I know. He was a *cunt*, Phil. Sorry."

"It's okay."

"I saw him last night outside my mum's front room window. Just standing there. He was grinning with a gob full of those glass teeth and his eyes were white and he was giving me the finger with a *claw*, man."

Trevena said, "When did you start drinking again?"

"No," Rob said, shaking his head, "No, I'm not having that. I had my first drink in seven years today. You helped me get off the sauce and I haven't had a drop in *seven* years. I wasn't pissed last night and it wasn't DTs. I didn't imagine it, Phil. He was *there*."

"It's fine, Rob. I believe you. I just need to ask."

"I was watching TV—some old film, can't remember what it was called—and was nodding off. So I switched it off and got up to go and crash and there he was. I froze. The streetlights were on and he was about a foot away from the window, looking in. He couldn't have been there long because I would have seen his shape behind the glass. It was as if he slid up the garden just as I stood up. Wallop. There he was. He had that Community Support Officer jacket on and it was all dirty with dry brown crap. Blood, I reckon. And he was grinning at me. I shot over to the window and hid beneath the sill. I reached up and yanked the curtains shut and crawled out of the room without looking back. I checked on mum but she was asleep—she's eighty-six now, Phil. I can't worry her with this."

"No, of course not."

"I still get three meals a day off the old girl. She'd be devastated if she knew I was hitting the bottle again. I spent the night on my computer in my room just fannying about with websites but I knew he was out there. I could hear his jacket rustling as he prowled around the house all night. I put all the lights on and locked up but, man, that was *very* bad."

"What happened this morning?"

"I fell asleep in my chair eventually. Must have been about four in the morning. When I woke up I was thirsty. Raging. I went straight to Balv's and bought two bottles. Went back to mum's and did the lot. Easy. Like coming home. But I stopped at two, Phil. When I went out,

Neil was gone. I legged it to Balv's and was back in less than fifteen minutes. Drank them on the sofa and then thought: no way. No way is he doing this to me again. So I made up my mind to come here."

"You did the right thing, Rob. What's it been, two years since I discharged you?"

Rob nodded. "Yes. Pretty much." He looked disconsolate.

"You've had a blip, mate. That's all. Any stress at the moment?"

Rob was silent for a while, looking out of the window in much the same way Chapel had earlier that morning.

"Well, I've been having some nightmares. Sleep paralysis. Something pressing on my chest as I'm struggling to wake up."

"Do you know what it is?"

Rob slumped back in his chair. He put his arms out, mimed carrying something heavy.

"It's like a dense black shape. It's awful, like time and eternity pressed into a single mass. And it's alive. It knows me, Phil."

Trevena was doodling on his pad, the strokes deliberate, the nib digging into the paper and pressing through the layers beneath. His teeth were clenched. He had drawn a shape, and the shape was a black polygon that was filled with eyes.

He held the pad up and showed it to Rob.

"Something like that?"

Rob's mouth hung open. He wiped a hand over his face, and nodded.

"That's it. That's the fucker."

Trevena had no choice but to readmit Rob onto his caseload.

They shook hands at the entrance to the hospital and Trevena was saddened to feel how weak Rob's grip was. It had been like receiving a handful of warm twigs. He shook gently then patted Rob on the shoulder.

"I'm glad you came, Rob."

Rob nodded and looked at his boots. "I'll see you tomorrow?"

"Yes, here, not at your mum's if you prefer."

"I don't want her knowing, Phil. I'll stay off the sauce."

"I know. Good fella."

Rob traipsed off and Phil hoped that there wasn't a pub somewhere in his immediate future. He watched Rob dwindle for a minute then returned to his office to write it all up.

DRUNK AS AN owl. That was one way of saying it. He'd heard it before and it had never made sense. It was wise as an owl. Wise as an owl made sense. Did it? It didn't. Owls weren't any wiser than they were good at blowjobs. A cunt was what owls were, round-faced starey little bastards. Gave him the creeps. Like that little fucker sitting over there in the corner with a half a lager in his mittened fist. Beanie. Beanie the dwarf. Like one of those little screech owls he'd seen once in a zoo, tiny but not one fuck given. Staring at him with enraged yellow mince pies, bastards.

Rob swung around on his stool and glared at the little chap sitting over by the fruit machine. Beanie was ignoring him, or perhaps genuinely hadn't noticed Rob sitting there in all his camouflage gear. Possible. There were two other men standing at the bar in The Macebearer. Rob squinted and tried to listen to their conversation. He recognised them. A formless, inebriated recognition that at once enhanced certain features and simultaneously leached them of any significance.

One was telling the other a story.

"I'm renting this room off this old girl on the estate, right. Cash—she needs it 'cause she's got this son with Down's syndrome and they've cut her benefits. He's alright. Big old boy, just sits in his vest watching fucking Harry Potter all day. Loves it. Morning, noon and night that shit's on. One after another. I come back after a day's work and go up to me room. He just looks up, tea round his chops, and grins at me. So one morning the old girl has to go out and get something from Balv's and says to him, 'Edward, I'm going out. I'll be twenty minutes. Watch your Harry Potter and if anyone comes to the door, don't open it, all right?' It's this routine she has to explain to him every time. She won't leave him as a rule but she was out of fags. Had to go, so she puts this rule in place. She puts his telly on and lays out snacks and drinks, warns him again about answering the door and then goes off to the shops. She gets back about twenty minutes later and he's turned the lounge over. There's drink all up the walls, crisps and biscuits everywhere. Pictures off the wall, sofa over, telly over, the curtains are down. He's standing in the middle of all this sweating, pointing at the cupboard under the stairs. He's terrified, poor bastard. Mum goes, 'What the fuck have you done, Edward?' Edward's going 'Goblin! Goblin!' like that. Pointing at the cupboard. Mum thinks he's been scared by something on his Harry Potters. 'You see goblins every day, Edward,' she says. He's going, 'Goblin! Goblin!' She goes to the cupboard and opens it."

The man stopped and took a slurp of his lager.

Rob leaned forward. He was hooked.

"There's this fucking dwarf in there. He's cowering at the back of the cupboard all covered in blood and bruises. The mum pulls him out and asks what happened, why is there a dwarf in the cupboard under her stairs? The little bloke's too terrified to talk, just tries to escape. She sees he's dressed smart, suit and tie, and he's still clutching this handful of flyers for a mobile disco. She twigs then and lets him go. He's too terrified to complain or anything, doesn't say a fucking word. Just legs it down the path."

Rob's mouth was hanging open.

"What's happened is Edward's gone to the door anyway, despite what his mum's said, seen it's this dwarf giving out flyers and he's dragged him in thinking he's being attacked by goblins. Grabbed him and pulled him in off the step. He's kicked this dwarf's arse all round the lounge for nearly fifteen minutes. Poor cunt couldn't get away. Edward's caught him and thrown him in the cupboard."

The man stopped as a chair grated across the floor. He watched as Beanie waddled out of the pub leaving half of his half untouched. The men looked at each other, and then they looked at Rob.

Rob was roaring with laughter.

* * *

Rob's new friends were called Dean and Mickey. They worked on one of the nearby farms as labourers. Their boots were caked in pigshit and they were two of the stupidest people Rob had ever met. But they were a distraction.

"You want another one?" asked Dean.

"Go on then," said Mickey, he of the Beanie anecdote.

"Wasn't askin' you," said Dean.

"You been poncing my fags all day," said Mickey. He slid his glass across the table.

Rob was suffused with their easy camaraderie, buoyed by their cretinous rapport. The horrors of the previous night had receded and now he wondered whether the whole thing had been a dream. He'd gone to see Phil today, hadn't he? Told him something bandy. How embarrassing. He'd have to ring him later and cancel their appointment.

Rob was experiencing the sweet diversions of early evening in a pub for the first time in seven years, and he was relishing it. People were coming in, the place was filling up. There was the pallid chicken soup aroma of an unpalatable carvery. A plump bird behind the bar was looking lovelier every hour that passed, despite her tattooed neck and a teasing glimpse of sallow belly that hung like an apron beneath her T-shirt and over the waistband of her taupe leggings. She kept glancing at Rob with an antagonistic kind of interest. Rob was beginning to fancy his chances with her.

Dean got up and lunged for the bar. He got his order in and came back with three more pints held deftly between his palms and splayed fingers.

"That bird fancies me," he said as he plonked the glasses down.

Rob felt a stab of jealousy and glanced up at the bar. The lusty wench in question was looking in their direction, but so crossed were her eyes that it was hard to tell at whom her interests were directed. Dean turned around on his stool and gave her a wink but she had wandered off, plucking at a bolt of leggings fabric that had been hoovered up by her bum crack.

"Nice," said Mickey, and by his tone it was impossible to tell whether he meant it.

Six hours later the chums left The Macebearer to go back to Dean's flat. A skinful of booze had allowed Rob to make the kind of rash yet inspired arrangements for the next day that he had excelled at when in his cups seven years ago. He'd missed that level of clarity of thinking. If life was words, he thought as they meandered across the plaza leading to Dean's flat above the shops, then pubs were brackets. Parentheses in the flow of tedious sentences where one could produce great works, illuminate new and important plans, do all the real thinking. He'd agreed to work on the farm tomorrow with Mickey and Dean. Fresh air and a bit of manual labour. Some laughs and then the pub again. Just what he needed.

Dean paused as they reached a gloomy stairwell. Light from a single orange sodium lamp in the middle of the square did little to illuminate anything besides the dirt in the concrete tubs beneath it. They looked like big pots of grubby marmalade.

"They never reopened that chippy," Dean said with regret, gesturing across the square towards a boarded-up shop front. A faded sign above the doors still advertised *Fish 'n' Chick'n.* "Not after that bloke working there topped himself jumpin into the fryer."

Rob made a face.

"Yeah. I saw it. Can't remember much about that night, though, it was a while ago," he said. "Terrible shame. I'd kill for a battered burger. Never mind. I've got some Ginsters under the sink."

They went up to Dean's flat. It was similar in many ways to Rob's old flat, where he had lived in squalor for years before Phil had sorted him out and he'd moved back in with his mum. He felt a prick of unease as he crossed the threshold and followed Dean and Mickey up the narrow hallway. The tiny kitchen was on the left as you came in, living room ahead and a bedroom and toilet on the right. No, it wasn't similar. It was identical. Were all council flats build from the same floor plan? It was like they'd tasked an architect to draw a cross on a piece of paper and make the lines a bit off centre. Great, thanks. How much for that? A *fiver*? Cheers. Won't be needing you again.

At least Dean had carpet, albeit, Rob suspected, from the remnant rolls. It looked like Dean had fitted them himself. They curled in ragged corners and up the skirting board. Rob could swear the carpet in the lounge was upside down.

There was a massive flat screen TV dominating the lounge. A pair of faux leather black two-seater sofas faced each other in front of it with a smoked-glass coffee table between them. It was all quite clean and tidy though. Rob was impressed.

"Make yourselves at home," Dean said, waving towards the couches. He disappeared into the kitchen and Rob heard him opening cupboards and the effortful sucking sound of an old fridge being yanked open. There were clanks and rustling sounds.

Mickey sat opposite Rob and let off a short blat of wind. Dean returned to the lounge cradling tins of beer and snacks.

"Oo grunted?" he said, snorting.

Mickey lifted a hand and grinned.

Dean put a tin of economy lager in front of Rob and lobbed another into Mickey's mephitic lap. He unloaded an armful of processed food onto the coffee table and sank down next to Rob.

"Ginsters," he said. "Food of the gods."

"Not Allah," said Mickey.

Dean looked at Mickey blankly. "Nutella? I'm not making fucking san'wichers." He ripped open the plastic around a sausage roll and slid it onto his knee. The meat protruding from the latticed pastry looked the colour of a compromised leg ulcer. Dean picked it up and ate it in two bites.

Rob popped the tab on his can and took a slurp. He sat back and looked around. The quality of the lager was so dismal Rob might have been swigging water that had been used to boil batteries. He examined the label. VAL-YOU Lager. Nutritional information: additives of which 97% He shrugged and had another mouthful.

There was a picture on the wall above Mickey's head. It was the kind of execrable poster art people with training but no talent liked to paint. A mad-eyed unicorn in a glade flamboyant with exotic plants standing by a static, solid-looking river the obstinate colour of toilet cleaner. A bird with massive tits was riding it and she had her hair pulled up into some kind of pointy topknot. There was reflected light everywhere but where it ought to be, mostly enhancing the undersides of her knockers.

Mickey reached over and snagged a pastie. "All-day breakfast," he said, his tone impressed. "Got beans in it?"

"And black pud," Dean said with a pride that suggested he might have sourced the ingredients himself.

Rob poked through the remaining pile, eschewing anything remotely containing chicken. He was hungry but couldn't face reformed beaks. Not tonight. He settled on a steak and onion slice.

"So how long have you been working on that farm?" he asked.

Mickey was compressing the sides of his pastie to get a better look at the contents. It belled open where he had bitten out a chunk and he fingered it with the professional curiosity of a gynaecologist. "This is fucking hollow," he said. "There's just a bit of sausage rattling about in the bottom."

"Just eat it, you cunt," Dean said.

Mickey shrugged, withdrew his finger and licked the juice off it.

"About six weeks," Mickey said.

"What is?" said Dean.

"I've been on the farm for about six weeks. Dean's been helping me out for a fortnight since he lost his licence."

Rob was starting to feel tired. He remembered that he'd had very little sleep the previous night and was beginning to wonder how he might be able to get out of going to the farm tomorrow with these twin idiots. He should go home and sleep this off. They didn't know where he lived. They'd probably forgotten all about it anyway.

He put his can of lager down on the table and sat forward. He yawned.

"I should make tracks," he said through the tail end of the yawn.

"It's early," said Mickey. "Have another beer. We'll drink through and take you in with us."

Rob did an elaborate stretch and yawned again. "You've been very hospitable, gents, but I'd better get some kip. I'm knackered."

Dean said, "We're goin' to watch *The Fast and Furious*, ain't we, Mickey?"

"One of 'em," Mickey said.

Dean reached down and took a DVD from beneath the coffee table. When he sat up he was too close and his eyes were bloodshot and watery. Rob felt himself pressed against the arm of the sofa.

"Get us some more beers from the fridge, Mickey," Dean said.

Mickey stood and edged out of the lounge. Rob saw him look back as he reached the door. He lifted a cupped hand and mimed drinking from a can. He nodded and Rob swallowed, his mouth suddenly dry.

"I need to go," he said with no authority in his voice. Fear had replaced boredom and it tweaked at his belly making him feel unmanned. Dean shook his head.

"We're watchin' a *video*," he said, and even in his agitated state, Rob was infuriated by the presumption and ignorance of the man.

"It's not a video, you prick," he said. "It's called a DVD." He was shaking. He was getting flashbacks, too, of a night seven years ago, in a flat similar—no, exactly the fucking *same*—as this one. Except with no carpet. The same level of threat he had felt and a commensurate notching up of terror. He pushed himself up off the sofa and tried to step past Dean.

There was the sound of the fridge opening: *pppfffffock*.

And Mickey screaming.

Dean and Rob bolted to the kitchen.

Mickey was standing hunched on trembling legs, a hand plastered over his mouth. He was staring at the fridge. It was an old make and the ceramic paint was chipped and stained around the handles. Rob peered over Dean's shoulder. He could see that Mickey had opened the large freezer compartment at the bottom by mistake and not the fridge. It was empty except for one object. Dry ice ghosted out across the lino and rose in tendrils around the object. It was a big glass jar.

Mickey turned, his face bleached with shock. He peeled his hand away from his mouth.

"It's a fucky *ned*!" he said, and collapsed.

ROB PUSHED PAST Dean and knelt by Mickey.

Mickey's complexion had gone from white to bluish. His eyes were shut, his mouth open. Rob put his ear to Mickey's mouth but his hair fell over his face and blocked it up. Rob flicked the hair out of Mickey's mouth and started pushing on his chest with his palms.

"What you doing?" Dean said from the doorway. Rob looked up. "You doing that C3PO?"

"CPR," Rob said through clenched teeth. "It's called CPR!" He raised his arms, fingers locked above his head and brought both fists down on Mickey's sternum

Mickey's eyes flew open. "Stop it," he yelped. "I fainted. I've got fuckin' asthma." He rolled onto his side and pushed himself up onto his knees. Rob helped him stand.

The three of them stood in Dean's tiny kitchen and looked at the jar sitting in the bottom of the freezer. Rob approached it and wiped a trembling palm over its curved surface. He cried out and toppled onto his backside, the buckles on his biker boots jangling like sleigh bells.

"What is it?" said Dean.

Rob was still staring into the freezer compartment.

"It's a fucking *head*," he said.

THEY GATHERED IN front of the freezer but none of them dared touch the jar. There was a head in it. It had been badly burnt. It was hairless and most of the flesh had melted away. Two livid, frosted eyes glared out at them. How hadn't they melted, Rob wondered. They looked almost alive. The mouth and nose were gone. All that remained was a thin rind of jawbone studded with a few black nubs of teeth.

"Is it a joke head?" Dean asked. "You know, like from a horror film?"

"You mean a special effect?" Mickey said.

Dean nodded, his mouth hanging open. "Yeah."

Rob withdrew to the doorway. "You're telling us you don't know why there's a head in your freezer?"

Dean shrugged. "Bloke who runs the farm give it to me."

Mickey looked at Dean with a perplexed expression. "Cookie? He gave you a fridge with a head in it?"

"I was moanin' I didn't have any money and mine had packed up and he said he had an old one I could have. It was in his barn, right at the back under some bales of straw. Plugged into an extension lead. He brought it over with his boy a couple of days ago."

Rob said, "You didn't look in it? *Clean* it?"

Dean's face remained blank.

"I told Cookie I don't use a freezer. Just fridge for milk and beer and a few pies. Cookie said I could have it anyway."

"You didn't even *look*?"

Dean shook his head.

"Does this *Cookie* know how stupid you are?"

Dean nodded.

"Oh, he knows," said Mickey, and punched Dean on the arm.

"You've been set up," Rob said. "They've topped someone and you're hiding the evidence."

"What am I going to do?" moaned Dean.

"You own up, don't you, you fucking cripple," Mickey said.

THERE WAS A sound, then, from outside and below. Something in the plaza. All three men jumped. It was an electric humming, like a generator building a charge. There was a sudden flash of light and they jumped again and closed their eyes against it. When they opened their eyes the light remained, a horrible, fatty orange-yellow glare as though the entire plaza was on fire and the fuel was bodies.

They pushed and jostled to the door and flung it open. They piled out onto the walkway and peered down into the square.

"Oh, not again," said Dean.

THERE WAS A hole in the air above the plant pots in the middle of the plaza. Light flashed and strobed, blinding the three men on the walkway. They turned away, their profiles lit up in hectic flashes. "What is it?" Rob screamed. Somehow the light was deafening, and he couldn't hear himself think. He edged back into the flat.

"What does it want?" Mickey wailed.

Rob glanced into the kitchen. He staggered and put a hand out to steady himself against the flimsy architrave around the door.

Inside the jar the head had begun to thaw.

Its eyes rolled and glared at Rob.

"I think they've come for the head," he said. "Dean, get a bag."

Dean and Mickey came back into the hallway. They were backlit by lurid, cycling flashes of blazing yellow-orange light. Dean went into the kitchen and opened some drawers. He produced a couple of small rumpled plastic bags. They were stained from the takeaways they had contained.

"Any good?" he asked.

"If I was picking up dogshit," Rob said. "I need a holdall, or a rucksack or something."

"Where you going?"

"It's for *that*, you idiot," Rob shouted, pointing at the jar in the freezer.

Outside something was pushing its way from the Gantry. Long wavering shadows whisked across the kitchen walls.

"Hang on." Dean went to his bedroom and pulled something from under his bed. He came back with a voluminous handbag the size of a small suitcase. It was burgundy and covered in jewels. "Bird left it here," he said.

Rob took it and looked inside. It smelt of celebrity body spray and tobacco. He stretched the top and measured it against the neck of the jar. He chewed on his bottom lip. "Should do," he said.

He reached into the freezer and pulled the jar towards the edge of the compartment. His breathing was coming fast and he was fighting panic. Just touching that cold, curved surface made him feel sick with fear. Condensation had fogged the inside of the jar, which was a mercy, because he could no longer see the head clearly. He slid it a third of the way over the edge of the compartment.

"Hold the bag," Rob said.

Mickey and Dean squatted either side of him and took a side of the bag each in their fists. They pulled it wide and held it beneath the jar. Rob eased the jar further until it tilted. He put a hand beneath it and rocked it. The head nodded forward and bumped the glass. Rob cried out but managed to hold on. An eye was pressed against the glass and it was glaring at him with a murderous fury.

Rob grunted and pulled the jar from the freezer. It dropped into the bag like a shell sliding into the chamber of a gun.

"Sweet," said Dean.

Rob couldn't close the bag because the jar was too tall. The top stuck out about six inches, but at least he could carry it. The bag had two big looping handles stitched to the sides.

Rob hefted it. The handles stretched against the stitching but held. "Is there a back way out of here?"

"Not like a back door or anything," Dean said. "You could go out the window. It's about a twelve-foot drop to the verge. I done it before when some gusset's bloke pitched up—"

Rob went into the lounge and pulled the curtains back across the window behind the TV. There was a sliding door opening onto a tiny concrete balcony. There was a spavined lawn chair out there and a plastic table covered in beer cans. A couple of pairs of thongs were drying over the rail. There was a satellite dish the size of a dustbin lid bolted to the wall. Rob thumbed up the latch and slid the door open. He carried the bag out onto the balcony and looked down. There was a sloping verge beneath edging a gravel path. Rob put a hand in his trouser pocket and pulled out a rubber band. He gathered his hair into a ponytail and fixed it with the band. He rolled his shoulders and bent his knees. He stood up too quickly and staggered against the low balcony rail. He was still pissed.

"Come on," he told himself, and squeezed his eyes shut.

He recalled that night seven years ago, when his nemesis Neil Gollick had come for him. He'd been drunk then, too, and could remember very little of it except what he and Phil Trevena had reconstructed for years afterwards. Rob had worked hard to recover from that and now he could feel it all going back down the shitter. He lifted the bag and put it on the table, knocking beer cans to the concrete with a clatter.

Rob stepped over the rail and turned to face into the flat. The wide steel toecaps of his biker boots balanced on a couple of inches of overlapping concrete. He leaned back and lowered his backside.

"Throw the bag down to me," he said. Dean and Mickey had come onto the balcony. One of them had closed the front door but Rob could still see flashes of light battering the kitchen, lighting up the hallway like a furnace.

Something hit the front door and a vertical split appeared in the wood. It lit up like a fork of lightning, widening as something applied pressure to the door.

"Follow me," Rob said. He looked down, measured the drop and let go.

He hit the edge of the verge and rolled down onto the gravel. As he got up, brushing his backside off and checking for sprains or grazes, the bag containing the head thudded to the earth beside him.

Rob stuck his head out and looked up.

"I meant wait for me to catch it. *Fuck*!"

He threw himself backwards to prevent his head being taken off as Dean plunged to the ground. They stepped up onto the verge and Rob checked the bag. The jar was made of thick glass and the lid was held on with a big metal clip. It was undamaged. Rob picked it up and carried it further onto the green at the back of the flats.

Dean followed him. They both looked up as Mickey cried out.

He was hanging from the balcony rail. Something was in the flat, blundering around. Mickey had closed the balcony door behind him and what looked like thick white tentacles were rolling across the glass, drumming against it in an attempt to break through.

"Let go," Rob shouted.

Mickey looked down. He closed his eyes and let go of the rail just as the balcony door shattered and blew outwards. Rob and Dean covered their heads as glass showered around them. Mickey squealed.

Rob stumbled over to him and tried to help him up.

"It's me leg," Mickey said. He pressed his lips together into a white line of pain. "It's broke."

Rob eased Mickey back to the verge. He looked up as the pale tip of a tentacle nosed through the balcony rail. He put his hands on his head and looked around.

Dean was gone. Rob could just make out a figure legging it across the green and into an alleyway between two blocks of flats.

"I'll carry you," Rob said. "Come on." He turned to put down the bag but as he did so a tentacle flashed down from the balcony, unrolling like a colossal party blower, encircled Mickey's waist and yanked him off the ground. Mickey screamed.

Rob reached out but he was too late. Mickey hung there for a split second, his expression imploring and terrified, and then he was gone, reeled back up, and disappeared over the balcony and into the flat.

Rob was stunned. He watched as more tentacles began to explore the lip of the balcony. He could hear Mickey screaming as he was flung around. He picked up the bag in both hands and set off across the green. He wasn't sure where he was heading but he wasn't going to his mum's. Not with this.

"Fuck you, Gollick," Rob muttered.

He had made a decision.

THE CAR PARK was still crowded with night-shift workers' vehicles when Trevena drove into work so he pulled up behind a canary yellow Audi TT and blocked it in. It belonged to one of the consultants so would probably sit there all day, but just in case he wrote his mobile number on a scrap of paper and put it on the top of his dashboard facing out. She'd have to ring him if she wanted to move her car.

He collected a few files from the boot and went around to the front of the Mental Health Unit. The doors hissed open and he walked into the foyer. He was early and the reception desk was unoccupied. He had wanted to be in first today to catch up with some paperwork and put his mind to the mysteries of Andrew Chapel and Rob Litchin. There was a connection, definitely, but was it his to make?

He stopped. "Rob?" he said.

Rob sat forward in the rattan chair and brushed a palm frond away from his face. "Phil," he said. "I've been here all night. I couldn't go home."

Trevena walked over to the doors leading onto the unit.

"Come on," he said.

Rob pushed himself to his feet and retrieved something that was lying under the chair. Trevena noticed that it was a huge burgundy handbag containing something bulky.

"Stylish," he said.

"It's not mine," Rob said, looking guarded. He followed Trevena through into the corridor that led onto the wards. Trevena opened the counselling room door on his left and they went in. They sat beneath the window and Rob put the bag on the low table between them.

"You've been here all night?"

"Yeah. Couldn't think where else to go. It's safe here and I needed to see you. I couldn't take this back to my mum's," he said, glancing towards the bag.

Trevena sat back and crossed his arms. He could see the top of a jar protruding from the neck of the bag. He wondered what was in it. It looked heavy. Maybe Rob was distilling his own moonshine. He wouldn't put it past him.

"What can I do for you, Rob," he said.

"I want to show you this," Rob said, and yanked the handles of the bag downwards revealing the jar and its contents.

Trevena froze, his arms still crossed. Very slowly he sat forwards and looked at the jar. When he had been a student, many years ago, he had used his ID card to get into the medical museum in St Bartholomew's hospital in London. He and his mate, Charlie, had spent a gruesome and fascinating hour peering into jars very much like this one. Things floating in preservatives; dead monsters, white and flaking, with Cyclops eyes and tubes for mouths, wounded, unloved flesh spawned from mother to bucket to labelled jar. There was no label on this one but if there had have been, Trevena knew what it would have said.

"That's Barry Cook's fucking *head,*" he said in a voice barely above a whisper.

"HE WAS ONE of your patients?" Rob said, aghast. "I knew it. I knew you'd know what this was."

Trevena nodded. He couldn't take his eyes from the jar on the table. The head was a ruin, little more than a charred skull, but he knew who it was. Who else could it be, come here to accuse him? To haunt him. He couldn't explain to Rob what he knew about the condition of the head, how one chill morning seven years ago he and Daniel and the others had executed this man in order to take control of the Night Clock and quarantine the devil-in-dreams to the perpetual hell of a burning Quay.

He needed to deflect Rob's curiosity.

"Where did you find this, Rob?" he asked.

"It was in a freezer in a bloke's flat."

Trevena stared at Rob.

"I'd been drinking. Phil. I met these two blokes in The Macebearer and we went back to Dean's and it all got a bit weird and then Mickey went to get more beers and he found this in the freezer."

"Why have *you* got it?"

Rob explained the rest of it, all-inclusive, up to the point where he had decided to come to the Unit and hide out there until Trevena came in. Under the circumstances he considered that Trevena was taking it all pretty well.

"Okay," Trevena said. "I'm betting these two characters were working at Cook's farm in Thetford."

"I reckon. Dean said that someone called Cookie had given him the fridge."

Trevena nodded. He pointed at the head.

"That would be Barry's dad. Evil old bastard. Somehow he's kept his son's head frozen for seven years and, coincidentally, just as you—and another chap I've been assessing—start to have visions of dark forces, he decides to move the evidence."

"*Seven* years?"

"Yes."

"How do you know that?"

Rob's question caught Trevena off guard.

"Oh, I can tell by the condition of the remains," Trevena said, not looking at Rob but keeping his eyes on the jar.

"Ah," said Rob, convinced.

"Can you leave this with me?" Trevena said.

Rob shrugged. "I don't want it," he said.

"That other stuff you said you saw," Trevena said. "The lights in the plaza and the tentacles. You believe you saw that?"

"I saw it with my own eyes," Rob said, his expression fierce with the declaration.

"You did say you'd been drinking heavily. Remember the work we did around Neil Gollick?"

Rob sat and pondered this. He stared out of the window.

"Neil's dead, isn't he?" he said at last.

"Yes."

"I hallucinated him."

"That's right," Trevena said with caution.

"And the tentacles?"

"What do you think, Rob?"

Rob nodded, a sharp assertion. "Mental," he said.

"Let's call it stress, Rob. You did well to bring that here. I'll get rid of it."

Rob sank back into his chair. He ran his hands over his head, pulled his ponytail through his fists. "I do feel better, Phil."

"So, I'll see you tomorrow. At your mum's. Stay off the pop, mate."

Rob saluted. "Absolutely," he said. He went to stand up. "Bloody fuck," he said.

"What?" Trevena watched Rob's expression change from relieved complacency to outright horror. He was staring at the jar.

The head had opened its eyes. They rolled in the ash-beds of their sockets and glared at Trevena. And then they swivelled and peered with an avid expectancy towards the office door. Trevena swung around. His hands gripped the chair's armrests. He stood slowly. Something was behind the door. He could feel it. There was a line of shadow beneath it, blocking the light reflecting off the floor of the corridor.

He crossed the office and gripped the handle. He looked back at the jar. Rob was cowering in his chair. He looked up at Trevena, saw his hand on the doorknob, and shook his head, his expression beseeching.

The eyes blazed in the remains of the face in the jar and Trevena could hear it now; could hear something calling from a cosmos away, sending out its signal like a black, probing filament. It made his mind feel cold and unable to resist.

He opened the door.

Andrew Chapel was outside.

"Hi, Mr. Trevena," he said brightly, and hit Trevena over the head with something that felt like a piece of iron.

As he collapsed to the floor, his vision blurring, fading, Trevena could hear Rob shouting for help. Whether for himself or for both of them, Trevena might never find out.

All went dark.

* * *

TREVENA CAME TO lying on his back on the office floor. Emily the receptionist was kneeling beside him pressing a cold, wet hand towel to the top of his head.

He tried to sit up but Emily scolded him and told him to stay put. There was a cushion behind his head and he sank back down with a groan and stared at the ceiling. His vision was blurry.

"Where's Rob?" he asked.

"Who?"

"The man who came to see me yesterday, the drunk in reception."

Emily shrugged. "No idea. Did he attack you, Phil? I've called an ambulance."

"No," Trevena said, and this time managed to sit up despite Emily's protestations. His vision swam and he felt nausea rise in his throat. "I'm ok."

"You've got a head wound! It's still bleeding."

Trevena looked around. The office was empty. The bag and the jar were gone.

"Help me up," he said.

Emily tutted. "You shouldn't have been seeing patients here on your own, Phil. It's dangerous."

"It wasn't Rob," Trevena said. He struggled to his feet and stood on rickety legs. He put a hand out and steadied himself against the wall.

"Did you see who it was?"

"No," Trevena lied. "Someone jumped us." His head was pounding.

They heard footsteps in the corridor and a green suited paramedic put his head around the door. He looked about twelve. "Emily Moneypenny?" he enquired.

Emily held out the towel. It was scarlet. Trevena staggered a little and made it to a chair where he sat, white-faced, gagging.

"Tell him," Emily said to the paramedic. "He's being all brave."

EMILY DROVE TREVENA home. The paramedic had recommended A&E for stitches, but Trevena had declined. The paramedic had been cheerful enough and whistled a toneless version of Walking On Sunshine while he patched Trevena up and did his best to hold his gashed scalp together with steri-strips. He had given Trevena a card with the signs and symptoms of concussion printed on it and then left, lugging a lime green medi-kit the size of a laundry bag over his shoulder.

Now Trevena sat in the front seat of Emily's tidy, fragrant little Golf with a huge dressing bandaged to the top of his head. His neck and ears were a washed out pink where they had tried to scrub off the blood. He looked sunburned. His hair was matted and crusty with dried blood. He felt like he'd been hit with an axe.

Emily was giving him the silent treatment. Trevena felt the urge to justify his decision not to go to A&E but kept fighting it, not wanting to get drawn into a conversation about what had happened. He'd have plenty of explaining to do to his boss soon enough. And the police wanted to interview him, of course. Emily had been thorough enough to let them know about the assault.

"Bollocks," he said, unable to contain his frustration.

"What?"

"My head hurts," he said.

"Well, you know what I think."

"Yes, yes, yes. It's good of you to give me a lift, Em. I'll make it up to you."

Emily glanced at him.

"Dinner and a show?"

Emily was about to reply but Trevena was saved the sarcasm as his mobile rang. He lifted it from his coat pocket and put it gingerly to his ear.

"Phil Trevena."

"Can you move your car? I've got a drug lunch."

Trevena closed his eyes against the onslaught of his headache.

Emily dropped him off and took his car keys.

"Thanks for all this, Em," he said as he got out of the Golf.

Emily shook her head. "I'll drop these back later, Phil. Have a rest."

Trevena gave her a weak smile. He patted the roof of the car and closed the door.

"Phil," Emily said, leaning across the passenger seat and looking up at him through the half open window.

"Yeah?"

"Maybe just dinner." She put the car in gear and pulled away leaving Trevena standing at the roadside perplexed and in a lot of pain.

TREVENA LET HIMSELF in and went straight into the kitchen. He sat on a stool at the breakfast bar and got out his mobile. He grimaced at the pain in his head and thumbed through his contacts until he reached the number he needed to call.

As the phone rang he leaned his elbows on the bar and closed his eyes.

"Hello," a young woman's voice said.

"Hi. Can I speak to Doctor Mocking, please?"

It had been six and a half years since Trevena had called the Doctor's office. He'd assumed the Doc had continued practising, but the voice on the other end made him sit up and open his eyes. The kitchen was bright with morning sunlight and he winced. He recognised the voice.

"Lesley?" he said.

"Is that you, Phil?" she said, and Trevena could discern the emotion there, the depth of feeling.

"Yeah, it's me, Lesley. How are you?"

For a moment there was silence and then Trevena heard Lesley's voice, muffled as though she was holding the phone away from her mouth. "*It's Phil*!" he heard her say. Then she came back on the line. "I'm fine, Phil."

Trevena caught the hesitation. "What is it, Lesley?"

Lesley began to cry.

* * *

TREVENA CALLED A taxi and stood on the pavement waiting for it to arrive. When it pulled up at the curb he slid into the passenger seat and gave the driver the address to Doctor Mocking's office.

They headed off across town in heavy mid-morning traffic. Trevena flipped the visor down to block the sunlight. He was wearing sunglasses. The dressing bandaged to his head felt damp and he hoped blood hadn't soaked all the way through. He reached up and touched it with his fingertips, but they came away dry.

Mercifully, the driver was of the taciturn stripe and they took the ride in silence. Trevena rested his head on the back of the seat and thought about what Lesley had told him. Doctor Mocking, her father, was dying. They were all there with him, awaiting his last wishes. If Phil had news, he should come fast and let them all hear it. Anxiety tightened his chest. It had been seven years. What was he going to say?

The cab pulled up on a tree-lined avenue. Trevena paid the fare and walked up to the gates of a large detached three-storey house set in private grounds. There was an apple orchard at the rear, he knew, and a little stream with two bridges. Not visible from the front was a small wing, an addition, where Doctor Mocking had his office. It overlooked the orchard. Trevena had sat and gazed out at that orchard at weekly intervals for two months following his divorce from Carol. They had discussed his dreams, and something had come for them, something ancient and unremitting and evil and he had been drawn into a battle the outcome of which might have been the end of everything. But they had won. Or thought they had.

Trevena walked up the path and rang the antique, push-button doorbell.

He watched the shadow of a figure approach through the stained glass window set into the door. There was the sound of a heavy bolt being drawn back and the door opened. He took off his sunglasses, folded them and put them in the pocket of his jacket.

"Hi, Lesley," Trevena said. "You've grown."

Lesley stepped out onto the porch and embraced him. The last time Trevena had seen her she had been a child, almost a teenager. She was beautiful. He looked into her face and smiled. "Are you hurt?" he said. As they had embraced he had felt Lesley tense.

Lesley patted her chest. "Bandages. Not broken but badly bruised."

"You've got to stop getting in fights."

"You haven't changed a bit, Phil," Lesley said and Trevena could see the tears in her eyes, catching the sunlight that glimmered through the trees, making them sparkle.

"Not bad for a fifty-five year old," he said. "All things considered."

"What happened to your head?"

"Had a work-related accident," he said. "It's why I'm here."

Lesley led him through the wide, panelled hallway into the living room. Three people were sitting together on a plump floral sofa. A child played on the rug near the French windows, her dark hair long and glossy. She was walking a toy tiger across the jungle pattern in the rug.

Trevena felt emotion overwhelm him and he reached out as the man and the two women stood to greet him. The child looked up and smiled.

Lesley said, "You remember Steve and Claire? And Elizabeth?"

"Of course," Trevena said. He gripped Steve Iden's hand and shook, and then was grabbed in a fierce hug by his wife, Claire, and then Elizabeth.

"This must be Chloe," Trevena said, smiling at the child by the window. He couldn't help feeling a sense of awe as he appraised the child, knowing how powerful she was, how precious. Chloe looked up and gazed at Trevena, her eyes wide, dark and direct. "Hello, Phil," she said. "Come and sit by me."

Trevena looked to her parents for some indication of Chloe's intent. Steve said, "I think she wants to look at that head." Claire seemed in agreement, her appealing face open and expectant.

Trevena went and sat cross-legged next to Chloe on the jungle-patterned rug. She put the toy tiger in her lap—it was a small, fierce-looking plastic tiger with a tail curled like a crook. Trevena knew him well; they had done work together—and then she said, "Lean forward and close your eyes."

Trevena hunched forward and his knees popped.

"I'm getting too old for yoga, Chloe," he said.

"This isn't yoga," Chloe said. "This is much older. Shush now and keep your eyes shut."

Trevena felt her small fingers touch his temples.

"Don't open the door!" Rob said to me.

I heard him but the urge was there, pulling through my brain like a black, barbed line. You know what it felt like, Chloe? It felt like an addiction to something terrible, something lethal. Impossible to resist even though you knew the next hit would kill you.

So I opened the door.

Andrew Chapel was there. He looked well. That's the first thing I noticed, even in that split second of recognition. He looked peaceful, flushed—satisfied. Nothing like the pale, drawn, deeply troubled man I had seen the previous day.

He spoke, a greeting, and then he raised his hand and it held something heavy. It was a hammer. I realise now that it was a stone carving hammer. He had been using it to sculpt something. I could see where the head was discoloured from pounding at the handles of chisels. I saw all this in great detail as his arm came up.

And then I heard your voice, Chloe. It was very clear. I knew it was you. You told me to stand aside. I stepped back, away from Chapel and watched as he lowered his arm, his expression suddenly baffled. Then he refocused and walked past me into the office. He bent slightly and peered at Rob. Rob was cowering in the chair. I don't blame him. Chapel had an aura, and it was as malevolent and compelling as that filament that had reeled through my head. Chapel snarled and said, "Get out!" like he was commanding a dog. Rob got up and ran. Again, I can't blame him. Chapel was horrifying in that moment.

I continued to watch from the door. Chapel grabbed the handles of the bag and pulled them upwards, concealing the remains in the jar, and then lifted it, holding it to his chest. He turned and I saw how his eyes were black holes. I couldn't look away, although I wanted to. I thought at first they had been scooped from his head and what I was seeing were the recesses of his empty sockets, but as he walked past me carrying the bag I saw that he still had eyes only they were like lenses looking into an infinity of living darkness. He might have wished he had been blinded, considering the things there must have been out there to see.

He went past me and turned and headed down the corridor. He went through the double doors and left the unit.

I closed the office door and followed him but when I got outside he was gone.

I went to my car and drove home.

I phoned Doctor Mocking and then I came here.

TREVENA OPENED HIS eyes.

Chloe sat before him. She looked pale.

"You okay, Chloe?" Trevena asked. He reached out and took one of her slender hands.

"Yes," she said. She stood and reached for his head. "Don't move."

Trevena ducked his head towards her as she pulled at the bandage holding the dressing to his scalp. She removed it and held it out to him. He took it from her, astonished. The dressing was dry and bloodless. He reached up and probed his scalp. The wound was gone. Not healed, but *gone*. It had never been there.

His headache was gone, too.

"What did you just do?" He asked.

Chloe sat down again and picked up Bronze John. She resumed trotting him through the fronds of the jungle.

"I changed what things I could," she said. "There was no need for you to get hurt."

"Did that really happen? Why didn't I fight?"

Chloe didn't look up. Bronze John paused in his roaming.

"You're not a puppet. I could only have asked you to fight and then you would have died. I needed to protect you. I couldn't stop Chapel, either. He was too powerful."

"Who *is* he?"

Chloe shrugged.

"I think he's a Firmament Surgeon," she said.

STEVE CAME OVER and knelt by his daughter. "Are you okay, sweetheart?"

Chloe nodded. She had regained her colour. She tilted her head and let her dad kiss her cheek. She touched his face, smiled.

"Very *composed*, isn't she?" Trevena said, getting to his feet.

"Very," said Steve.

"You think Chapel's a Firmament Surgeon?"

"Yes," Chloe said. "He's being corrupted. He's not an Autoscope yet. He hasn't entirely fallen. Something is stopping that happening. I could feel it, his resistance."

Trevena looked around the room seeking confirmation or denial from the others, but they all looked as perplexed by Chloe's revelation as he felt.

"I think it's time to see Doctor Mocking," Trevena said.

ELIZABETH LED TREVENA up a wide staircase onto an airy landing.

"They're in here," she said. It had been seven years since Trevena had seen Elizabeth. Those years had been kind to her.

"You look happy," he said.

"I have a good man."

"I know that for sure. It's going to be strange seeing them all again. I'm not sure how I feel. I'm not like them. I might implode or something."

Elizabeth laughed. "*I'm* like you," she said. "And I've been bringing them all snacks and drinks all bloody day since they arrived. If anyone's going to implode, it'll be me. Go on in, Phil. They're all looking forward to seeing you."

Not entirely mollified, Trevena opened the bedroom door and went in.

THEIR GREETING DISPELLED any fears he might have had. Bismuth lifted a hand from a huge leather armchair in the corner of the room and nodded. Alex and Eliot stepped up and shook his hand with the firm grips of boys on the edge of manhood, heartening, testing squeezes. They looked strong and fit and just a little wild. A big hug and a kiss from Anna, Lesley's younger sister. She grabbed him by the neck and put her head on his shoulder and Trevena was transported back to a time on a benighted promenade when she held onto him like that, a little girl terrified but finally safe. Jon Index gripped his elbow as he shook and Trevena was suffused with relief that the man's presence hadn't brought on a stroke. Of them all, Index made him feel as weak as a kitten. John Stainwright smiled and nodded from where he stood in the recess of the bay window; Trevena knew him least, a quiet, peaceful, introspective man whom he nonetheless respected as much as he did the others.

Trevena muttered *hellos* and did his best to keep his dignity, but when Daniel stepped around the bed and hugged him, Trevena's resolve broke and he felt tears well up, prickling and uncomfortable. He swiped the back of his hand across his face and sniffed. He looked at Daniel and saw, to his surprise, that he, too, was fighting back the tears. The harmony of their emotions gave Trevena back the dignity he felt he was losing.

"Thanks for coming, Phil," Daniel said.

"Look at you," Trevena said. "Pull yourself together, man." He sniffed again and laughed.

"Phil."

Trevena walked up to the side of the bed.

"Hi Doc," he said. He took the doctor's proffered hand. There was still strength to the grip, but Doctor Mocking looked frail and tired, propped up with the pillows against the cast iron headboard of his modest single bed.

"Sit down here beside me."

Trevena sat on the edge of the bed.

"It's good to see you again," Doctor Mocking said. "Are things well?"

Trevena felt a surge of strong emotion again and willed it down, suppressing it as best he could. "I'm good," he managed to say. "Thanks to you."

Doctor Mocking closed his eyes and patted the back of Trevena's hand.

"I'm pleased," he said. Then he opened his eyes and looked around the room. "Right. Help me sit up a bit. We need to talk."

THINK OF IT like a handover, thought Trevena. Keep it simple and be professional. He swallowed, his mouth dry. The expectant faces of the people surrounding him made him feel inadequate to the task of conveying his information. He knew something of these extraordinary beings, but he realised that it was at best patchy. There were few of them left and those that remained had been scattered, almost destroyed by the devil-in-dreams and his ruthless Autoscopes in a war over aeons for control of Dark Time. Trevena had watched them come together, rally themselves, and become the Night Clock, taking command of Dark Time and the dreams it made possible. It needed all ten of them to make it theirs, otherwise they did not have the cohesion to possess it and the Autoscopes would gain authority over the Night Clock, as sickening as that sounded, and dreams would cease. Dark Time would run down forever, evaporate, its phantasmagorical infinity obliterated. And the Quays, those cities and lands woven by the Firmament Surgeons for the purpose of safety and the principles of plenitude would be destroyed, laid waste and consumed by entropy.

If Doctor Mocking died, what of the Night Clock?

Trevena looked down at his hands. The room was hushed, deferential.

Imagine they're all Consultants, he thought. Which, he supposed, they were.

Speaking with care, keeping to the facts, Trevena told them everything that had happened since Andrew Chapel had come for his first assessment.

DOCTOR MOCKING WAS speaking.

"We've spent the last seven years trying to destroy as many of the Autoscopes as we can. A task made easier because they are confused, disorganised without the influence of the devil-in-dreams. But they greatly outnumbered us so progress has been slow. We are starting to encounter more of the Higher Ones, though, which could mean one of two things. They are perhaps depleted to the point where the generals are being flushed into battle, or the containment we set up to hold the devil-in-dreams is failing. I imagine it's probably both, based on the evidence you gave us, Phil. It confirms what I theorised.

"In anticipation of one of us dying, or being killed, we have made every effort to weaken the Autoscopes' power, but with the threat of the devil-in-dreams breaking out it would have been for nothing. It is imperative we seal the breach and arrest whatever is causing it.

"Chloe is correct. Andrew Chapel is key to this. He's fighting whatever is happening to him. Both by his suicide attempt and by coming to you, Phil. He is, however, *incredibly* conflicted and we need to find him before he is lost forever.

"What do we think about Barry Cook's head?"

"It's simple," Daniel said. "We fucked up."

Doctor Mocking nodded.

"We did," he said. "Do you want to elaborate, Daniel?"

Daniel was sitting on a blanket box at the foot of the doctor's bed. He ran a hand over his face.

"We left his body burning in a field. We made *assumptions*. We assumed that his family would conceal evidence for form's sake. We thought they would accept it as suicide and that the police would be disinclined to investigate thoroughly because of his history. Relief for the family at last and one less sex offender for the force to worry about. But they obviously didn't report him dead and probably told the police and probation he'd gone missing. Phil, he'd been one of your patients. Did you get an alert?"

Trevena shook his head. "He wasn't on the books at the time. Slipped through the net. Nothing new. Maybe, because I knew what had happened, I didn't look out for it."

"Not your fault. This is down to us. I think the devil-in-dreams managed to reach out to Barry's family before it was contained. They were in a hypnopompic state but I was casting it very wide, much wider than I have before, and I think it must have given the devil-in-dreams a split second to send a message or implant a beacon."

"Both. The family heard the message. The head's the beacon," Jon Index said. "They kept it frozen for seven years. We sealed the devil-in-dreams in a Quay in a dead man's dream and we thought it had burned. It didn't. Something remains and it's gathering its forces to break it out. Doctor Mocking's approaching death has weakened us and strengthened them."

Trevena wondered at the frankness of Index's comments but he considered the ways of these beings and put his ethics in perspective. Doctor Mocking spoke again, and confirmed Trevena's thoughts.

"We need to make a decision. I'm sick and I'm dying. If I die here then I will be reborn. But what use will I be to you as a baby? And you will have to track me down. Chloe might be able to do it faster than all of the rest of you put together, but that is untested. While you're distracted looking for me, the devil-in-dreams would break out. If I go back to my Quay I'll live on but I won't ever be able to come back through, and without the ability to travel between times I will be a weakened component of the Night Clock and this will empower the devil-in-dreams to come after me there. If I die in my

Quay I am gone forever, never to be reborn.

"So, I have a theory, and it entails a request and your faith." He paused. Trevena looked around the room. Everyone was standing, pressed together around the bed. Anna and Lesley were by their father's side. "I am going back to the Compartment. I might die there, but the result is unknown. It is worth the risk. There is someone there I need to find. And, because I am so weak, I will need one of you to come with me."

EVERYONE HAD AN opinion on that and the confusion of their voices brought Elizabeth, Steve and Claire to the door. Chloe stood between her parents, holding her mother's hand, listening intently as the discussion continued. The voices died down when Chloe spoke.

"Doctor Mocking's right," she said. "I'll go with him."

She let go of her mother's hand and approached the bed. Doctor Mocking smiled and held out a hand. Chloe climbed up onto the bed beside him and looked into his eyes.

Daniel came over and stood next to Trevena.

"We don't know what happens if a Firmament Surgeon dies in a Gantry. It's something that has never happened. The Gantries take us from linear time through to the Quays and give us access to the Dark Time flux. They're portals, but they're neither part of this world or the world of the Quays. They're immense, unfathomable even to us. It's all the dimensions of God and we're allowed narrow paths through it."

Trevena knew some of this but the enormity of these portals had escaped him. He'd imagined them as gateways but his mind was too paltry to grasp their incalculable scope.

"Do you remember the name Robin Knox?" Daniel asked.

Trevena thought for a moment. The name was familiar. "He was one of you. He died before you could all get together."

"He was attacked in a Gantry by Ray Cade. Cade burst through as it opened and Robin confronted him. The others got away but, as you know, Cade found a way into the Quays and snatched Anna."

Trevena's expression was grim. He remembered it all too clearly. The red castle, and the beast in the mirror, standing over the dying Doctor Mocking. "Cade's dead." He spoke it as a fact to calm himself, not as a question. He knew full well the fate of Cade, torn to shreds by the tiger, Bronze John.

"Doctor Mocking thinks Robin may still be there, trapped between the two worlds. Unable to be reborn and unable to return to the Quays. Lost."

"How long have you known this?" Trevena was shocked, horrified to think of Robin wandering the chambers of God for the last seven years, in limbo, alone.

"It's always been a theory. But there's no way of knowing. Not until one of us goes back to the Compartment to find him. And that's something we felt was best avoided." Daniel was looking askance at Trevena as if reading his thoughts. Trevena felt abashed.

"We do have *some* evidence, though."

It was Bismuth's time to speak.

"I WAS LOST. Lost in a labyrinth of golden Looms. The paths were everlasting and the light a desert brightness. The Looms were immense, like cathedrals and they wove and wove and wove, on and on, the blistering fabric of God. He creates, and creates, and all I could hear was a thundering sound I knew was a Word. A Word that drove the shuttles and pedalled the Looms. There was clockwork, too, cogs the size of Saturn's rings, all turning in spirals a million miles away towards a terrible, blinding rim. The rim was no end to the place. It was like the wall of a cell, and beyond it an infinity of others like it. I wandered, lost in grief. A grief that had unhinged me and sent me out into this vastness to go insane. I wanted to go insane because that thing, that devil-in-dreams, had broken me. I had been locked into a loop of Dark Time and relived the loss of my father forever. I loved my father. I had thrown myself from the path of the Gantry to thwart the devil-in-dreams and break free of the loop. But I was lost. My friend searched for me and found me. Doctor Mocking risked himself, his sanity, to walk the labyrinth and save me. Without him there would be no Night Clock. There would be nothing. We must trust him. I was not dead and my life force led Doctor Mocking to me, but if we can breach the threshold and survive then perhaps Robin has survived, too. It is pure creation energy there. How can anything truly die?"

"CHAPEL IS CAUSING ripples," Doctor Mocking said. He was sitting up against his pillows. Lesley and Anna had helped him get dressed. He was wearing a black suit and tie, and a long black coat. His shoes were black and shiny. Everyone stood in anticipation around the bed. Chloe sat beside Doctor Mocking and held his hand. "If we can find Robin and free him from beyond the Gantry it might give us enough power to find this breach and seal it. I leave the rest of you to find Andrew Chapel and take care of the remains of Barry Cook."

They said goodbyes then. Doctor Mocking and Chloe were kissed and held. Claire and Steve had a moment to hold Chloe but they were so distressed Lesley and Elizabeth took them from the room and away to comfort them. Chloe had gone into a semi-trance; her eyes shone but did not focus on anyone in the room.

Doctor Mocking closed his eyes. He squeezed Chloe's hand. "Are you ready, my angel?" he said.

"We're there," Chloe said.

DOCTOR MOCKING OPENED his eyes.

He and Chloe were standing on a golden path. Ahead the Gantry was open, the portal to a Quay. The portal was a few steps away. It was a billion miles away.

Chloe was holding his hand. He smiled at her.

"I don't feel dead," he said. His voice had a quality of brightness, a belling of sound both divine and unfamiliar. He realised he had

never uttered a word in transit before.

He laughed, and that sound was truly enormous, a shofar sound, haunting and booming. He moved his lips in a musician's embouchure, tightened the muscles of his cheeks, and the sound of his laugh lengthened, bugled, and Chloe laughed beside him, and Doctor Mocking had to cover his ears because the sound was so lovely he could hardly bear it.

"I don't think you can die here," Chloe said. "In-between. You can get lost, but not die." Her voice was gorgeous, the World's songbirds' entire twilight chorus.

Doctor Mocking pointed outwards, beyond the shimmering wall of light that was the margin of the path.

"Can we find him, do you think, Chloe?"

Chloe walked to the edge of the path. She put out a hand and the light pattered and jumped on her palm, parting in a gleaming, brazen tear where she touched it. They could hear the sound of the Gantry, the enormity of it, telling of unendurable distances beyond and forever.

"I know where he is," Chloe said. "I can feel him."

Doctor Mocking went to her side.

Holding hands once again, they stepped through the wall of light.

THEY LEFT DOCTOR Mocking's house and travelled in two cars through Norfolk to a caravan park near the coast of Invidisham-next-the-Sea. John Stainwright lived there in a refurbished static caravan, and they agreed it would make a good base from which to plan their next moves. It also gave Elizabeth the space she said she wanted for Steve and Claire. They wanted to be at the house, close to where they had last seen their daughter. In case she returned there, alone, frightened, hurt; they were in shock, devastated, but allowed Elizabeth to console them. Index withdrew to Doctor Mocking's study. He, too, would stay, to protect and monitor.

Trevena rode in John Stainwright's antique white Hillman Minx. It smelt of dog and old leather. Alex and Eliot sat on the big bench back seat rattling about without the advantage of seat belts. Trevena had pulled a couple of old fabric straps across his lap and fitted them together with a hinged clip.

"Is this even legal?" he asked as they pulled away from the curb outside Doctor Mocking's house with a lurch. He held onto the armrests.

"Not particularly," John said.

Daniel followed in a muddy green army jeep. It suited him, with his short grey beard, creased, sun-swept face, desert boots and long khaki coat. Bismuth sat beside him looking grim and uncomfortable with Lesley and Anna in the back.

They pulled off the main road and turned down a smart, well-kept tarmac drive. The sign at the entrance read RESERVOIR END CARAVAN PARK.

They pulled up in a car park in front of a long single-storey building advertising gifts, coffee shop and reception. Ahead, broad boulevards stretched off into the park bordered by ranks of colourful static caravans. Most of them had small decking areas and bright, fluttering awnings. The grass was cut short and interspersed with tidy flowerbeds and shrubs.

"This is nice," Trevena said, climbing stiffly from the Minx.

"We like it," John said. "It suits us."

Daniel swung the jeep in beside them and they all followed John along one of the boulevards. They came to one of the caravans and stopped. Trevena appraised it. It was painted an ocean blue and covered with sea-going paraphernalia. There were fishing nets, creels and lobster pots, red and white striped life buoy rings and multi-coloured floats and spinners. Portholes had been painted on the slatted wooden sides. Trevena thought it was another gift shop, but when John led them up into the cool of the interior he realised how wrong he was. He pushed through the rainbow strips of a fly blind and found himself in a small, shady clubhouse. There was a tiny bar in the corner lit up with fairy lights.

There was an old man standing behind the bar, wiping a dented tin pub ashtray with a chequered cloth. He must have been in his early seventies. He had the courageous remains of a thin grey ponytail hanging down his skinny back. He was wearing a T-shirt with a palm tree on it. He looked up as they came in and grinned with enormous and palpable joy. He didn't have a tooth left in his head. As he threw down the cloth and made to come around the bar a dog barked and stood, wagging its long, feathery tail, from where it had been snoozing behind the bar stools.

"A coach party, Bix!" the man cried. "Just what I need."

TREVENA AND DANIEL sat at Colin Dack's fragrant little bar. It had been a perfume counter decades before, in one of the old department stores in Invidisham-next-the-Sea. Colin had salvaged it from a skip. It still held the memories of all those perfumes spritzed across it; they had sunk into the wood and lingered there. Colin liked to think of the bar as an instrument, an olfactory piano, constantly giving off motes of fragrance rather than notes of sound. A seductive, timeless symphony of scent.

He was explaining this to Trevena. It just made Trevena want to sneeze.

"All those happy customers," Colin was saying. "All those lovely ladies!"

Trevena thought about the lovely ladies he'd seen working at perfume counters on the few occasions he'd had to go near them. Faces stiff with mortuary-grade makeup and eyes that went dead the moment you showed disinterest in their stall.

"You still doing those caravan towing courses, Colin?" he asked.

"Not so much these days. Not much call for it. You interested, Phil?"

"Frankly, no, Colin."

"Well, the offer's there. You want another pint?"

Trevena shook his head. He had only choked down a couple of mouthfuls of Colin's home-brew so far. How did he get a licence for this place?

"I could make punch?"

"This'll do me, Colin. Thanks."

Bismuth came up to the bar. He had to duck beneath the low ceiling and peer through the string of flickering lights above the bar. He put his empty pint glass down.

"I've got a taste for this," he said.

Colin beamed, delighted and refilled Bismuth's glass from a steel barrel beneath the counter. "Crusader," he said. "Been brewing it for years. It's my best seller, isn't it, John?"

"Yes, Colin. It flies out of the door," John said. He was sitting at a small table in the middle of the clubhouse floor with Alex and Eliot, playing cards. None of them had touched their pints. Lesley and Anna had gone for a walk around the park, declining Colin's generous offer of a free bar for the day, in search of ice creams. Bix looked contented, lying at John's feet with his nose in a packet of crisps.

Daniel said to Trevena, "You know this Andrew Chapel, Phil. You're the only one who has met him. What do you think?"

"I don't think he knows himself. He reported having visions of black polygons, all tethered together across the sky. Very nihilistic. He thought he had seen the real fabric behind reality and it was just mathematics and chaos, all utterly meaningless. It didn't feel completely delusional. It was very *angry*. Angry in a suppressed and unconscious way."

Bismuth put his glass down on the bar. Trevena looked up at him. He put a hand on Daniel's arm and indicated with a glance that Daniel should look, too.

Bismuth was standing stock-still, his head touching the ceiling of the bar. His eyes were wide and his mouth was trembling behind the untended curls of his beard.

"What is it?" Daniel said. He got off his stool and looked up into the giant's face. "Bismuth!"

"Black polygons," he said. "Blocks of darkness."

"Yes," Trevena said. "He was obsessed by them."

Bismuth relaxed. He refocused, looked around the room. Everyone was staring at him. He put a hand on his belt, where his levers were held in loops at his sides.

"I know who Chapel is," he said. "He's the boy in the refrigerator."

THEY DREW THEIR plans, sitting around two of the clubhouse tables that had been pushed together. Lesley and Anna had returned, their lips red and shiny from the Rocket lollies they had bought at the gift shop. Bismuth was agitated. He wanted to get on with things, but Daniel and John managed to calm him sufficiently to get him to sit with the rest of them at the tables. He sat scowling, perched on a stool, looking like an adult at a child's tea party. He had declined Colin's second pint and had left it on the bar, to Colin's visible disappointment.

Before Bismuth had been reunited with the others, he had been lost, wandering, seeking the oblivion of insanity. But before that he had been caught, trapped and deceived in a loop of Dark Time, made to relive bereavement and loss, over and over again. His gift as a Firmament Surgeon had been his ability to enter the dreams of the bereaved, the broken and those stuck in denial, and free them, removing them from the dream and allowing acceptance to replace the devastation. The devil-in-dreams had used this ability against him and manipulated Bismuth's loss to perpetuate his cycle. He had become stuck, unable to realise what had been done to him. Doctor Mocking had saved him and brought him back to the fold.

Bismuth had been lost, but his powers had remained, and before he cast himself from the Gantry he had seen something amongst the bombsites of a mother's dream: a refrigerator, old and rusty standing in the distance, on a dais of concrete. It shone, he recalled, in that concrete greyness, and he called to the mother not to open it, in God's name. As he had scrambled over masonry and cables he knew he would be too late, and she reached out and opened the door.

Her screams had done for him, Bismuth had said. It was the last time he travelled and he threw himself into the brazen, consuming magnitude of the Gantry with her screams still howling in his head.

After the Night Clock had been assembled he had made it his mission to find the residue of the dream, track down any echo of it remaining in Dark Time. It had become his obsession, to find the boy in the refrigerator and set him free. Because, as the mother had opened the door and seen the child dead in there, blue and cold and cramped into that shallow space, Bismuth had seen something else. The child had opened its eyes. They were black but far from dead.

He had found it by chance, in a dump, tracking down and killing an Autoscope that had fled there during the Firmament Surgeons' purge following the gathering of the Night Clock. He had stood before it, the remains of the Autoscope beneath his boots, already rotting into the filth, and reached out a trembling hand.

It had been empty. It was always empty. Seven years and over a thousand battles across that dump but at the end, it was always empty. Until the last time.

"It was a block of darkness," Bismuth said. "Living. The boy was in it. I could see his eyes. I thought I had lost him."

"Why do you think it's Chapel?" Lesley asked.

"Synchronicity, archetypes. They're what we work with, isn't it. The architecture and calculus of the Night Clock. I think the boy was trapped, lured there in childhood. He was a reborn Firmament Surgeon as lost as the rest of us, but never grew up to be found and become a part of us. Chloe said she thinks Chapel is a Firmament Surgeon but in the throes of corruption. I *feel* it's him. They're the same person. The devil-in-dreams has kept the boy in a loop, feeding off him, making him relive his nightmare the same way he made me relive mine.

"Chapel's depersonalisation and visions of dark blocks, polygons. He's externalised the darkness within the fridge, that cold, blind hell, into his art. He's communicating with himself."

Trevena spoke, "That makes sense. But how can he be in two places? Trapped in a refrigerator and alive and growing up as Chapel?"

"Chapel the boy is trapped in Dark Time, in a dream, or part of a Quay. Chapel the man was allowed to grow up for the purpose of being controlled and corrupted, to be turned before we could find him. He has been saved for a mission. The devil-in-dreams has tried to outthink us. It has almost succeeded."

* * *

"He's probably felt like shit his whole life," Daniel said.

Trevena agreed. "When I assessed him that was what came across in his history. I thought at first he had a personality disorder, something narcissistic or schizoid. An emptiness. It explains the depersonalisation and detachment."

"Something essentially missing."

"Yes. Exactly. There's one other thing, though. It bothered me at the time and it's bothering me now. He spoke of having a child. Male. He never referred to him as his son, though, or called him by name. Just *his child*. It was odd, but I put that down to the lack of emotional involvement. I was going to ask him about it, next time I saw him."

"I don't think he's got a child," John said. "The child's *him*. A projection. He's holding them both together. He's been doing it all his life."

Bismuth stood up, the stool scraping across the lino.

"And he's just broken the connection. We need to move. Now."

Part Four

Unease

CHAPEL AWOKE ON his bed, in the dark, close to panic, everything feeling loosened by emotion and misrepresented. He had done something terrible, had hurt someone. The memory was vague, pressure against the back of his eyes like a headache.

He remembered leaving the hospital and hiding in the recesses of an unlocked garage overnight, feeling cold and disoriented, not knowing where to go next or why he was there. At some point in the night he had fallen asleep squatting against the wall and something outside had been trying to fumble the door open, but without the strength to lift it. He had jerked awake from a thin and grainy sleep, and had sat frozen while the fumbling continued. And then it had stopped, and he was able to exhale a long-held breath, his ears ringing in the sudden silence, hyper-vigilant. The voice had spoken from outside and he had had to bite down on his bottom lip to prevent a scream, because he recognised it. He listened wide-eyed, and eventually, when it became too much to bear, he agreed to do what it was asking of him. When he crept to the garage door and pulled it open he saw that it was first light. He remembered going back to the hospital. He remembered hurting someone and taking something. He remembered the taxi ride home, huddling in the back seat clutching what he had taken, sweating and confused, his thoughts no longer his alone. He had let himself into the cottage and gone straight to sleep, exhausted, shaken.

The dark bedroom pulsed, the furniture seeming to pull away from his eyes when he darted them around, trying to focus on something reassuring, something real. They looked like alien objects and he struggled to find names for them. He awoke to the immediate sensation of weeping. Tears were teeming down his face even as he was opening his eyes, flowing from the well within him that untapped when he slept. He sat up on the side of the bed and sobbed, unable to locate anything; his memories shuffled like the pages of a book in a cold wind, and he couldn't trap a page, make it settle on some comforting and happy image that might complete him for a while, might take away this awful feeling of loss and disconnection.

He felt his mind groping and sobbed again, hating the sensation but unable to stop it. He stood up and walked on unsteady legs around the bed.

He was certain that nothing was real, his memories vague fabrications, and that everything was a film he had been ghosted out of. He groped about, feeling translucent, panic rising, just trying to grasp something that would make his world three-dimensional again. There was an elusiveness to the *sense* of everything and everyone, an evasion of solidity. He even tried to use his imagination, to disarm the horrors of unreality by peering further, stripping things down to what he knew they were; but there was only absurdity to the molecules that made him and atoms made his mind reel with their racing, terrible spaces.

The first time it had happened he had awoken in pitch darkness, blind and mindless. He found himself blundering around a formless place, expanding without boundaries into that space and all of him a part of it, stretching forever, until he brushed against something soft and reached out and grasped it. He pulled on it and the heavy curtain drew back from the window and moonlight switched everything back on in his head. He stood staring out into the night, heart racing, eyes wide and startled, and at last began to recall who he was and where he was.

Now he waited until his eyes became more accustomed to the darkness and then made his way out of the bedroom. He paused on the landing and glanced around. He still felt alarmed by the dismaying scale of consciousness. He could feel his heart beating tightly in his chest and pressed the palm of his hand over it, feeling the pain in the muscles there, and the tingling in his fingers

He wanted the toilet, but couldn't face the stark light in the bathroom. It would throw his face back at him in the mirrors and he couldn't stand to see himself and not be certain at whom he was looking. And the bath and sink and the toilet bowl would all glare white, gnashing out at him like huge teeth in a shiny mouth, and that would be awful.

He felt everything in him drawn down into his heart, and he tried to locate himself there in the throbbing chambers, but the darkness of the rushing blood submersed him and drove him back out so that he was standing at the top of the stairs listening to it rushing and beating in his ears.

He went downstairs in his boxer shorts and let himself out into his back yard. He stood in dim twilight and urinated into the drain beneath the gutter downpipe. When he had finished he went across the yard in bare feet and stood outside his workshop. He could hear whispering from inside, cunning and insistent. He looked up into the sky. The light remaining on the horizon was brown and exposed a black mountainscape of jagged, tilted vertices.

Chapel turned his back on the polygons and went into his workshop. The bag was there, with the jar still inside, placed on his workbench that morning before he had gone inside the house. He couldn't have stood having it in the house, not seeping that awful, constant invocation.

But now he listened, and began acting on what he heard.

BISMUTH STOOD AT the edge of the boulevard outside Colin's clubhouse. It was already getting dark. Trevena figured they had been at the caravan park for about five hours, thinking, talking, planning.

Bismuth was holding a lever in his right fist. In his left hand he held a compass. It was antique-looking, silver, and seemed to be without cardinal points.

He slid the end of the lever into the soft earth of the verge at the foot of the clubhouse steps. He compressed the handle and a line of light the height of him opened in the air. It glowed an iridescent, electric silver and widened to the width of a man's outstretched arms. Trevena felt the hairs rise on his arms and the back of his neck, not entirely from the effect of Gantry but *because* of it.

Bismuth wanted John and Bix to go with him, for their enhanced sight and sensitivity. Daniel and Trevena would try to locate Andrew Chapel. Alex and Eliot would stay at the caravan park with Colin, and Lesley and Anna would go back home to talk with Index and gather any information they could about Doctor Mocking and Chloe.

"Good fortune, everyone," John said.

Bismuth stepped through the Gantry, and John and Bix followed.

The rest of them watched the Gantry close. Colin ushered the boys into the clubhouse. He looked troubled.

"You okay, Colin?" Alex asked.

Colin wiped a hand over his face. "I really like that big fella," he said.

"He'll be all right," Eliot said. "Come on, tell us about that time you blew up those Toyceivers with a gas heater."

Colin beamed. "Good lads. A Crusader for all of us!"

Daniel, Trevena, Lesley and Anna returned to the jeep. "I'll drop you girls off at home," Daniel said. "Have you got Chapel's address, Phil?"

"It's on file. We'll have to go back to my office. He's not likely to be at home, though. The police did a check when he went missing from the ward."

"It's a place to start. It might throw up a clue. Coppers just knock and have a look through the window. We both know that."

They got into the jeep and drove away from the caravan park.

* * *

BISMUTH, JOHN AND Bix stood on a snow-blown street at the entrance to an abandoned arcade.

"This used to be a pretty place," Bismuth said. "When dad was alive."

John put a hand on Bismuth's shoulder.

"What happened here?"

Bismuth gazed the length of the arcade stretching ahead of them. All the units on either side of the arcade were empty and full of shadows and dry leaves that had blown in off the road. The roof was high and arched, corrugated, and the ornate iron struts that reinforced it and the flues that ran between them looked skeletal with the dried droppings from birds that no longer roosted and flitted there.

"I used to help my dad in his shop when I was a boy," Bismuth said. His expression softened for a moment with nostalgia. "It was an ironworks. He made ornaments and furniture, and repaired things for people in the tiny stockroom at the back of the shop." He pulled open his coat and put his hands on the levers in his belt. "He made these but he didn't know what they were for. He used to experiment with things. He liked to make things that looked arcane but had no function. I didn't know why, I just assumed he was happy shaping metals. But I think he was being guided. When he wasn't making things to sell or fixing someone's typewriter, he made piles of unfathomable things."

Bismuth walked into the arcade. John and Bix walked alongside him. It was cold and melancholy in the arcade. They passed what had once been a flower stall. John could smell the ghost fragrance of its history.

Bismuth said, "I think he wanted me to run the shop with him when I was older. I would have, gladly, but I became consumed by my calling and lost myself in it. I was alone, with powers I barely understood, and it obsessed me. And then he died. He died in my arms on the floor of his shop, and my heart broke. I recreated this arcade in my Quay, as a memorial to him, but it was foolish. The devil-in-dreams trapped me in my grief, and I had to relive his death every time I came here. I couldn't do my calling without coming here and seeing him, and watching him die."

John stayed silent. He had never heard Bismuth speak for so long, about such personal things. They reached the end of the arcade and stopped at the door of a small shop built into the facing wall. Next door was a derelict café. John could see the dusty blue tabletops and a copper urn behind the counter through a grimy window. On the corner was a barbershop. The door was gone, wrenched off its hinges some unknowable time past and he could see chrome fittings in the floor from which the chairs had been ripped out. The walls were covered in perforated display board, yellowed and peeling.

"After Doctor Mocking rescued me from the Gantry I found this place derelict. Any life I had put into it was gone. My dad was gone."

"How did you feel?"

Bismuth looked back along the empty arcade.

"I felt strong again. I'd let go. Accepted it. I stopped wasting energy on this."

He turned to the door of the shop and opened it.

TREVENA AND DANIEL took Lesley and Anna back home. They watched the girls walk up the drive. They turned and waved. Trevena wondered how they were feeling about losing their father. They had been quiet on the journey back from Invidisham-next-the-Sea, sitting together in the back of the jeep. They had drawn close, their relationship sustaining them in privacy and introspection. Trevena couldn't believe the doc was gone.

"He's not gone," Daniel said.

"Are you reading my mind, now?"

"In a way. If you weren't thinking about Doctor Mocking I'll give you my jeep."

"Jeep's safe. What's going to happen to him?"

"He's got Chloe with him. *Anything* could happen."

* * *

Daniel stopped outside the Mental Health Unit and Trevena went to the sliding doors that led into the foyer. He pushed the buzzer and after a few seconds there was a crackle as the intercom was activated on the ward. Trevena looked up at the CCTV camera above the doors and grinned.

"It's Phil Trevena. I need to get something from my office."

The intercom buzzed and the doors slid open.

Trevena went through the foyer and headed for his office. He walked past the untenanted reception desk, and thought about Emily and her surprise comment about dinner. Was she taking the piss? Trevena couldn't be sure; she was a sarcastic cow sometimes. But he was very fond of her and there was a certain edgy chemistry between them. She was a bit younger than he was and there was nothing spinsterish about her prolonged unattached status. She liked low-cut tops and a bit of makeup. She was a looker, Trevena reminded himself. He also had to remind himself that with Chloe's intervention, Emily would have no memory of driving him home and tending his injured head. It would keep things simpler between them, he thought, with a touch of regret. Let's get business out of the way first. Maybe he'd ask her out if he survived this.

He opened the office door and went to his desk. He shuffled through his notes, stacked in an untidy pile beside his computer. He hadn't got around to writing everything up and still had Chapel's details written on a sheet of A4. He grabbed the address and left the office.

"Got it," he said. "It's outside a village called Holt off the King's Lynn road. Be in the middle of nowhere. Probably some artistic retreat."

"Tell me when we get close," Daniel said, and they pulled out of the hospital grounds.

They arrived at Chapel's address half an hour later. It was, as

Trevena had suspected, off the beaten track. A road through the village of Holt took them onto a country lane that wound through a flat region of farmland.

"It's up there," Trevena said, his face illuminated from the glow of the satnav on his phone. The jeep bumped over potholes. Daniel swung the jeep onto a driveway and guided it between narrow ranks of bushes until they reached a detached cottage. It was unlit and had been hidden completely from the road. There were no neighbouring houses, Trevena estimated, within a quarter of a mile of the cottage. The huddled, indrawn aspect of the cottage provoked in Trevena a sense that it had been discovered trying to hide from something intent on preying on it, and had failed, and knew it. As the headlights from Daniel's jeep slid across the front of the building, the glass in the darkened windows appeared to blink quick, pale membranes.

They went to the front door and knocked. While Trevena was waiting for any response, Daniel made a circuit around the outside of the cottage.

Trevena knocked again. He squinted through a panel of frosted glass set into the door and saw movement. He stepped back from the door, suddenly alarmed. They had talked about what they were going to say to Chapel if they found him. They knew he might be dangerous, or distressed, or both, and Daniel had assured Trevena that he would be able to deal with him. He could be very persuasive. But where was he?

"Daniel!" Trevena hissed.

The latch rattled and the door opened.

Daniel stood there. "Back door was open," he said. "There's no one here."

THEY WENT THROUGH the cottage, but Daniel was right; there was no sign of Chapel. The rooms were dark and cold. The bathroom was missing toiletries and drawers were open in the bedroom. Chapel had packed and gone elsewhere.

"He's got a head in a jar and he stopped to get his toothbrush,"

Trevena shook his head. "Fastidious."

"Fits the bill," said Daniel. He was standing by the bedroom window, looking out over the dark plot of land at the back of the cottage. "There's a big shed down there. Might be a studio of some sort. Let's check it out."

They went downstairs and through the kitchen. A cold Aga cooker took up most of one wall and they had to skirt a small pine table in the middle of the room set with only one chair.

They went across the yard and approached the shed. It was a solid-looking construction with a sloping roof and a single door. It had no windows but Trevena could see a cable running from the corner of the cottage that disappeared into a hole in the side of the shed, so he assumed an electricity supply.

Daniel tried the door. It opened onto darkness. Daniel felt around for a switch and found one. A fluorescent strip hummed and came to life in a fitting above the door. They went in. The floor was bare and covered in rock dust and chips of stone. A small bench in the corner was covered with stone-working tools, and Trevena recognised the hammer Chapel had brought with him to the Unit. There was a pile of black stones, each about the size of a loaf of bread, tumbled beneath the bench. They looked rough-hewn, possible debris chiselled off from a larger piece.

"Nothing here," said Daniel. "Not now, anyway."

They returned to the kitchen. Daniel looked around, his expression unreadable to Trevena. He might have been frustrated or furious, Trevena couldn't tell. Daniel went over to a telephone plugged into the wall above the sink.

"Have you got his details there?"

Trevena took the pre-assessment form from his pocket and unfolded it.

"He hasn't got a mobile," he said. "Or wouldn't give me the number."

"I've got an idea," Daniel said, and picked up the landline. He pushed a few buttons and brought up the last number Chapel had dialled.

"0208. That's London, right?"

"Outer London. You think he rang one of his arty mates to hide him out?"

"No. It's not a friend Chapel needs right now. He doesn't want to hide out, either. He's on a mission. Is there a next-of-kin on that form?"

Trevena put the form flat on the worktop. Daniel read out the number, matched it.

He put the phone back in its cradle.

"He's gone to his mum's," he said.

TREVENA USED HIS mobile to phone Doctor Mocking's number. Index answered on the first ring.

Trevena filled him in on the situation with Chapel.

"Go," said Index. "It's all quiet here. Steve and Claire are asleep. I think Elizabeth gave them something."

Trevena hung up and he and Daniel walked to the jeep.

"I feel like we're being played," Trevena said. "Or led into something. Do you feel that?"

"I think there's only so much Chapel can tell us," Daniel said. "But he's leaving clues. The part of him that's fighting the corruption wants us to find him. Did he talk much about his parents?"

"I got the impression he wasn't close to his mother. I think he blamed her for the way he felt. That's not unusual in my field. Most of the blokes I see with long-standing depressive illness have mummy issues." Trevena noticed the set of Daniel's jaw, the tension there.

"Sorry, mate. That was a bit poorly phrased," Trevena said.

Daniel's expression softened. "It's okay. It's the truth. When you see what's behind the hopelessness, it's easier to understand. It just makes me more determined to help Andrew Chapel, if I can."

Trevena put Chapel's mother's address into his satnav.

"North Cheam," he said. "Around the M25, over Dartford Bridge and round to Reigate. Three hours max this time of night. Should we call ahead and warn her?"

"No. I don't think she's at risk from him. Besides, I want her to be asleep when we get there."

They left the cottage in darkness and headed for London.

JOHN AND BIX followed Bismuth into the shop. It was empty, bare and cold. There was a small counter facing them with a door behind it and another at right angles to the back wall.

Bismuth went around the counter and opened it. "Stockroom," he said. John waited while Bismuth was in the cubbyhole. Bix sat at his feet.

John stroked his head.

"You okay, chap?"

"It feels sad in here," the dog said.

John fussed his ears. "I know," he said. "Sadness never entirely goes away."

"But we learn to live with it?"

"We have to, don't we?"

Bismuth returned from the stockroom and stood behind the counter. He looked huge and suddenly rather poignant, a giant shopkeeper with strange metal goods in his hands. He placed them on the counter top and, to John's surprise, said, "Take these and go back. The boys are in danger. And Colin."

John looked at the objects. One looked like a small brass telescope and the other was a lever of some kind, not dissimilar to the ones Bismuth carried, but shorter and thicker with a bolt attachment at the base of the rod.

"What's happened?"

"I heard these calling to me from the stockroom. Sometimes I find things here, things dad made and I forgot about. The boys will know what they are. They need their instruments back. It's the Despatrix. I can sense it. It likes to go for the young ones."

"Will you be all right?"

Bismuth pushed the Instruments towards John. He moved towards the door set into the back wall. When he opened it, John saw a vast landscape of dereliction and ruin. Bombsites from the Autosomachy, the war with the Autoscopes that had raged for so long. This was Bismuth's Quay, and none had fought the war harder.

"I'll stay," Bix said. He followed Bismuth out into the grey, blasted rubble. Bismuth put a huge hand on the dog's neck. He looked up at John, who still stood behind the counter.

John nodded. He picked up the objects and came around the counter, stepping out onto the edge of the debris at the back of the arcade.

Bismuth took a lever from his belt and put it in the ground. He opened an egress Gantry for John, one that would lead him back to the caravan site. As the Gantry widened to become a shining band of light, John went through without a backwards glance at his dog.

"I love you, John," said Bix.

The Gantry closed.

IT TOOK THEM three hours and seventeen minutes to get to Chapel's mother's house. Daniel had rigged a canvas roof over the top of the jeep but it was still cold, damp and uncomfortable.

"Why didn't we go back for my car?" Trevena said as he climbed out, stretching his cramped back and massaging his frozen buttocks.

Daniel ignored him. He had allowed the question to become rhetorical after the third time he'd heard it. They'd have lost too much time swapping vehicles and Trevena knew it. On the way down, Trevena had asked other questions, less rhetorical ones, and Daniel had been happy to answer them.

Wrapped in his coat against the weather, Trevena had asked, "Why didn't you just open a Gantry and spring us to London?"

"There's a limitation to what we can do. We all have different abilities and to be honest, I'm pretty sure we don't all know what they all are yet, even now. Seven years we've been together and we've been getting stronger, more connected, but I don't think we've *optimised* fully."

Trevena was aware of the organic nature of the Night Clock, of the Dark Time it controlled. It was as fluid in places as a dream but fixed by rules that became evident even as they were being discovered. It was a paradox, its totality glimpsed but always immediately beyond his grasp.

"Bismuth can travel like that, but only if he senses either one of us or an Autoscope in the region, and even then it's not an exact science. I think the emotional investment he has with his Instruments connects him somehow, grounds him like a lightning rod. Index, too. He can pretty much do anything. The rest of us need these." Daniel tapped his palms on the steering wheel.

"Ever take the bus? A number 87 to the nearest Autoscope, please, driver?"

"Elizabeth likes the bus. Sometimes we go into town on it. Saves paying for parking."

Trevena studied Daniel's profile, looking for anything that might give away the joke, but there was nothing in Daniel's expression other than a slight frown of concentration as he peered through the windscreen. Another paradox: this man had embraced a simple life, finally accepting the love of his woman, and fought demons with a tenacity and courage Trevena could only marvel at. It was enviable.

"Okay," Daniel said. "You're the psychiatric nurse. I've been having a recurring dream. I'm walking in some woods and come to a clearing and hanging from the branches of the trees are all these old tin cans. They're full of water and swarming with mosquito larvae. They repulse me and I pick up a branch and start smashing them up. Then I wake up. What's that about?"

"You should ask the Doc, he's the shrink."

"I never got a chance."

Trevena took out his phone and waved it at Daniel. "Wonders of the modern age," he said. He brought up Google and searched for *dream analysis*. He typed in *mosquito*. "Passes the time," he said. "When I was a kid we used to have spotter books. Here we go: *To see mosquitoes in your dream suggest that some situation or someone has been draining you of your energy and resources.*

Alternatively, mosquitoes indicate that your resistance to attacks will be in vain. To dream that you are killing mosquitoes denote that you will eventually overcome your obstacles. Happiness and fortune will be in your grasp. How do you like those apples?"

"I like the last bit. I think it's more than that, though. I get a sense that those larvae are going to become something more than just mosquitoes. I have to kill them all before that happens. If they germinate in the dream they'll infest Dark Time."

"And do what?"

"Feed on more than blood? Feed on dreams? Draw off fragments of the collective unconscious, combining all the eternal variables of the human dream state. To make a monster from the transcendental molecules of the imagination. A host body for the devil-in-dreams."

"You won't get that on Google."

Trevena turned off his phone. "How do you know when you're dreaming and not just in a Quay?"

"Same as anyone else. I don't have control."

"Here's one for you. If you're dreaming could another Firmament Surgeon enter your dream and change it?"

"I suppose so. I don't think anyone's done it though. Kind of an unwritten rule. It might fuck up the Night Clock."

CHAPEL'S CHILDHOOD HOME was a small mid-terrace on a side road off the high street. Trevena remembered what Chapel had told him during the assessment, how the road must have been pretty once. There were echoes of the past still – in the low walls and front gates that remained and the tree-lined alleyways that separated the houses at intervals – but most of it was gone, crammed and cramped by families with more cars than garage space, dropped curbs, paved front gardens and extensions erected on every end-terrace plot available. The road itself was a chicane of bollards and speed bumps. Trevena felt hemmed in. There was just too much here; it was a municipal palimpsest where ghosts of the original features could be glimpsed beneath the endless pouring of concrete and tarmac, the buckling of the pavements by constant laying and re-laying of pipes and cables, and the grasping enlargements of properties once meant to be appealing and that now just looked tumorous with home improvements.

They walked up the path and stood outside the house.

"Do we break in?" asked Trevena.

"No need," said Daniel. "She's asleep." He looked up, towards the small bay window overlooking the garden. He sighed and smiled. It was a reassuring smile Trevena recognised.

"It's all right," Daniel said. "You're dreaming."

He wasn't speaking to Trevena. Daniel was The Hypnopomp. He was speaking to Chapel's mother.

Upstairs, a light came on.

A FEW MINUTES later a frail-looking woman opened the front door. She was in her late seventies. She was wearing a shabby pink dressing gown over a tatty red cardigan and fluffy slippers. Her thin grey hair was pressed flat against her head on one side and stuck up in a fan on the other. She had dribble on her chin. Her face was pinched with sleep but her eyes shone out from beneath her crumpled, speckled brow with a cold, determined vigour.

"May we come in?" Daniel asked.

The woman stood aside and Daniel and Trevena stepped past her into a bare, narrow hallway. The house stank of stale cigarettes.

"Is your son home, Mrs. Chapel?"

The woman stared past the two men.

"I was dreaming about him," she said. Her voice was a dry rasp, toneless.

"Do you know where he is?"

She frowned. "Where he always is," she said.

"Can you tell me?"

The old woman shrugged her thin, bony shoulders.

"He's at the dump," she said.

* * *

Bismuth and Bix crossed the dereliction. Bismuth trod over the rubble and the pipes and craters with long, heavy strides. Bix stepped more lightly but kept up, jumping over steel cables and an endless dry shore of rocks that might lead eventually to a terrible black, metallic sea. The air was thin and dusty and had the unremitting smell of minerals and the smoke from scorched buildings.

Eventually they could see a wall rising from the rubble. It could have been the walls to a mythical city, a sanctuary in the midst of a desolate plain, but there were no lights, no life, and no guards at the ungated entrance. As they approached all that was visible were towering pyramids of rubbish and a maelstrom of gulls wheeling above it all, crying like a nursery of forsaken children.

They went through the gates and entered the dump. The ground was white with gull droppings and wet slurry. The stink of scorched masonry was replaced by the fetid odour of rotten waste. It was overpowering and Bix growled, unable to keep his distress contained. Bismuth stopped and said, "Breathe through your mouth, Bix. You'll never get used to it."

Panting, Bix followed Bismuth through aisles of refuse. Muck welled between his paws. His tail was low, clamped against his back legs.

They rounded a mountain of junk and came to a space at the rear of the dump. It looked like it had been cleared by a bulldozer. There were caterpillar track marks in swoops and rucks but the ridges were hard, ossified, like work done an age ago.

Against the far wall, perched on a platform of flattened, saturated cardboard boxes, leaned the refrigerator.

As they stood together before it, waiting, hushed, the insubstantial night-shadows of airborne gulls flickering across the dirt and the ivory ceramic door of the fridge, a crimson light blazed suddenly at their backs.

Bismuth and Bix turned to face it, and what came out from it.

Trevena found a coat hanging on the back of the kitchen door and helped Chapel's mother into it. She complied without issue, and Trevena couldn't help feeling that he was partaking in a form of abuse. Daniel caught his expression.

"You know what it's like, Phil," he said. "She thinks she's dreaming." He tapped his temple with a finger. "No trauma."

"I know," Trevena said as he ushered the old girl to the front door. "But it's kind of against her will."

"No it isn't. This is what she's always wanted. You know it. Freedom from the nightmares, the fear. All the shit she projected onto Chapel for decades. All the self-defeating, repressive crap."

"Who's projecting now?" Trevena said. He lifted Chapel's mother's feet, one at a time, and took off her slippers. He replaced them with a pair of soft zippered boots that Daniel handed him from a corner of the hallway.

"Fuck off," Daniel said mildly.

Trevena took her arm and led Chapel's mother down the path to the jeep. He helped her into the front seat and put the belt around her.

Daniel started the engine.

"Give me directions to the dump, Mrs. Chapel," he said.

The old woman was staring ahead, her eyes fierce with native scorn.

"Turn left at the bottom of the road," she said. She sat back in her seat and smiled, the look of a woman being taken on a surprise trip somewhere nice during the entire course of which she would carp and disparage incessantly.

"Can she hear me?" asked Trevena from the back of the jeep.

"She won't remember it," said Daniel.

"That's a nasty old cow, isn't it?"

CHAPEL STOOD INSIDE the grounds of the recycling centre. He had climbed the gate regardless of the CCTV cameras situated around the vicinity. What he had to do would not take long. This was no longer the dump he had played in as a child, grubbing through the mountains of rubbish looking for treasures with his friends, but it was built on the same site. Now everything was divided up into huge containers, all ranked along one side of the recycling centre. Everything was swept and tidy. Officials patrolled the skips in green uniforms and watched for recycling misdemeanours with an eagle eye. When he had been a boy there had been an old, crumbling wall at the back of the dump leading onto allotments and alleyways and he and his friends would drop down into the back of the dump and scoot about dodging the old man who guarded the entrance. Sometimes they found transistor radios that still worked, and once a pile of mouldering dirty magazines that they divvied out quickly and shot straight off home with.

He had done something bad here. He had done a cruel thing. He had been playing with a boy called Peter who had learning difficulties. Peter had died a year or two later of a brain tumour. They had found an old refrigerator at the base of a pile of rubbish and Peter had climbed into it. An impulse of pure and unanticipated spite had made Chapel slam the door shut on him. He had stood there, breathing hard, a coil of fierce excitement in his belly, for over a minute and then he had snapped back to himself, horrified at what he had done. He had torn open the door and pulled Peter out. Peter was in some kind of shock. His face was slack and his lips were blue. His eyes were staring off into the distance. Chapel apologised, expressed his regret at his sudden cruelty but Peter was unresponsive. In an attempt to show Peter how sorry he was, Chapel climbed into the refrigerator himself and shut the door.

The door locked itself and Peter had never opened it.

In the night, long after Chapel's screams had ceased and the air had mostly gone, something else opened the door.

And got in with him.

JOHN STAINWRIGHT EMERGED from the Gantry and it was raining there on the caravan site. He stood in a fine drizzle and recalled the squall that night seven years ago, when Colin had come to him and explained to him who he really was and what his calling was. He looked up into a sky almost dark brown with low cloud, an unsettling storm-colour polluted by the sodium lights of the surrounding town of Invidisham-next-the-Sea.

There had been a Gantry up there then, revolving above the site, some kind of monstrous rig out of which emerged a raiding party of Toyceivers, falling from the clouds to search for him and destroy him. But he and Bix had escaped, opening a Gantry for themselves to Quay-Endula. There he had found Lesley in mortal danger and had rescued her from an Autoscope called The Flyblown Man.

He wondered about the Gantries the Autoscopes used, and how they constructed them. He had seen them open, watched things emerge, and always there was a terrible red light, or an abyss forced out of the earth, or sometimes, when Toyceivers were unleashed, that colossal scaffold of assembled, twisted metal excising chunks from the air. What he sensed was the application of awful *effort*, a breaking out, rather than a passing through. John's experience of travel was the ease of it, the effortless passage to the Quays. The Autoscopes must be contained somewhere hellish and given authority to travel but with limitations, a principality from which they drew a certain amount of influence, or *rights*, until the war was finally over.

There was nothing overhead now, except that industrial-looking cloud cover, and he ducked into the blowing drizzle and made for Colin's clubhouse.

He stopped outside. The door was open and the interior was dark. The fly blind had been knocked from its hooks and lay tangled across the top step. John went up the steps and looked inside. As his eyes became accustomed to the dark he was able to see why the fairy lights above the bar were out. They had been yanked from the top of the bar and were looped around the two bar stools, themselves tumbled over onto the floor beside the bar. Some of the tables and chairs had been scattered and overturned, and there were pools of spilt beer and broken glass across the floor. John walked in and went over to the bar. He put the Instruments

Bismuth had given him on the bar and then he put a hand flat on the worn but lovingly polished surface. The bar top was split lengthways. John could smell perfume on the air, dry and antique, but pungent, as though the splitting of the bar had released a fresh reserve, or emptied it through trauma in an aromatic abreaction.

On impulse, John placed both hands on the top of the bar and closed his eyes. He pressed his palms flat against the wood and ran them over the surface. He lifted his hands to his face and inhaled.

Then he picked up the Instruments lying next to him and ran out of the clubhouse into the rain.

LESLEY AND ANNA were sitting in their father's study with Jon Index when the windows on the top floor landing blew in.

They ran into the hall. Elizabeth came out of the kitchen to meet them.

No one spoke. Index led them to the stairs and they followed him up to the first floor. Index pointed to the bedroom where Steve and Claire were asleep.

"Anna, go with Elizabeth," he said. "If you have to, take them all out of here. Go to a Quay."

Anna nodded and she and Elizabeth opened the bedroom door. There was no movement from inside, just the sound of two deep sleepers breathing. They went in and shut the door.

Index and Lesley went around the banister rail to the bottom of the stairs leading up to the top floor. They could hear the wind gusting through the shattered window but could see no movement.

They heard something, though, above the sound of the wind and rain. And as they stood there, something appeared over the top step and peered down at them, the sagging oval of its face grinning with mad, awful effort.

Index switched on the light and the shuddering bulk of Nurse Melt was thrown into sharp relief on the landing. Behind her, folded and crumpled in a terminal pile, the wreck of her old cloudbike lay in a heap on the landing.

Melt toppled towards them and thudded down the stairs headfirst, arms flung out in an attempt to slow her descent. Her fat, white palms thumped against the steps and her shoulders shuddered and she shrieked, the red mat of her hair trapped beneath her, knotting around her throat making a dirty flaxen bonnet out of which her bloated, tattered face bulged.

Lesley and Index stepped backwards and let her come. Melt fetched up in a heap on the landing between them and tried to roll onto her back. Index helped her with a boot to the ribs. Melt collapsed onto her back and stared up at them. Her torn mouth—ripped and hanging in a wedge from an old injury at Lesley's hands a decade before—worked but made no sound. Her small black eyes roved between them, fixed in a furious dilation, and she tried to sit up but her legs were too heavy and too twisted. Still, a hand groped for Lesley. Fingers flexed, plump as grubs, reaching for any final, lethal purchase.

Lesley knelt before the stricken creature. She took Melt's hand, grasping it, and closed her fist around the twitching fingers. Lesley looked down at Nurse Melt and considered her ways. Melt made a small, questioning hoot, her whole body trembling.

Lesley put a hand on Melt's wide, bovine brow, brushed strands of wiry hair from it. The flesh was cold and lifeless as tripe. Melt's eyes rolled and again she made a small sound in the back of her throat.

"Are you afraid?" Lesley asked.

Melt sneered and lunged upwards, her other arm coming around fast.

Index was faster, and caught it. He twisted and wrenched the arm from its socket, dislocating it like he was pulling a cork from a bottle. Melt howled and the arm dropped to the carpet.

"Are you in pain?" Lesley asked.

Melt rolled her head and stared into Lesley's eyes.

"I wonder what you were? Did you want this, or were you made?"

Melt grunted.

"*No...choice...*" she said, and closed her eyes. Lesley felt the fingers trapped in her fist grip her own.

Lesley looked up. "Is dad's bag still in his room?" she asked him.

"I'll look," Index said. "Are you all right?"

Lesley nodded and looked back down at Nurse Melt.

Index went to the Doctor's bedroom and returned with a large black leather bag. It was soft and creased with age and had a large brass clip holding it closed. Index put it down next to Lesley.

"Thank you." Lesley opened the bag with one hand and sorted through the contents until she found what she needed. She withdrew a large glass syringe and an ampoule of clear fluid. She let go of Melt's hand and unwrapped a needle from a strip she found in the bag. She fixed the needle to the end of the syringe and used it to draw up the entire contents of the ampoule. There was a sharp, disagreeable odour.

"Paraldehyde," Lesley said. "100 milligrams. Lethal at a third of this dose. It's vile stuff. They used to use it in the old asylums as a sedative. It caused abscesses, and had to be given in a glass syringe because it melts plastic."

Melt eyed the syringe.

"It's as if dad was keeping this just for you," said Lesley, and she pushed the needle deep into the sagging flesh beneath Nurse Melt's chin.

She felt no mercy as she depressed the plunger, merely relief.

THEY WRAPPED MELT'S body in a blanket and dragged it to the top of the stairs. Elizabeth and Anna came onto the landing and together they got the corpse downstairs and into the hallway.

"She can't stay there," Elizabeth said. Her face was flushed and had an expression of immense aversion writ large there. "It's *seeping.*"

Melt's remains were breaking down quickly. The blanket, which they had wrapped taut around her body was now noticeably slack where Melt's flesh was collapsing. There was a large brown stain spreading from the head end of the shroud the size and shape of Melt's face.

Index opened the front door. "Get it outside," he said.

Index got a grip of two handfuls of blanket and dragged Melt out onto the porch. Lesley and Anna took a leg each but the going was easier. Her stout calves were becoming pulpy and their hands could feel bone through the material. There was another smell, too, above the institutionalised tang of the Paraldehyde. Decomposition. Melt was dissolving with monumental speed, and by the time they got her out onto the drive she was little more than a hammock of slops. They cast her to the gravel and watched as the saturated blanket deflated further in the rain.

Lesley stood with her hands on her hips. Her expression was reflective. Her eyes shone with emotion. She thought of the times this creature had come for her over the past two decades, and how each time she had bested it, made Melt look inept. She wondered why Melt had latched onto her with such savage and determined resolve when Lesley had such a history of victories. Melt was bungling, incompetent, senseless, yet still she came, like a stooge to be battered. Lesley realised that her feelings for Melt were ambivalent. She had finally done to Melt what Melt surely would have done to her, but still, there was a complex symbiosis between old foes and Lesley had been a component of it for most of her life. Looking down at the putrid blanket, Lesley felt a pang of... what? Pity? Remorse?

"Forgive her," Index said.

"Huh?"

"You have a chance to forgive her. Take it."

They all looked up as headlights lit them up like the shock of sudden judgement, and a car turned into the drive. Melt's body looked liked the shucked, still wet skin of something awful that had crawled away into the night.

It was a white Hillman Minx. It shuddered to a stop and John Stainwright got out.

"The boys are in trouble," he said. "We have to find them." He was holding something in each hand, strange looking brass objects he had scooped from the front seat as he got out of the Minx. He held them up for the others to see.

"I know what that is," Lesley said, pointing to the Instrument in John's right hand. "It's Eliot's kaleidoscope."

"And that's Alex's," Index said as he indicated towards the other Instrument. "It's *Railgrinder's* throttle."

"I think I know where they've gone," John said. "We have to regroup. The devil-in-dreams is trying to separate us again."

JOHN TOLD THEM about the clubhouse and the missing boys as they headed up to the room in which Steve and Claire were sleeping. Elizabeth went in first and roused them while the others stood on the landing outside and talked.

"When I touched Colin's bar," John said. "I saw what had happened. The Despatrix attacked them while they were sitting playing cards. I saw it in a series of broken images. I saw the boys' faces when they looked up and saw it standing inside the clubhouse. I think its beauty caught them by surprise. They were still staring at it when it attacked them. Alex grabbed Colin and pushed him towards the bar. I could see his expression, too, as he stumbled into the stools and pulled the lights down around him. He couldn't take his bloody eyes off it. He went and hid around behind the bar while Alex and Eliot fought back. Tables went over and Eliot caught the Despatrix with a blow to the side of the head. They came around to protect Colin and the Despatrix launched itself over the bar. Its eyes were blazing, speckled with awful lifeless pupils. Colin was terrified but he was pissed off too and he grabbed it by the arm and yanked it across the bar. Alex took its head in both hands and smashed it facedown into the bar. The bar top split. He'd used enormous force, he was so angry. Then light streamed from the split in the wood, a huge silver fan of light. His beloved bar had absorbed so much positive energy, it became their Gantry and the boys took Colin through it. It gave up every last ounce of its power to take them away. When I touched it I smelt something else. Something other than perfume. It was coal dust."

"What of the Despatrix?" asked Index.

"I don't know. I saw it blown backwards by the force of the light. There was no sign of it when I got there."

Elizabeth opened the door. "They're awake," she said.

They went in. A single bedside lamp lit the room. Steve and Claire were sitting next to each other on the edge of the bed looking rumpled and disoriented.

Anna sat next to Claire and took her hand. Claire's face was white and still strained despite the sleep, but she managed a smile for Anna. Steve ran a hand over his face and yawned. "What did you give us?" he asked Elizabeth.

Elizabeth said, "Trade secret."

Steve shrugged. "Takes me back to my youth," he said.

Index said, "I'm going to open a Gantry and we are all going through it. I suggest that Steve, Claire and Elizabeth close your eyes."

"Now?" said Steve.

"Now," said Index.

And they were gone.

Coal dust. Sparks. *Firebox heat. Steam.*

Colin opened his eyes and blinked. It was dark. As his eyes accustomed he saw that he was standing on the edge of a platform in a small train shed. He realised that his eyes were not adjusting to darkness within the shed but were adjusting to daylight after being blinded by the light from the Gantry.

He felt chilly. A cool breeze ran the length of the train shed and intruded up the legs of his shorts. The light was pale, early morning light. The doors at the end of the shed were open and a wedge of dusty radiance was creeping up the weed-choked rails. A skylight made from semi-transparent fiberglass let in a little more light and Colin was able to see clearly now the wonderful and mythical thing that waited on the tracks in front of him. He put his hands on his bony hips and whistled.

Alex appeared on the footplate, his face and hands already blackened with streaks of soot.

"You alright, Colin?"

"Survived worse," Colin said. He took a step nearer the edge of the platform and peered into the cab. Alex had begun shoveling coal into the firebox already. "Can I come aboard? I want to see it for myself. What a beauty."

"I don't know if it'll still work," Alex said. His tone was hopeful, but Colin could see the flicker of doubt in his eyes. "There's a piece missing."

"Let's take a look," Colin said, and stepped over into *Railgrinder's* cab.

"It's the throttle lever," Alex said, and pointed to a large, greasy nut above the driver's seat. "It's gone."

"Maybe we can find a spanner or something, rig something up?"

"That's what I thought. We can have a try, but I've got a feeling it needs that lever."

"I'll have a look around," Colin said. "I've heard so much about this beast. I've always been a bit of a train spotter. Can't believe I'm actually standing in its cab."

Alex shoveled another pile of coal into the firebox. There was a yellow flutter of flame from within and a burst of embers. "I thought *Railgrinder* was wrecked," he said. "Someone must have brought it here and repaired it. Kept it ready for us. I'll get it fired up."

"Where's Eliot?" Colin asked.

Alex gestured back towards the platform.

"He's getting breakfast."

Colin was surprised to see Eliot emerge from a small door set into the wall of the shed carrying bacon rolls wrapped in cellophane. As Eliot opened the door, Colin could see that behind it was a small but busy café. A brass urn sat on a narrow counter at the back of the café and filled the place with steam and all the tables were packed with people eating and drinking and reading newspapers. Colin frowned. Voices were raised.

"Are they all speaking French?" he asked as Eliot stepped into the cab.

Eliot handed him a roll. It smelt wonderful.

"It's a *Lacan-café,*" he said, and put a roll in Alex's reaching hand. "It can appear anywhere in the Quays where there's a vacant lot or an empty shop. It's for people to get together and process stuff, make sense of their dreams. Everyone speaks French because it's the language the Autoscopes hate the most. It's too *elegant* for them."

"I can't speak much French," Colin said. "I can ask for a beer or the toilet but that's about it."

"You're not dreaming, Colin. *They* are."

Colin considered this as he bit into his roll.

"Actually," he said, "I could do with a wee. The old bladder's not what it was and this chill isn't helping. I'll nip in and ask. *Ou est la toilette*, right?"

Eliot was looking past his shoulder.

"Too late, mate," he said.

Colin looked around.

"*Merde*," he said through a mouthful of bread.

The door stood open, askew on broken hinges. Inside all was dark and stripped bare. The room looked burnt out. The café was gone.

"I'll go behind a bush," Colin said, and lobbed his empty cellophane wrapper underarm into the firebox.

John Stainwright and the others emerged from a Gantry inside Bismuth's arcade.

Elizabeth staggered and Steve caught her. She looked dazed and her face was flushed.

"First time for me," he said, "I came out on a beach in Quay-Endula and spent half an hour standing with the sea up to my knees just staring at the horizon. I thought I was dreaming. Are you ok?"

Elizabeth reached out and put the palm of her hand against Steve's bearded cheek. She closed and opened her eyes. "I'm fine, dear."

Steve had to wonder, "Hasn't Daniel ever...?"

Elizabeth laughed. "I've never asked," she said.

Index led them through the arcade, past the dark and empty units. As they approached the end where Bismuth's father's shop was they began to hear a lively murmuring sound.

"That's voices," John said. Above his head came a sudden muted flapping as a pair of gray doves settled onto one of the slender support rods high in the roof.

"Look," Elizabeth said. She was standing at the entrance to one of the units. In the rear stood a stainless steel pail full of orange roses.

"This place likes life," Index said.

The arcade was responding to something and as they came around the side of the last unit that ran up the center of the arcade they saw what it was.

The derelict café that stood between Bismuth's father's metal workshop and the old barbershop was no longer empty. The windows were misted with steam and the shapes of people could be seen clustered around tables and sitting at the counter. They were all reading newspapers and speaking French in loud voices.

Index opened the door. Immediately the arcade was filled with the sound of people arguing, shouting, and laughing. They went in and made their way to the counter. There was a radio playing in the back of the café, tuned to a French station and broadcasting what might have been news or a variety of educational program; the voice was smooth, cultured, and seemed a calming background against which all the other voices were raised. French newspapers rattled and were thrown down, or changed hands, each emblazoned with their own cryptic headlines. A voluminous urn atop its brass burner hissed and blew jets of steam against the low plaster ceiling. Condensation gathered in wobbling droplets. There was a tall, slender man standing behind the counter wearing a blue apron. He had small, very dark eyes, slicked back hair and a pencil moustache. When he saw Index he threw down his dishtowel and yelled,

"*Jon Index! Bienvenue a mon café! C'est Index! Jon Index, tout le monde!*"

Broadsheets were lowered and conversations went quiet for a moment. Curious faces peered at them. Cups of coffee and pastries paused on their way to and from mouths.

"Bonjour, Johnny!" Index said and reached across the counter to embrace the owner of the café.

Index turned back to the others. They were clustered in the

middle of the floor in a negligible aisle that ran from the front of the café to the counter. Everyone had gone back to reading, eating and making a noise. A short man wearing a wide-brimmed black hat and a loosely-wound paisley cravat stood to make room for them, pushing his chair beneath his small cluttered table. He gave Lesley a rakish wink and said something to her in French that made Steve take her arm and glare at the man. Index smiled.

"Elizabeth how's your French?"

"Mediocre," she said.

"I can speak pretty passable French," Steve said, still frowning at the man in the black hat. "Learned it on my travels. Stayed with a couple in Languedoc for six months picking figs."

"I want you all to stay here. Make yourselves comfortable. I'll come back for you."

John said, "I'm going with you. I want my dog."

Index nodded. They went to the door while the others found a table that abutted the counter. Johnny was taking their orders as the two men left the café and went back out into the arcade.

John looked up towards the roof. A group of pigeons had joined the doves in the struts and as they watched, four sparrows darted in through the entrance and sped low along the aisle. They landed on the roof of the flower stall and hopped about, pecking at the felt.

They walked over to the metalwork shop and went inside. It was gloomy and cold. The counter was bare, as were the shelves behind it. Index followed John to the rear of the shop and John opened the door that led onto the bombsite.

There was a figure coming towards them, treading with slow, heavy steps over the rubble, and he carried something limp in his arms. The sky was a pale, sick purple bandaged with wide strips of high gray cloud. The air was thick with particles of masonry dust.

"Oh, no," John said.

THE INCURSION GANTRY blazed at their backs. The chipped ceramic door of the refrigerator blushed a hot pink, reflecting the crimson light and seemed to lurch backwards as the shadows fled. The edges of the flattened boxes beneath it glowed like filaments in a gas fire and looked like they were about to combust.

Bismuth and Bix span around to face the Gantry. Bix lowered his head and snarled. Bismuth took a step forward, a lever held in each fist. The Gantry was a vile gash exposed immodestly in the night air, glistening with putrescence and hot with infection, and it pushed the beast from it with a great, rippling contraction that sent it spewing onto all fours in the dump's slurry.

It was titanic, at least twice the size of Bismuth, and covered in a moldering black cape with a hood that covered its head and hid its features. Its forearms, piston-straight against the ground, ended in hands with fingers fused and covered with horn, hoof-like and heavy as clubs.

It lifted its head and began to stand, the hood of the cape peeling back to reveal a huge elongated skull covered with the flesh from a boar's head. The meat had been crudely stapled to the bone; heavy black jowls hung and the pointed, interrogatory V of its mouth lolled, thick with a bulging white tongue, beneath a short, broad snout.

Morgoder had joined the War.

Its stench was incredible. The vileness of the already putrid air increased by an order of magnitude. Morgoder seemed to emit the pestilence like an aura.

Bix whined and put his front paws over his muzzle, burying it in the wet, gray dirt, smothering it in a filth that was preferable to the mass grave reek coming off the Autoscope.

"Don't let it touch you, Bix. It's death." Bismuth said, and as he said it, Morgoder charged.

Bix lifted his head. Filth dripped from the fur around his mouth. His eyes were half shut but he saw the monster charge towards them. His paws slipped in the dirt and he felt Bismuth's weight against his flank as the man tried to push him aside with his leg, but it was too late.

Morgoder hit them like a wrecking ball. A caped shoulder hit Bismuth and sent him spinning, staggering against the wall at the back of the dump. He found his feet and slammed the ends of his levers against the crumbling brickwork to thrust himself forward, pushing off from the wall in a shower of golden sparks. His boots thudded in the dirt.

Morgoder was standing over Bix, a hoof raised to bring it down on the dog's head. Bix lay against a pile of junk, his chest heaving and his muzzle open. He rolled an eye that was full of fear and pain and fixed it on the creature that towered over him.

Bismuth shouted, changing direction, and instead of running to attack Morgoder, he ran back to where the refrigerator stood on its dais of rotten cardboard.

Morgoder swung its foul, heavy head. The boar-skin mask slid on the bone of its skull, quivering. The white tongue slid from the side of the lolling mouth, across ridges of blunt, brown teeth. It made a sound; a deep, feral grunt, which clapped against Bismuth's eardrums and made him wince. Bix shuddered and his feet paddled as though he was dreaming.

Bismuth grabbed the refrigerator's handle and threw open the door.

Morgoder lowered its arm. The bulging, viscid pig's eyes gazed blindly at what had been revealed but Bismuth could see a light somewhere behind them, thin filaments of *nihillumination* deep in the monster's head, watching with sudden caution from behind the dead bulbs in the boar's face. The light hurt Bismuth's head and he looked away, looked back towards the refrigerator and to what had been hidden inside.

It was a boy.

Bismuth slid his levers into his belt. Tears blurred his sight and he felt himself trembling. Here was the boy.

He bent and lifted the boy into his arms. He was no weight. He was pale and did not breathe. He was like a ghost in the crook of the giant's arm.

Morgoder made no sound as it stepped away from Bix and moved towards the Firmament Surgeon.

Bix opened his eyes. He was cold. His fur was slathered with filth. There was a great pain in his side from where Morgoder had clubbed him against the junk. He could taste and smell the overwhelming odour of death, and it was black and nightmarish with not so much as a pinhole of light at the end of it. It was the collapse of everything, the absolute stemming of the fountainhead of light, the silencing of The Word forever. The closing of the slot.

Bix lifted his head from the dirt and barked.

Bismuth turned, the boy light as sticks in his arms. Morgoder lumbered towards him, fused fists raised to bring them down on the back of Bismuth's neck.

Bismuth ducked and sidestepped. Morgoder charged past him and thundered into the refrigerator, slamming it against the back wall of the dump. It fell sidelong, its door dropping shut against the emptiness within.

Bismuth watched as Morgoder lifted itself from the ground. It fumbled at the handle of the refrigerator with its bonded fists and lifted the door like a car bonnet.

There was a new darkness inside, a darkness full of eyes. It welled against the opening like a vat of tar too dense to pour, seeming to coagulate against the stinking atmosphere of the dump.

Bismuth held the child tight against his chest. This was what he had come here for. This was what he had *always* come here for. It was a terrible decision, but one he would have always made.

Bismuth ran, his long coat swaying and his heavy boots slamming through the dirt, and took the child away from the dump.

Behind him, Morgoder roared. Bismuth glanced back, sure it would be in pursuit, but it was still hunched at the door of the refrigerator. It was watching him, though. Bismuth felt his retinas itch as he looked into the vicious sockets that smouldered behind the mask.

Bix was unmoving, whatever dream he had been having now over.

Morgoder shouldered the door open, bending the ancient hinges until they snapped. The door crashed against the side of the fridge and broke off, sliding onto the ground behind it. Morgoder wrestled the refrigerator upright again, hugging it like a bear; urgency in its purpose, and Bismuth could see the eyes sluicing in the blackness, welling against the border of the darkness.

Morgoder stood sentry, the bulging rim of the devil-in-dreams straining against its containment, a remorseless predator pressing against a wall of curved glass.

Bismuth ran.

INDEX PUT A restraining arm across John Stainwright's chest and held him firm.

John was devastated, his eyes wide and flaring with fury, but his voice was steady and firm.

"Let me go, Jon. I want my dog."

Index softened his grip on John's shoulder but stood in front of him, blocking his way.

"We have to see to the boy."

"*You* see to the fucking boy."

Index closed his eyes.

"Morgoder will kill you. You don't want to die in this Quay."

John stepped to the side, like a child trying to see past a father protecting him from a sight of carnage.

Index raised his hands. They were huge hands, the palms deeply lined.

"I'll stop you if I have to," he said.

John clenched his fists, but now his eyes were wet with tears and he was trembling.

"Take the boy inside. I'll get your dog," Index said.

BISMUTH CARRIED THE boy through his father's shop. John stood at the door and watched as Index trod across the bombsite towards the dump. He felt hollow and very afraid. Old feelings of isolation and exclusion rose from a part of him he had long forgotten and he closed his eyes tight against the hideous panic threatening to unwind him. He should never have let Bix go.

Bismuth had stopped at the door that led out into the arcade. He was watching John, his face lined with ancient compassion.

"I had no choice," Bismuth said. "But I am so sorry."

John let the door close against the bombsite. He looked into Bismuth's tired eyes, at the boy curled in his arms. He felt the coldness of the empty shop around him. He looked down at the counter and saw something that had not been there before.

It was a thin, silver curl of metal—a ringlet of swarf from a lathe—and he picked it up and twirled it in his fingers. It was serrated and sharp as a blade. He put it down again and stepped around the counter, the sensation of alienation and anxiety ebbing slightly. He walked over to Bismuth and put a hand on his arm. Bismuth nodded, and John knew he would never be alone again, not in this life or the next.

"Let's see to this boy," he said, and they left the shop and walked into the arcade.

11

THE ARCADE WAS a carnival of life and colour.

Overhead there was light, weak, watery snow-light. The blackouts had been rolled back and there was opalescence to the air. It was cold and dream-like and frosty but there was activity everywhere. There were floor tiles, jade green marble with Art Deco swirls, and now dust and leaves and shadows had been swept, they shone like something excavated, precious, all the dead years brushed carefully away. Throughout the arcade the units were full, working again, and there were flowers in the stall in bunches in buckets, on shelves and in rows at the front, displayed on the jade tiles, and the scent was blissful and extraordinary

John turned to Bismuth and whispered, "Are you doing this?"

Bismuth shook his head, an expression of wonder on his face. "This is how I remember it. As a boy."

Lesley and Anna came out of the café to meet them. They saw the boy in Bismuth's arms. Lesley reached out and touched his pale cheek.

"He's alive," Bismuth said, "but catatonic. I can't wake him."

Anna was looking around, peering past the giant. "Where's Bix?"

John explained. Anna and Lesley were distraught for him. Lesley held him, the curls of her hair soft against his cheek. John closed his eyes and cried.

Bismuth carried the boy to the flower stall. Away from the throat-closing stench of the dump and the staleness of the bombsites, he could smell the boy now, the musty airless smell of thousands of nights spent in that refrigerator as a part of Chapel stored away in oblong darkness, like something fossilised in a chamber of black amber. The scent from the stall drew him. He could hear the voices of his friends, John's sobs, the clatter and bustle of the working stalls around him. Birds fluttered in the skylights. He could hear the people in the café, their voices constantly raised. He stooped beneath the low, sloping roof and stood amongst the garlands and bouquets. He inhaled, clearing his nose of the noisome dregs still clogging his sinuses. Gradually his head cleared.

There was a bench at the rear of the stall and he placed the boy on it, laying him so that he was curled on his side, with one arm gently arranged beneath his head to support it.

He stepped back and waited.

ANDREW CHAPEL BEHELD the refrigerator.

It stood, as it had always stood, on its platform of rotting cardboard boxes, its heavy door shut against the existent darkness clamped inside, the true polygon of his deepest nightmares.

He held the burgundy handbag tight against his chest and tried to breathe. Panic froze him, rising in great distorting tremors through his guts, palpitating his heart. Depersonalisation gripped him, reworking his surroundings into something flimsy and absurd, without the substance to sustain an illusion of reality. Everything threatened to collapse, and in that frailty became itself threatening, teetering, a mockery. Only the refrigerator behaved. Its solidity grew immense, a sarcophagus containing the stirring ruin of a god.

He could hear it calling. It was incessant, a black, smoking cable being drawn the length of space, reptile-cold and subtle as a concealed blade, and into the ventricles of his mind.

Now he had the jar and the remains it contained he could no longer resist it. He sobbed and took a step closer to the refrigerator. As clouds gathered overhead, great strokes from a dirty brush on a canvas scorched black, he reached out and took hold of the handle. He felt agitation within the jar and dragged his eyes away from the trembling hand that gripped the handle. He cried out as the light burning inside tore at the backs of his eyes. Fire and nightmares, silhouettes of savageries dancing in rooms boarded from the light.

Inside the refrigerator they would become one and the containment would break. *Wouldn't you like to be whole?* the voice said.

"*Yes*," whispered Chapel, and opened the door.

DANIEL SWUNG THE jeep off the A217 and into the car park of a small McDonald's next door to the recycling center. He pulled up in a space at the far end of the car park and switched off the engine.

"Hungry?" asked Trevena.

Daniel ignored him. He got out and walked around to the back of the jeep. He lifted a roll of canvas and took something from beneath it that he slipped inside his coat, and then he went to the passenger side and opened the door. He helped Mrs. Chapel out of the jeep. She stood staring ahead without focus, pigeon-toed in her furry boots. Daniel took her arm and led her onto the path that ran around the outskirts of the car park. Trevena followed them.

Daniel stepped off the path and approached a row of high bushes that bordered the recycling center. He pushed through a narrow gap and took Chapel's mother through with him. Trevena stuffed his hands in his pocket and glanced over at the McDonald's, unease gnawing at him. What did they look like? Two men dragging an old lady into some bushes. Fucks *sake*.

He ducked through the gap. There was another path running behind the bushes, untended and buckled with weeds. A long palisade security fence ran the length of it. It was at least twelve feet high and each pale ended in a sharp triple-pointed notch. "We'll never get over that," Trevena said.

Daniel winked at him and reached into his coat. He withdrew a formidable-looking crowbar and twirled it in his fist like a baton.

"Not over," he said, and knelt down by the bottom of the fence and inserted the crowbar between two of the steel pales. He leaned into it and Trevena could hear him straining. He took a step forward, but heard a sharp crack and two of the pales popped from their rail.

Daniel looked up and grinned. "Security implications," he said. "There's always a way in." He moved the crowbar along and did the same with the next three pales. He stood up and took hold of the first pale he had forced off. He pulled upwards and Trevena was surprised to see how easily it bent against the high fulcrum of the top rail. He stepped in and helped, pulling the last rails loose.

Daniel edged through the gap and gently helped Chapel's mother step over the jagged lip of the bottom rail. Trevena bit his lip, fearful of her catching the backs of her legs on the metal. The parchment skin would tear like an economy bin bag. She made it through unscathed and stood staring into the depths of the recycling center, her mouth half open, dry and soundless.

Trevena followed and they stood together beneath the glare of the security lights. Daniel took Chapel's mother's hand and they walked across the smooth, swept concrete towards the back of the lot.

CHAPEL STARED AT the interior of the refrigerator, at the yellowed plastic shell discoloured by mould and scuff marks, the rusted freezer compartment built into the top, and saw a sky beyond it, red and streaked with smoky cloud. The image shuddered and shifted sideways as though the fridge had been struck with great force and made to pan across the sky, but the fridge remained there, unmoving on its stack of boxes. Chapel stumbled backwards, still clutching the bag. He couldn't bring himself to remove the jar even though he felt its desire to be free of the bag. What would it do to his flesh if he pressed his palms against that roaring glass?

Then the image tipped again and he could see shadows moving against the surface of churned muck. Something blotted the light and Chapel saw the black, draped shape of a monstrous figure as it crashed to the ground and rolled towards the back of the fridge. He apprehended its mass and his skin crawled as it lifted its head slowly from the ground, and the bare skull stapled with shreds of dark flesh hung in the gap. It seemed to gaze through at him, stunned and insensible, the great arms that pushed it up from the ground trembling like the legs of a foal. Its fists ground the dirt.

And it leapt through the gap.

Chapel fell backwards and dropped the bag. It hit the concrete with a padded thud, but the heavy Kilner jar didn't shatter. He kicked his heels and raked himself away from the thing lunging from the refrigerator with the heels of his hands, grazing the flesh, breaking fingernails.

The creature was trying to force itself through, its great size wedging it between two worlds. It twisted and bellowed and wrenched an arm through, and this time the refrigerator did move. It rocked and trembled as the creature reached a huge fused fist towards the bag that lay on its side between them. Chapel covered his eyes as the faux-leather began to bubble and melt, turning black and peeling off of the jar. Shafts of diseased light burst from tears in the material and strobed across the yard.

The creature stopped moving. Its arm froze and its fist stopped reaching and hung, wavering, in the air above the jar. Its skull lifted and peered at Chapel, tilted slightly, the mouth open and baring double rows of teeth. A sound came from the back of its throat, not a bellow, but a whine, and then it was bucking again, the entire refrigerator lifting feet from the ground and slamming down onto the cardboard, as something seized the creature from the rear and gored at it, picking it up and dragging it back to the place with the red, fuming sky.

Chapel sat forward, his eyes wide and watched as something huge and made of mechanisms of light cast the monster about on colossal pearlescent tusks, winnowing it hollow. It tossed its head a final, exultant time and the monster blew apart. Chapel witnessed this as an abrupt upheaval of brown, wormy meat bursting from the shredded confines of the cape. The elongated skull hit the ground and split along the frontal suture line and the toxic light bled out, dissipating like embers from a smoldering plague pit.

Chapel glimpsed the creature of light again as it passed across the aperture and stood over the remains of the monster. It lowered its great, blazing head and stirred its tusks through the muck, drawing the cape aside, and seemed to ponder the dissolution for a moment.

And then it turned and looked at Chapel. Chapel gasped and fell back onto his elbows. The creature was changing. The plates of light that made it and the thrilling wheels that revolved at its heart were fading, powering down. In a moment Chapel found himself looking at a man.

The man held out a hand.

Chapel got to his feet. The jar lay on its side. The bag had burned away almost completely and the jar lay on a bed of melted plastic. He approached it, shielding his eyes from the awful light that pulsed within it. It was weaker now, fluttering, but still wormed at his retinas. And he could still hear the call, desperate now, imploring, promising meaning and wholeness. Wholeness in hell, but wholeness nonetheless.

He touched it with the toe of his shoe, rolling it away from the remains of the bag. He took off his jacket and threw it over the jar, concealing its contents, and the light that blazed from the eyes of the thing inside.

The man was still standing on the other side of the refrigerator. He was beckoning. He stepped forward and was about to reach through the aperture but as he did so, Chapel heard a voice.

"*Andrew.*"

Chapel turned slowly, his flesh crawling. His hands clenched into fists and his chest tightened with the old anxiety, a strain of trepidation more primitive, more ingrained than anything generated by these fresh horrors.

His mother was standing ten feet behind him. She was with two men, one of whom he recognized. His presence there was so surreal, so unexpected that for a moment the shock of seeing his mother was neutralized.

And then she was coming for him, her dressing gown peeling open to reveal a tatty red cardigan and veined bony shins visible beneath her knee-length floral nightdress.

Chapel recoiled. The two men were coming for him, too. One held a crowbar in his right hand and was lifting it, a look of bleak purpose on his face. The other man was watching his companion raise the crowbar, and his hands were coming up in a gesture of dissent, his eyes wide and his mouth open to say something, perhaps shout a warning.

Chapel stumbled backwards, catching the jar with his heel.

"Andrew," the old woman said again, and he cowered, a child again, all the decades of bitter criticism and pious scruples she had projected onto him for no-one's sake but her own burst into his head and he clenched his eyes shut and held up his hands. The tone of her voice *exhausted* him.

"You're dead," he whispered.

The man swung the crowbar.

"GOOD GOD," SAID Trevena.

Daniel swung the crowbar again and this time took a chunk of the back of the head off like a divot. It sailed across the yard and landed a few feet away from a metal container labeled *Hardcore only*.

The old woman collapsed. One of her fluffy boots had come off and sat next to her white, twitching foot like a petrified and useless little pet, hollow and unzipped as if it had abruptly shat its back out in shock.

Daniel stood over the woman and clubbed her again and she stopped twitching. Andrew Chapel was moaning, his hands still raised, trying to ward off the horror. Trevena circled the body of his mother and went to him.

"She's dead," Chapel was muttering. "She's dead."

"Fuck me, Daniel," Trevena said as he knelt next to Chapel. "I think you got her."

Daniel stood up straight, his expression serene. He looked down at the old woman and let the crowbar drop from his fingers.

Trevena put a hand on Chapel's trembling shoulder.

Chapel looked up, his eyes wide and full of tears. His hair had fallen across his brow and he looked to Trevena like a man half his age.

"She's dead," Chapel said.

"Yes," Trevena said. "How long has it been?"

"Two months," Chapel said.

Trevena held him while he wept.

TREVENA HELPED CHAPEL get to his feet.

"How long have you known she was a Toyceiver?" Trevena asked Daniel, glancing at the body of the old woman. She was already liquefying, rotting away inside her garments.

"As soon as I saw her," Daniel said. He used his boot to ruck the clothing into a pile. The movement seemed to agitate the process and in a moment there was nothing left of her but what had soaked into the material. Daniel bundled it up and took it over to a waste container. He lobbed it over the side.

"Why didn't you kill her then? It would have saved Andrew having to see that."

Daniel was wrapping the jar in Chapel's jacket. He picked it up.

"Closure," he said.

"I've seen that done more therapeutically."

"I only did what he wanted to do himself. He needed to see her. It makes it real."

"But it wasn't her."

"Yes, it was. As much as it needed to be."

Trevena and Daniel looked at Chapel as he spoke.

"I didn't see her when she was dying. I didn't go to the funeral.

Whatever that thing was had taken her essence from that house, whatever was left of her seeped into every fucking surface. I could *feel* it, all through the meat of that thing. She's gone now."

"You phoned her, from your house."

Chapel laughed and shook his head. He looked at both men and Trevena saw that the amusement was sour.

"You're clever, but just lucky," he said. "I made that call over two months ago. A son's duty call. I haven't used the phone since."

FLASHING BLUE LIGHTS lit up the entrance to the dump.

"It's the rozzers," said Trevena.

Daniel spoke to Chapel.

"Do you know what you are?"

Chapel shrugged. He looked worn out, drained. "I have an idea."

"Come with us."

Daniel led Chapel to the refrigerator. He felt Chapel pull back, withdraw from the opening. The irony was not lost on Daniel. To find freedom Chapel would have to trust them and step into the thing that had haunted him his entire life. The aperture trembled and the figure on the other side, the tall blond man, appeared to flicker like an image on a screen that was about to lose resolution.

"What about the police?" Trevena asked.

"What are they going to find?" Daniel said.

"CCTV?"

"Three blokes disappear into the back of a fridge. We both know what's going to happen to *that* tape."

"You clubbed an old lady to death," said Trevena. "Technically."

"There'll be no evidence. Besides, I waited until we were in a blind spot."

"You worked that out?"

"It's not the Tower of London, Phil. It's a tip. Camera on the gate, couple on the fence. Probably caught Chapel when he was going over the first time."

Daniel stepped up into the refrigerator, ducking beneath the freezer compartment. He backed through the gap and held both hands out. He felt the rubble beneath his boots and smelt the stink of the dump. Trevena stood behind Chapel and put his palm in the small of his back.

"Go on," he said.

Chapel took a deep breath. He squared his shoulders. He turned and looked at Trevena and his eyes were a little wild. Trevena could feel him shaking, could sense he was ready to bolt.

Daniel nodded and reached out and grabbed Chapel's arms. Trevena shoved.

Chapel went through and Trevena followed.

AS THEY CROSSED the bombsite, Trevena appraised the man they had rescued. Chapel walked with his head down, picking his way with great caution over the rubble. He walked between Index and Daniel but seemed uninterested in their presence or what they carried. Daniel held the jar; Index held Bix.

Trevena considered what he knew of the man, which didn't amount to a great deal besides what Chapel had told him of his childhood and what Trevena had himself discovered. Trevena could identify with much of what Chapel had told him. They were of the same generation, and most of what Chapel had spoken of resonated with Trevena. Trevena's childhood had been poor but happy. He had grown up in a village in East Anglia just outside Cambridge, typically plain and pastoral, and holidays had been taken in Hunstanton, Southwold, and—if it had been a particularly lean year—Great Yarmouth. Holiday camps and caravans, hot summers and the cold North Sea. But Trevena had been spared the endless revisits; his parents had died within a year of each other when he was in his twenties. No routine obligatory trips to see the folks, struggling to find a role, or a persona to project back into their unchanged world, a transaction to negotiate in order to remain something preserved for them, for their sake. He had been set free. Chapel had never known that freedom. His past was a set to which a part of him must always return, to enact a crippling role. There must be places and people there, unchanged in outlook but older, superimposed like the structural modifications made to the road he had grown up on, constantly there, constantly reminding him of the tyranny of his mother, of the fractured childhood that had been taken from him.

Trevena never went back, never went home again. There were too many memories there, good ones he was better off keeping in his head, and some bad ones safely boxed away and repressed, too many people still around with no ambition or drive, drinking in the same pubs and shopping down the same aisles. Trevena shuddered. Sometimes the ghosts that haunted you most were the ones that were still alive.

THEY WALKED THROUGH Dark Time-light. Chloe could feel it forever generating, self-sustaining, and they were at once a part of it, illuminated and eternal.

Once she saw a shining thread stitch through the fabric of the air an astronomical distance away—a Gantry opening and closing, like a neuron firing— and she thought, *John*, and wished him well. Another, closer but still immeasurably distant, tore through the firmament, the jet stream from a twinkling, alien machine, and Chloe realized it was the great Looms that were weaving them.

They walked a labyrinth of monumental brazen machines, an endless factory built for archangels. The floor they crossed was the rim of it, the cytoplasm of a cell, and the Looms were its organelles, shuttling, clacking, from edge to unimaginable edge, flying, jagged cathedrals weaving Gantries like protein strands.

Bismuth, Index, Alex, Eliot.

She could sense them the instant their Gantries opened, each a unique resonance that she felt like a gravity wave, sending ripples throughout the great Compartment. She felt pain, fear, exultation, and sadness. Their emotions were forces as powerful as anything nuclear, prayers offered up in darkness unknowing of the immensity of light through which they passed. It was *faith*, she realized, that flung these Looms, faith that fuelled them and knitted their equations.

Chloe looked at Doctor Mocking. They were walking in silence, he following her lead as they negotiated the shining, golden boulevards. He had been here before, or in some region similar, and she wondered what he had seen. What had he intuited of this place? Of what might lie beyond it?

Doctor Mocking smiled at her.

"How are we doing?" he said.

Chloe took his hand again. "Are you tired?"

"Not at all."

"Are you going to die?"

"No," said Doctor Mocking. "Not here. Nothing dies here."

WHEN THINGS END, *is that moment all that remains? An image blasted onto rock, everything that has passed over its surface before nothing more than the wind or water from a stream, fading forever as it moves away. All we have left to hold is a shoreline pebble stamped with fossils of loss, intaglios of grief, turning it inconsolably in our fingers, while we howl at the sky? Is the future built against such ever-mounting cairns, foundations pressing us towards the dark?*

And while he thought this with a cold and undirected fury, Index laid Bix's body on the floor of the flower stall, amongst the sweet bouquets, with great tenderness, and stood aside as John Stainwright knelt and wept.

Others knelt with him, so that he didn't weep alone, Index amongst them.

THEY WERE CONTENT as they walked. There was time here, but no sense of the duration of it. They might have been there forever. They might have just arrived, landing lightly from the Gantry on a shallow slope of brass, rolling laughing between the crags of two soaring

Looms and into the labyrinth. Time was both a now and an always, issuing in pulses and ripples from every point simultaneously.

Chloe stopped walking. Doctor Mocking stood beside her. They both looked left just as the ground trembled beneath them and there was the sound of thunder. A million servers clicking over, a million shuttles racing, flying, rods and lathes blurring as the power station cycled. And up it went: a Loom an aisle away. Firing into the air like a rocket bathed in desert sunlight, weaving a Gantry behind it.

They watched, open-mouthed as it sped away, its wake staggering them, its noise deafening.

Chloe squinted, watched it go.

I don't know you, she thought.

They walked on.

"LOOK," SAID LESLEY. Her eyes were red-rimmed and her face was pale. She gently touched John's arm.

John looked up and saw that the boy was awake. He was sitting on the bench at the back of the flower stall. He was staring at the group of people clustered around the entrance to the stall with a look of fear.

"Hey," Lesley said. She stood up. The boy flinched, his white face trembling.

"Don't be afraid." She took a step towards him.

Lesley held out a hand. The boy looked at it, looked up into Lesley's face. She smiled and he took her hand.

As she turned to walk the boy out of the stall, Chapel came forward, his face as pale as the boy's. The boy saw him and his grip tightened painfully on Lesley's hand. She squatted next to him and put a palm softly on his cold cheek. "It's ok," she said.

And then the boy let go of Lesley's hand, pressed both of his own over his eyes and screamed.

Chapel turned and blundered into Daniel. He tore at the jacket covering the jar and ripped it away. Daniel gasped and stumbled backwards, away from the group. Chapel had his hands around the jar and as Daniel stumbled, Chapel pushed and wrenched the jar from Daniel's arms.

Lesley was holding the boy, trying to comfort him. Bismuth moved, Index and Trevena behind him, but Chapel was already halfway down the arcade. He turned, suddenly indecisive, the jar molten in his arms, a fuel rod of sick light. Chapel's eyes were black. He opened his mouth, said something, but could not be heard over the sound of the boy's continuing screams.

The air trembled around him. He took a step backwards and a Gantry opened and he was gone.

The boy stopped screaming and fell sobbing into Lesley's arms.

CHLOE AND DOCTOR Mocking reached the end of the boulevard and turned left onto another. Doctor Mocking had the sense they were traversing the surface of a vast circuit board and the Looms were its valves and capacitors, plugged in and bristling with energy. The hum was perpetual, but choral, enchanting, and their ears had accustomed to it quickly and now they barely noticed it.

"Were you married?" Chloe asked.

The question didn't seem to surprise Doctor Mocking.

"Yes," he said. "She left when the girls were young. She couldn't accept what I was."

"Did it frighten her?"

"I think it did. I loved her very much, but I understood. I threw myself into the work afterwards. It was Lesley who pulled me back. She wasn't much older than you are now."

"And then you came here, to find Bismuth."

"Yes. I suppose I displaced my grief. Instead of letting it destroy me, I thought, if I could do something good, something useful—"

Chloe pulled on Doctor Mocking's hand.

They stopped. "Listen," said Chloe.

Above the eternal sounds of the Compartment they could hear a sound at counterpoint to them, something arrhythmic, industrial.

"It's him," Chloe said.

* * *

INDEX LEFT THE group and went to the window of the café. He gestured through the window and Johnny appeared at the door, a dishcloth in his hands. He stepped out into the arcade. In the café, voices were raised as usual but there was an apprehensive tone to them. Pale faces peered through the steamy glass.

Outside the café, Johnny spoke perfect English.

"I saw the others, Jon, at a train shed in Quay-Fomalhaut. I gave Eliot breakfast. They seemed well."

"Can you take us back there, Johnny?"

"Of course! Come inside and I'll set the coordinates." Johnny winked, conspiratorial.

Index thanked him and went to gather the others.

Lesley was still holding the boy. He was looking around with dark, startled eyes. She soothed him. Bismuth, Daniel, Steve and Trevena were talking in a huddle outside the flower stall. There was a lot of swearing. Trevena put a hand on Daniel's shoulder and Daniel shook his head, raised his hands as if to say, *how the fuck did that happen*? Anna stood with Claire and Elizabeth inside the stall and tried to comfort John Stainwright.

The boy disengaged from Lesley and stepped over to John. John was kneeling at Bix's side, stroking the dog's flank. He had tried to clean a lot of the dirt from Bix's fur, but it was still matted in places. John was talking to the dog in a quiet voice.

John looked up as the boy approached.

The boy squatted and put a hand out. "I'm Andy," he said. "What happened to your dog?"

John took the boy's hand and gave it a quick, loose shake.

"John," he said. "He was helping to rescue you. He got hurt and died."

"He's not dead," the boy said, and laughed. John stared at him. Lesley came over. "Andy, shhhh," she said, a little astounded that the boy should be so insensitive. John's lip curled.

The boy turned to Lesley. Some of the others were standing

around now, faces registering concern. Anna knelt and put an arm around John's shoulder.

"He's not dead," Andrew Chapel said again, "Not yet. I've spent a long time in the dark. I know what death is. Close your eyes."

John Stainwright placed both hands against Bix's chest. He lowered his head and closed his eyes.

They connected.

John stood at the foot of a low mountain. The rock was red, darkening to purple as the sun set beyond the forest at his back. The earth around his feet was rich, loamy, and soft. It smelt of autumn. He heard something, and looked up.

There was a small cave about thirty feet above his head. It made a dark, shaded indentation in the rock, a cool niche like an archway leading into the mountain. An aluminium extension ladder leaned against the rock face, its steps flaked with mud and leaves. John saw paw prints.

He heard the sound again, a scratching and clatter of pebbles, and looked up to see Bix poke his head out of the entrance to the cave.

"Hi John," Bix said.

"Hey, Bix. Should I come up?"

Bix looked back over his shoulder. When he returned his attention to John, he said, "Better not. I'm okay here. Safe. Got someone to look after for a while."

John raised a hand.

"Good to see you, fella. Do you need anything?"

"I'm good. I love you, John."

"Love you, too, Bix."

John opened his eyes and rubbed his face. He looked around at the concerned faces of his friends. He smiled.

"Hey, Claire," he said. "How long have you known you were pregnant?"

Claire's eyes grew very wide.

Steve said, "What?"

John carried Bix into the café. Johnny cleared some tables and indicated that John could make a bed for the dog in the corner. A couple of diners gave him their coats and an elegant-looking woman with a dramatic and tottering beehive of graying blonde hair took off her black mohair sweater and handed it to John with a shy smile. John nodded, "Merci, merci," he said. He laid Bix on his bed and settled him, stroking his muzzle with gentle, trembling fingers.

The group stood around and waited as Johnny went behind his counter and placed his hands flat on the blue Formica worktop.

"Et maintenant," he said, and clapped his hands.

The café began to fold in on itself. It was disorienting and Trevena staggered and sat down on a spare stool. He leaned against the counter and watched as the window slid towards him. The customers all froze. Their faces slackened and their eyes unfocused. Index tottered over to where Trevena was sitting, like a sailor negotiating a deck in a rising storm. "Just fitting ourselves into the new place. It's quite a bit smaller."

Trevena swallowed and gave Index a weak smile. The counter retracted and he lifted his arm, watching with apprehension as the urn at the end tilted beneath gas pipes that were kinking themselves into a more compact arrangement. The stool slid away from Index taking Trevena with it. Trevena shrugged and waved his fingers as he slid across the floor. Index roared with laughter.

The stool rotated once and Trevena watched his reflection revolve through a speckled, steamy mirror fixed to a wall that wrenched suddenly away from him, crimping like foil. As the mirror slid through ninety degrees, Trevena saw Steve and Claire holding each other, their eyes tightly shut, in the middle of the room as chairs and tables rotated around them like rides on a carousel. Elizabeth was holding onto Bismuth's arm, her face white, while Bismuth patted her hand and stared impassively out of the window.

And then all was still. Trevena turned around and looked across the café. Johnny stood behind a much shorter counter. He clapped again. "C'est fait!" he said, and all around the customers began speaking again. Cutlery rattled on plates and in cups, chairs scraped as people adjusted themselves to the new dimensions. It was certainly more snug in there now. Trevena heard the radio come back on in a series of static bursts and faltering signals, the voice of the newscaster gaining strength and integrity as the café settled.

Index went to the door and opened it.

COLIN ZIPPED UP and turned to go back into the train shed.

He heard something move on the cinders behind him, a gritting step, and he whirled around.

The Despatrix stood between the rails, her hair hanging in a fringe across her eyes. Her full lips parted.

"Take it out again. Let me see what you've got."

The Despatrix reached down between her thighs and loosened the thong of flesh covering her groin. She slid long fingers beneath the flap of skin and lifted it aside, revealing a discreet slit curving beneath the hairless mound. She took a step closer, her hand still pressed against her sex.

Colin stared at her as she came across the tracks. He felt a sudden and long-forgotten pulse between his legs and was dismayed to discover he was getting an erection.

"Oh bloody hell," said Colin. "Not *now*."

The Despatrix kissed the air with her wide, wet lips, and flipped her fringe away from her eyes with a toss of her head. Colin staggered backwards, his hands raised, the mistimed bulge in his shorts subsiding the instant he saw those diseased sockets blazing from her otherwise perfect face.

He turned and ran, his flip-flops smacking against the soles of his bony feet. He could hear the Despatrix following, treading more slowly up the tracks.

"Alex!" Colin shouted, his voice hoarse with exertion. "*Eliot!*"

The boys' faces appeared as they leaned out of *Railgrinder's* cab. They saw Colin running towards them with the Despatrix following, and both leaped from the cab. They came around the front of *Railgrinder* and went to help Colin the last few yards. He was red faced and panting. He clutched at the boys' arms and let them drag him the rest of the way along the tracks and up the slope that led onto the platform.

Eliot watched as the Despatrix approached. Her long hair fell in lush waves across her narrow, pale shoulders. Long thighs, slender ankles, naked feet picking their way over the cinders.

"It's beautiful," he said, and there was an unmistakable note of regret in his voice.

Colin was leaning forwards, his hands on his knees, gasping for breath. His ponytail had come loose and a loop of thin gray hair hung over his shoulder.

"Yeah," he said. "If you don't have to look at the mantelpiece."

Alex went to the edge of the platform.

"We can't keep dodging it," he said. "We'll have to kill it ourselves."

"It's too powerful." Eliot said.

The Despatrix had reached the front of *Railgrinder's* engine. She stood gazing up at the boys, her head cocked, a hand cupped between her legs, fingers deep and kneading. She ran the palm of her other hand over the warming metal of the engine.

And then the long muscles of her thighs tensed and her back arched. She uttered a guttural, drawn-out moan, and driven by the power of her revolting climax, she leaped from the tracks, arms outstretched, and plucked Alex from the edge of the platform.

INDEX EMERGED FROM the café into the train shed in time to see Alex disappear over the edge of the platform. Eliot had already made to leap down onto the tracks and had time to register that the others had arrived before momentum took him over and he landed on the cinders between the rails.

They crowded the edge of the platform as Eliot—the stockier of the two and with more muscle developing in his arms and chest—piled into the Despatrix and wrestled her away from Alex. Alex looked stunned, but picked himself up and headed back into the fight.

John Stainwright reached into his coat and pulled out the Instruments Bismuth had given him. He was about to step down onto the tracks but Index held out an arm.

"Wait," he said.

John turned to look at the others but they all appeared to be heeding Index's command, and were waiting, tense and poised, while the boys fought the creature.

Colin put out a hand. "John," he said. "Give me that lever."

John handed it over and Colin trotted over to *Railgrinder's* cab and climbed in. He tapped the lever on his palm, thinking.

"This must be it," he said, and slotted the end of the throttle lever onto the awaiting thread and tightened the nut with his fingers.

The Despatrix shrieked and backhanded Eliot across the cheek. He staggered, dazed, with blood pouring from his nose. The Despatrix rounded on Alex but he was already charging in, and caught her a blow to the stomach with the sole of his boot. The Despatrix howled and fell to her knees. She pressed a hand against her belly and glared up at Alex from beneath her swaying fringe. Black blood squirmed between her fingers, slow and heavy, and when she stood again Alex could see a wound, reopened by the force of the blow, where the white edges of an old scar were gaping.

"Eliot!" shouted John, and lobbed the other Instrument towards him. Eliot caught it and, despite the situation, held the brass cylinder in his hand for a second, a smile spreading across his face. He wiped blood from beneath his nose with the back of his hand and walked towards the Despatrix.

The Despatrix was crouching at the far side of the tracks. The tops of her thighs were sheathed in cold, congealing blood. She moved her head back and forth from the boys to those standing crowded on the edge of the platform. She snarled. She wanted one of these boys very badly. She darted forward, slender hands hooked into claws, and went for Alex. She would have the small one, tear out his throat. She would take one of them with her.

Eliot stepped between them and swung his arm in a low arc. The Despatrix barreled into him but he braced his legs and leaned his shoulder into her. The Despatrix's face registered shock. Her mouth opened wide and she squealed. Alex jumped forward and seized one of her flailing arms. Eliot pushed again, and slid the entire shaft of the kaleidoscope into the hole in the Despatrix's belly.

The Despatrix bucked and flailed with her other arm, but Eliot ducked beneath it and grabbed hold of the end of the kaleidoscope with both hands. He twisted the object chamber and heard—above the scrape of feet on cinders and the agonised mewl of the Despatrix—the familiar and always oddly wistful sound of the tiny coloured beads falling into new and unique patterns: *churrrr churrrr*.

The Despatrix screamed and clutched at her gut. Eliot shoved a final time and the end of the kaleidoscope disappeared inside her, thrusting upwards beneath its ribs. He grabbed her other arm and he and Alex held the Despatrix in a restraint as her legs buckled and she sank to the rails in shock.

Colin was peering down at them from *Railgrinder's* cab. His face was grim but he had a resolute look in his eye. He reached up and pulled on the chain whistle.

The Despatrix lifted her pointed chin and glared at him as the mournful note rose, fell, and echoed through the train shed.

Colin released the brake and grasped the throttle lever. *Railgrinder* hissed and belched a great raft of furious, white-hot steam against the roof of the shed. It jolted forward and the grinding wheels beneath its engine carved sparks off the rails.

"Step away from the dirty bitch," he said.

The boys let go of the Despatrix's arms. They went to the side of the platform and were helped up by Index and Daniel.

The Despatrix was shaking, her hands in the hole in her belly, trying to pull the kaleidoscope out, but there was too much heat, and she slid her burning, blackened hands from her guts and held them before her face in despair. The kaleidoscope was glowing, filling the Despatrix's trunk with good, clean light. She sank further onto her haunches and put her smoking fists in the cinders. Her eyes bulged and flared as the light filled her, and then ruptured as *Railgrinder* bore her into the ground and passed over her.

Nobody rejoiced, no voices rose in cheers as the body was folded over itself and turned to paste beneath the grinding wheels. Those that watched did so with white faces. The others turned away. Colin was hunched down in the cab and only engaged the brake when *Railgrinder* had gone a yard past where the Despatrix had been kneeling. The engine fumed and trembled, the remains concealed beneath it.

Eliot had watched, Alex had not.

Doctor Mocking and Chloe walked on, passing Loom after Loom, each one towering over them and throbbing with unlimited energy, until they reached an alcove set between two of the Looms. The area was wide as a building site, its surface scarred and pitted. It contained the relic of a Loom, the walls that remained blackened and jagged. They stepped off the road onto the crumbling bay and stood beneath the bulk of the Loom.

It was cool in the sudden shadow, the shafts and pillars that remained were dull and lifeless. It had been hollowed out, so that it looked like the shelving remains of some great, ancient fortress, crenellated and empty of parts essential to its function.

They went further inside, beneath a high lattice of bare stanchions, while all around them the Loom clacked and hummed, dormant, vast and alien, its servers jammed, its power re-routed.

There was a sound from the rear of the Loom, a crackle, and a sudden discharge of sparks. The floor beneath them shuddered.

Doctor Mocking peered into the depths of the Loom, his neck bent and his eyes narrowed.

There was another brief display of sparks and a man shouted,

"*Shit!*"

Doctor Mocking saw someone coming towards him, shaking his right hand as if to rid it of dirt, or dispel a sudden pain. The man was slight of build with short, dark hair. He was wearing glasses, which reflected the Compartment light behind them and looked like gold coins in his face. His shirtsleeves were rolled up to past his elbows and his trousers, particularly the knees, were blotted with oily handprints and powdered with dust. In his left hand he carried what appeared to be a soldering iron.

Doctor Mocking exhaled a long breath and went to meet the man, to embrace him, all the time laughing with astonishment and blessed relief.

Robin Knox smiled a small, crooked smile, and hugged the Doctor in return.

"SEVEN YEARS," ROBIN said. "Wow. It doesn't feel like I've been here a day. Cade's dead?"

"Yes. We got him."

Robin looked relieved. "He was strong, enraged. He caught me by surprise. After a struggle he threw me off the Gantry and into the Compartment. That's when time stopped for me."

Doctor Mocking looked around, at the blackened shell of the Loom. Robin watched him for a moment, anticipating his questions, and then spoke.

"That's how the Autoscopes travel to and from the Quays. They fire one, it burns out like a bulb in an old radio. They aren't meant to use them, but they're allowed certain latitude it seems. I think it expends tremendous energy and effort. I've only seen one other like it. I saw it take off, and it burned and smoked and screamed. It was miles away but I imagine there are hundreds of thousands amongst the trillions here in this Compartment alone but the chances of finding another are equal to finding a precise atom in an ocean of seawater."

Doctor Mocking turned to face Robin, his expression curious.

"I wanted to keep busy," Robin said with a small smile and a shrug. "Doing what I do. Trying to make myself useful if I was going to remain stuck in here. Tinkering."

Doctor Mocking smiled too, at the thought of Robin *tinkering* with the great Looms of Dark Time. Of them all, he had always been the bravest and most pioneering engineer.

"I wanted to find out how the Autoscopes used these, how they *forced* them to operate, and whether I could stop them. But the golden Looms were flawless and impenetrable. I needed to find one of these."

"How did you find it?" Chloe asked.

Robin knelt by her side and put a hand on her cheek. "I'll show you something, but you'll have to be brave. You might feel very sad."

Chloe looked into Robin's eyes, saw the gravity there and gave him a solemn nod.

"Come with me," Robin said.

Doctor Mocking took Chloe's hand and followed Robin into the dark recesses of the Loom, and the wreck of the thing that was concealed there.

IT WAS A camper van. It sat on four wheels tilted on buckled axles. The windows were gone, shattered by whatever had befallen the vehicle. Chips of glass still protruded from the perishing rubber sills. The sliding door in its side was gone, lost from its runner, and the interior was bare, stripped of its original furnishings. Beneath its sagging chassis a pool of oil had spread out across the floor of the Loom. Despite the dents and scrapes, and the lack of light this far back in the body of the Loom, Chloe could see, where paint remained, that it was green, and had once been bright and cheerful.

"Oh," she said. She let go of Doctor Mocking's hand and put her fingers to her face, to cover the trembling of her lips. Her eyes blurred with sudden tears. She felt a wrench in her belly, a sensation of loss as though something had reached a cold hand inside her and stolen a chunk of her core. "*Babur*," she whispered.

"It's his van," Robin said. "It was here when I found the Loom. It called me here. Before I gave it to Babur, I fitted it with a device that could track us all when we were in the Quays. When I reached this Loom, after what might have been days, minutes, centuries – I have no way of knowing—of walking, my beacon was alight and flashing."

"Despite the wreckage?" Doctor Mocking asked.

Robin shook his head. "The van was beaten up, but I've stripped most of it for parts. There were tools here, and water in the bottle beneath the sink, which was welcome. Pleasant, if not entirely necessary. I don't get hungry or thirsty here." He indicated a dark corner recessed into the wall of the Loom. There was a couch and table there. "Took those out and made a camp. I can sit there and think. The battery was fine, so I've salvaged that, but everything else was fried when Babur hit the EMP."

"The alternator," Chloe said, still staring at the van. "Plays havoc with it."

"Yes," said Robin. "I sent Babur to find you, before you were born."

Chloe nodded, still looking towards the camper van. She remembered being in a town full of bookshops, being older than she was now, but innocent and unknowing in a way even more profound than her present child-state. All was new, and she recalled the sound of the van as it came into town, and the sight of it, bright and hackled with antennae and dishes and devices; the *thump* of the EMP as it discharged, destroying the advancing spiders; the first sight of the old man climbing out of the cab, stretching his back and going around to the rear of the van; the sound of his voice; the rush of emotion at his first touch – a handshake and a reassuring pat on her shoulder.

"I only met him once," Chloe said. "Not for long. But I loved him."

"He loved you, too," Doctor Mocking said. "He did this for you. For all of us."

"My parents told me what he did," Chloe said. "But it's hard, seeing this here. Was he...?" She left the question unasked, but Robin answered it for her.

"No. He was gone. I don't think he suffered. There's no sign of him, no sign of injury. I hope to meet him again, one day, in a Quay somewhere. When this is all over."

"*That* will be wonderful," Chloe said.

ROBIN HAD ONLY been able to theorize what had happened, but Doctor Mocking was able to complete the story for him. How there had been a battle in the road outside a pub in Daniel's Quay, and how Babur had driven the camper van into the Autoscopes' Incursion Gantry, sacrificing himself to close the Gantry.

"The EMP shut it down," Robin said. "I knew it was powerful, but I wasn't sure if it could do that. Awesome.

"And this was the Loom they used to force their way into the Quay. Either the EMP blew it apart or this is what's left once they've used it. Can't tell at this point, although the one I saw taking off was certainly breaking up. It looked like footage of a shuttle disaster."

"What have you discovered?" Doctor Mocking asked.

"Well, I don't think I can get this to work again. It's like the van's alternator. Knackered. But I have had better insight into how our whole system works. It came to me when I first saw the van. How what we do is about simultaneity, coincidence, the faith in quanta and how dreams are an effect of a kind of limitless energy we are able to use and modify. Me finding this van was more than blind luck. What do you call it, temporally coincident occurrences of acausal events?"

Doctor Mocking looked impressed. "That's Jung," he said. "Synchronicity."

"That's right, of course. The *Unus Mundus*. It's what we deal with, isn't it? The unified reality from which everything emerges and to which everything returns. That's this place, the source of all things. I have been able to estimate a measure of the energy that self-exists here." He held his thumb and index finger a sliver apart in front of his face, squinting through the tiny gap. "A square micron of the fabric of this place contains more energy than a thousand suns. It's the zero-point energy of God, the ground state of the Creator. Imagine converting that energy to matter and you could grow a galaxy on the palm of your hand.

"It's why the devil-in-dreams wants control of the Night Clock. To blacken these Compartments, burn them out like cancer spreading throughout eternity. It's heat-death in perpetuity. The razing of all creation-energy. Think about it. A God that can no longer create is no God at all."

Doctor Mocking looked around, at the landscape vast yet once familiar.

"We need to get out of here," he said. "Any ideas?"

Robin shrugged. "I've been trying for seven years, apparently, without any luck. Without any *synchronicity*, I should say. I understand more, but I can't translate that understanding into practical use. What I think is, this place isn't responsive to intellect or physical *work*. It needs something more… creative."

Doctor Mocking agreed. "Things need to come together at the right time. It's what happened before."

"Tell me," said Robin. "It might set something in motion. It might be what we need to move this on."

Doctor Mocking told him.

HE STOOD BEFORE the giant, his friend Bismuth, with the golden light of the Compartment all around. Doctor Mocking considered the terrible sadness borne on the other man's face. Exhaustion had discouraged his features of expression, his eyes of focus. He stood, hands loose at his sides, the levers in loops on his belt, head lowered, defeated.

Doctor Mocking reached out and took hold of Bismuth's arm, guided him away from the edge of the boulevard, embraced him.

"Come home," he said. "Old friend, come home with me."

Bismuth shuddered, and Doctor Mocking realised that the man was sobbing.

"There's no way back," Bismuth said. He stepped away from Doctor Mocking, his eyes blazing, wet with sudden pools of reflected gold.

"We go together," Doctor Mocking said. "The same way we came in."

Bismuth threw his arms wide. "And find an open Loom in all of this?"

"We walk until we find one."

Bismuth laughed, a defeated exhalation. "I've not seen one in all my time here. Leave me to wander. You've come here for nothing."

"There are others like us, waking up, coming together. We're being called."

"We are all lost."

"No. Not any more. We are being found again."

Bismuth turned, started to move away.

"Wait."

Bismuth stopped but did not turn.

"Take out your Compass."

Bismuth did not speak, but his head lifted at the command.

He put his hand into the right pocket of his long coat and withdrew an object. He held it tight in his fist.

"Show me."

Bismuth held out his hand, uncurled his fingers. Doctor Mocking approached him, came to his side. He said, "Look."

Bismuth looked down. His Compass, the Instrument that led him on his journeys through the Quays, lay against the deep lines of his palm. It was small and silver, its face parchment with no cardinal points. A slim silver needle span slowly, drawn not by magnetism, but by a force far greater and more mysterious: faith.

"Trust it," said Doctor Mocking, "Follow its lead."

They walked together, Bismuth watching the needle, his eyes never leaving the Compass on his palm. He felt its pull, and cupped his fingers around it as if expecting it to fly out of his hand. As they walked, the needle settled, and pointed them ahead.

In this timeless space, they walked, the great and fathomless distances turning above and around them. They passed by a million Looms, all vast but silent, unfired, awaiting engagement that might never come.

Without time, frustration existed without the protraction into an unknowable future and so was mitigated each moment by their progress throughout the Compartment and the seeming urgency of the needle.

And at last they turned a corner and felt the ground tremble.

They both looked up from the Compass, their legs unsteady. Bismuth closed his hand and returned the Compass to his pocket. It had brought them here and could do no more.

They waited, tense and expectant, unsure what was to come, or from where.

Then, to their left and perhaps half a mile away, they saw it blast into the air.

They stumbled, grabbed at each other to keep their feet. Already, the Loom was miniature against the wheels and nebulae that turned parsecs above them, but the trail it drew behind, the thread of the Gantry, was there, pulsing up from the labyrinth in its spectrum of metal colours.

They had no way of knowing how long it would stay open, so they ran.

They ran, and they were laughing.

THEY HAD AGREED, *breathless on their race towards the Gantry, that they would not stop, would not wait. As they reached the glittering shaft of light they joined hands and threw themselves between its teeming, upravelling curtain of atoms, and into it.*

AND CAME TO, *as if from sleep, standing in an orchard that overlooked a narrow stream between two bridges.*

A hot air balloon lay deflated across the grass, its basket and burner upright beneath an apple tree.

Doctor Mocking and Bismuth trod slowly across the grass. Bismuth blinked and wiped his eyes, looked around at both the beauty and ruin of this part of the Quay. There were bombsites, and the blackened, collapsed shells of buildings all around, and decay evident, but there was also this place, and across a canal beyond the balloon, a sunken row of tenements leading down to a dark and churning sea.

They approached the basket, and Doctor Mocking held his breath, and looked over the side. The bottom of the basket was covered in pieces of torn cloth and small, sharp-looking wires were jammed and pinned between the weave. Otherwise it was empty.

Doctor Mocking looked up, scanned the far bank of the canal, feeling panic rise.

Then he turned, as Bismuth touched his shoulder.

A man was walking towards them through the trees. He was tall, and broad, and fair-haired, perhaps even bigger than Bismuth, scale giving the impression by way of comparison with the girl that walked beside him and held his hand.

Doctor Mocking gasped, felt his heart clench with sudden relief.

The girl let go of the man's hand and started to run. She carried something, a round silver object bigger than Bismuth's Compass, but too similar not to be of the same mould.

Doctor Mocking fell to his knees and let Lesley race into his arms.

"It worked," she said, out of breath and elated, "It worked, dad!"

She pulled out of his grasp and held the Compass so that he could see. Its needle trembled, tipping towards the two men.

Doctor Mocking looked up at Bismuth, who was smiling. It was a small smile, and enigmatic, but it was there on his face, concealed beneath his beard, and reached his eyes nonetheless.

The fair-haired man had approached but stood at a courteous distance. He leaned against the trunk of a tree, reached up into the branches and picked an apple. As he bit into it, watching the others gathered near the collapsed balloon, something small and silver glittered on his tongue.

Doctor Mocking took the Compass from his daughter's hands. It was the same one Bismuth had given her on the day of her birth, the twin of the one he carried. He was her Godfather, and had loved Lesley from the moment he had first held her, gentle and fiercely protective.

"Bismuth," Lesley said. "It worked!"

She hugged him, too, and Bismuth bore it with the same tenderness he always summoned for the girl. He huffed, and patted her back.

Lesley laughed. She turned and pointed to the man she had been walking with.

The man saluted, tipping the hand holding the apple towards the three. He pushed off from the tree trunk and sauntered over.

"He had it!" Lesley said. "He found me asleep in the basket and gave it to me. He said I would be able to bring you back if I trusted it."

"And she did!" said Jon Index, with a good, deep laugh, and someplace dark —some flux above the linear—the Night Clock began to tick again.

Part Five

Autosomachy

WHITE-FACED, COLIN CLIMBED down from Railgrinder's cab. Bismuth helped him up onto the platform.

"Thanks, big lad," Colin said. He walked over to a cast iron bench and sat down. John Stainwright came and sat next to him.

"You okay, mate?"

Colin shrugged. "That was grim," he said. "I reversed a caravan over a pheasant once. Burst like a football. That was bad enough."

John smiled and patted him on the shoulder. Colin looked up and scanned the group standing on the platform.

"Where's Bix?"

John told him, and Colin said, "Oh shit," and stood up. The café was still there, its door shut, but the sound of voices could be heard coming from within. "Can I see him?"

"Don't see why not," John said. "He's asleep, though."

Colin went to the door of the café and went inside. John settled back against the bench but a moment later Colin came charging out from the café and grabbed his arm.

"John, you need to see him!"

John felt the ferric sensation of fear in his mouth but Colin said, "Don't worry, he's fine."

"What is it?"

"He's dreaming," Colin said. "Come see."

BIX STOOD AT the corner of the street. The road wound up through the village. He could hear the silvery rush of a stream through a culvert that ran alongside the road. He poked his head around the side of the building against which he stood, a bookshop, small, timbered, leaning against its neighbour, one of many that lined the sides of the road. There was a meadow to his left, high grass tipped with soft fronds, ripe and ready to gust away on the breeze. Beyond the meadow was a forest, deep and cool, and the low mountains, red as dried blood, rising in a perimeter above the trees. Bix lowered his head and sniffed. There was something in the road up ahead. It had called him from the cave in the red rock side of the mountain. He hadn't wanted to come, but the call was insistent, and he had left the sleeping child on its pile of rugs at the back of the cave and trod slowly down the ladder to investigate. The woods were dark but familiar and he emerged at the edge of the meadow with his paws stained brown, and leafy from the soft, fragrant loam.

And now he stood there, a worm of anxiety twisting in his belly, and watched as the man stumbled down the road towards him.

Bix waited until the man stopped in the middle of the street. The man appeared distressed and disoriented, his eyes wild. Bix could smell his sweat, sharp and redolent of panic.

But the smell and appearance of the man did not concern Bix as much as the thing he carried, the thing from which the call issued in a constant, imprecating whine.

The man started walking again, hesitant steps, his head switching about as though trying to find something familiar on which to focus. Bix shuffled backwards, hiding himself against the side of the bookshop. There was nothing to be gained from confrontation, not at this moment, not unless it became necessary. Bix turned and slipped away into the high meadow grass and ran back towards the forest leaving the man who carried the jar full of darkness and eyes to continue his aimless, faltering journey through the town.

"You have to connect, John," Colin said. He stood with his hands clasped beneath his chin as though begging John to act. "Bix needs you."

John squatted next to the sleeping dog and put his hands flat on Bix's flank. The dog's breathing was rapid, and his lips curled and his muzzle twitched. Occasionally his paws made a frantic paddling motion.

"He told me to stay here," John said.

"You can't leave him, he's been through enough." Colin's voice had an edge now, and John looked up at the old man. Colin was staring at him and there were tears in his eyes. "I'd go, if you'd let me," he said.

John shifted his weight and sat next to Bix. He put his face close to Bix's ear and whispered something to him, soothing and full of love. He closed his eyes.

Colin stepped backwards, his hands still clasped at his throat. The café was quiet again, the people hushed and expectant. Johnny had switched off the radio.

And then all was commotion again as newspapers were opened and coffee cups and cutlery resumed their clatter, conversations started up and Johnny flicked the radio back on.

Bix's agitation subsided. Colin thought he looked peaceful, now John had gone to find him.

John Stainwright opened his eyes. He was sitting cross-legged in the middle of a cobbled street that ran through a small town. He stood and looked about. Small shops lined both sides of the road. They all seemed to be bookshops. Above the sky was a clear blue. He felt a chill, and turned. A wind was rising and it moved through his hair, lifting it from his brow as he squinted back along the road. He felt gooseflesh crackle like static up his arms and across his belly.

Something was coming, and it brought dread to John's heart even before he saw it, slouching and crashing up the road.

John heard something else: a bark, sharp and adamant, and he turned on the sight of the Autoscope army, coming in their black machines, and ran, headlong, towards the meadow and the forest, and the low iron mountains beyond.

DOCTOR MOCKING PAUSED and glanced towards the cavernous opening to the Loom. Robin followed his gaze. Chloe was standing beneath a viaduct arch of broken metal looking out onto the Compartment. Her head was tilted slightly, as though she were listening to something above the endless hum and song of the Looms.

The two men approached Chloe and stood, one either side of her, and waited.

After a moment, Chloe frowned and said, "We have to go now."

"What is it?" Doctor Mocking asked.

"It's the devil-in-dreams," she said. "It's trying to kill my brother."

"HE'S ONLY THIS big," Chloe said, smiling. She held her hands an inch apart. "But as soon as I knew mummy was pregnant I put him in my Quay, to keep him safe like I'd been."

"You knew Claire was pregnant?" Doctor Mocking said.

"Straight away," Chloe said. "Mummy and Daddy don't know yet. Or maybe they do now, but they didn't. It wasn't for *me* to tell them."

"Very wise," said Robin.

Chloe's expression darkened. "But now that man is there and the devil-in-dreams wants to kill my brother."

Doctor Mocking put a hand on his forehead and looked over Chloe's head at Robin. "Can you get us out of here," Doctor Mocking said.

Robin shook his head. "I don't see how, not without an activated Loom."

Chloe reached out and took Doctor Mocking's hand in hers. "I can do it," she said. "With my brother's help. The same way Lesley helped you last time."

Doctor Mocking held his hands apart an inch, said, "But he's only…"

Chloe said, "Not here he isn't."

Robin was staring at Doctor Mocking.

"Robin knows," Chloe said, and squeezed Doctor Mocking's hand.

"He's you," Robin said.

Doctor Mocking felt himself go pale. He was suddenly, and not inexplicably, afraid.

"Yes," Chloe said. "He's you. Waiting to be reborn."

"PHIL?"

Trevena was still looking down at the tracks. He had watched it all and was wishing now that he hadn't. His stomach grumbled and his mouth was suddenly secreting saliva with too much generosity.

"Phil?"

Trevena turned and saw young Andy Chapel standing at his side. The boy's face was serious.

"Yes, son?"

"Can I talk to you?"

"Sure," Trevena was glad of the distraction. Since Colin had driven *Railgrinder* over the Despatrix everyone had seemed to retreat into themselves, as if wondering what to do next. Trevena certainly didn't have a clue.

He followed Andy away from the others until they stood a few feet away from the opening to the train shed.

"What do you know about him," Andy asked. "The other Andrew Chapel. The man."

Trevena thought for a moment and said, "He's empty. I couldn't get anything from him except his script. It was way beyond a personality disorder. He didn't *have* a personality to get disordered. That's what I think, now you ask."

"Is that unusual?"

"It's not unusual, it's impossible. He described a *temperament* but without any of the unique effects his perceived upbringing would have had on shaping a personality. Even his sculptures are a constant repetition of the same theme, dull and unimaginative. Shows how easy it is to pull one over on the *intelligentsia*. But I suppose he wasn't even an artist, really. You were using him to project yourself into the world through him." When Andy nodded, Trevena went on, "He was one of the most unengaging men I've ever assessed, if I can put it like that. Characterless. I'm sorry."

Andy laughed. "Don't be sorry. You're not insulting me!"

Trevena liked this lad already. He was bright and easy-going and had a good heart. Trevena resisted the urge to pat him on the head. There was something familiar about him, though. He felt like he'd known him all his life. Companionable, that was it. The lad was *companionable*. Like the son he wished he'd had.

"Phil?"

"Huh?" Trevena came back to the boy, from his strange but pleasant ruminations. He didn't feel nauseous any more, either.

"We both can't exist now," Andy said. "You know one of us has to die."

Trevena pointed towards Bismuth, who was standing talking to Colin in the doorway of the café.

"He's spent the last seven years looking for you," Trevena said. "I don't think he's going to let anything happen to you now."

"No, but what if he was only meant to free me? Just so I could be at peace?"

Trevena shook his head. "I don't believe that for a minute. And leave that soulless adult version wandering around until he's completely corrupted? He hasn't stopped causing problems since he pitched up for that assessment. It's *you* that's one of this lot, not him. I'm sure of it. I think you've been his conscience all this time. Now you're free and integrated, he's spiralling. There's nothing left in him to resist the darkness."

Andy was biting his lip. "I hope you're right," he said. "Because there's something else I need to tell you."

"WE HAVE TO go to my Quay," Chloe said. Doctor Mocking was holding very tightly to her hands. "Me and Robin. You have to go back home."

"To die." Doctor Mocking uttered this as a statement and not a question. He stood up straight and brushed dust from the lapels of his coat.

"Yes. So you can be reborn. And so my brother can help us defeat the devil-in-dreams."

"Do you know what to do?"

Chloe walked out from beneath the crags of the Loom and crossed the golden boulevard. She stood facing an unfired Loom, its gigantic bulk soaring above her in gleaming tiers and slabs. She approached its flank and put a hand against it, a pink orchid lying against all the gold ever mined from earth, and turned, and called across to the two men:

"This one," she said.

"You can tell?"

"No. I can fire it."

"You know how to do that?"

"Yes. It's easy."

Doctor Mocking laughed. "Easy! Chloe, you're incredible."

Robin was lingering in the shadows beneath the blackened Loom. He was digging about in a pile of machine parts and a snake's nest of wires.

"It's intuitive for her," he said. "There's no way to get inside these Looms and fire them. They have to be fired from outside, in the Quays or the Waking World. She's linking up with her brother. They'll do it together. Hang on, Chloe, I just need... this!"

Robin yanked a device from the midst of the pile of junk and carried it with him across the boulevard. He stood next to Doctor Mocking and Chloe.

"Ready," Chloe said.

"Yes," said the two men.

Chloe put both palms against the Loom and closed her eyes.

BIX FRETTED. THE child was restless.

The dog sniffed the air at the entrance to the cave. He could smell the man. He was close now, stumbling through the forest. He had crossed the meadow, the wind behind him, on a wavering course. Now he was amongst the trees and he was coming, coming carrying death.

Bix left the opening and went to the back of the cave where the child lay curled up on a pile of furs. Bix thought back to when he had first been here, seven years ago, protecting Chloe. Dangers then had been real, but located elsewhere. Now the danger was present, and closing. Bix whined, low in his throat.

The boy on the bed of furs flinched and cried out. Bix nuzzled the child's hand as it lay, fingers uncurled, against his flushed cheek.

What's your name? Bix wondered. *Do you know?*

When he had first met Chloe, here in her Quay, unborn but full of power, she had been a young adult, bursting with words and forming thoughts, but this child was young, no more than a toddler. Bix began to despair. What could he teach this boy? How could he protect him? He began to pant, tail pressed between his legs. He turned to go back to the entrance to the cave. There was a ladder there, and no one to pull it up. They were so vulnerable.

And then the boy spoke.

"Adam," he said.

Bix lowered his head. "Bix," he said. "Dog."

The boy was awake. He smiled, and his eyes were an incredible shade of slate gray. Tiny rainstorms circling his dilated pupils.

"Bixdog," he said. He reached out an arm and touched Bix's muzzle with a tiny, soft hand.

"You're safe," Bix said. "Safe, Adam." But he glanced away as he said it, looking towards the opening to the cave.

The boy sat up. He was looking in the direction of the opening.

There was a look of great interest on his face,

He turned to look at Bix, and said, "Chloe."

Bix was so surprised, he barked. Adam toppled backwards onto the pile of furs. He lay on his back and grinned. Then he chuckled, a rich, sweet sound of delight.

"Sorry," said Bix. "Sorry, Adam." He put his nose against the child's neck and licked him. Adam squealed and sat up, still laughing. He pointed towards the cave's entrance.

"Chloe," he said, again.

"Yes," said Bix. "Yes. Chloe."

THE GROUND TREMBLED. No; it buckled.

Doctor Mocking staggered backwards, and Robin caught him before he fell. Chloe was still there, pressed against the Loom with her eyes closed. She appeared unyielding, almost an extrusion of the great sheet of gold against which she stood. Her arms glowed, brazen, as the light poured through her.

"Chloe," Doctor Mocking cried, but Robin was dragging him away, back across the rippling surface of the boulevard.

The Loom shuddered, and a line of light, brighter than anything shining within the Compartment, appeared around its base. It was neon, radiant, fearsome.

Doctor Mocking and Robin stood with shadows long and brilliant black behind them, withdrawn to the opening of the blasted Loom again. It shook around them, and great stanchions of clotted metal broke away and thundered to the ground somewhere deep within it. Robin stood with the mechanism he had salvaged between his feet, its wires and circuits glittering in the sudden and enraged light. Doctor Mocking closed his eyes and clenched his fists, conscious of the intolerable clockwork spirals of untold galaxies pressing with every micron against his presence there in the Compartment.

The Loom broke free from the ground. The line of light grew into a white dais and then it was gone, and the Loom was gone, and all that remained was a silent geyser of metallic particles in its wake.

Doctor Mocking shielded his eyes and watched the Loom blast like a shuttle through the firmament. He saw Chloe, arms raised, head back, hair flying, as she urged it on, and he grabbed Robin's arm and yelled, "Go!"

Robin scooped his machine from between his feet and ran with Doctor Mocking across the boulevard. Chloe turned, bathed in sheets of pulsing light, flecked with sparkling embers from the ascending Gantry. They gathered her in their arms and plunged into the Gantry.

JOHN STAINWRIGHT FOLLOWED the man across the meadow. He kept low, his head level with the tops of the tall grass. The sound of the Autoscopes was growing as they came through the village, their black, crumbling vehicles and walking machines drawing nearer. Something tore through the air above the meadow, and John ducked down as it flew overhead. He got a glimpse of something ridged and jointed, with tatty wings soaring towards the forest. It made a loud clanking noise, the sound of foundry hammers striking iron rods. John raised his head and watched as it disappeared above the trees and then circled back, low across the meadow, and sailed away over the village, skimming the pitched and leaning rooftops.

Back bent, John continued forward, following Chapel at a distance of about two hundred meters. Chapel was nearing the edge of the forest, hunched over, carrying the jar. John waited until Chapel disappeared into the tree line, and then he stood up and ran.

BIX WAITED. THE child was sitting on his rugs, silent and seeming to be in a trance. His eyes were open but unfocused. His hands were clasped in his lap. His breathing was very slow.

Bix padded to the entrance to the cave and looked out across the treetops. He couldn't leave the child in case he decided to get up and wander about. He could fall so easily to his death. Bix could hear the man now, stumbling through the forest, and the wheedling imprecations from the thing he carried. Bix curled his lips and bared his teeth at the sound. Bix wanted to fight it, tear into it with mouth and claws and rip its blackness to shreds. It was calling its army, its corruption now fully integrated into the soul of the man who carried it. The man was carrying the beacon directly to the child. Bix scraped his claws against the rock, the desire to leap down the ladder almost overwhelming.

And then he sensed something else, a new sound, feet racing through the soft earth, a body crashing through branches. And a new smell, carried on the breeze. A familiar smell, good and comforting to his tensile nerves.

"John," he said.

The child spoke, "Go to John," he said. His face was very pale. Bix went to him. The boy's gray eyes were wide, his delicate red lips turned down. He looked sad, close to tears, but he reached out and stroked Bix's neck. "I won't fall."

Bix lowered his head, turned, and went to the ladder. He looked back once, and the child waved, his face white and tiny in the gloom at the back of the cave.

Bix bounded down the ladder and headed into the forest.

JOHN STAINWRIGHT RAN into a small clearing. Chapel had reached the middle of the shaded patch of rocky earth and turned with a clumsy half step as John emerged. He clutched the jar to his chest, and his eyes were black and fuming with insane hatred. John stopped a few meters from Chapel, alarmed by the change in the man. There would be no reasoning with this thing. He stepped towards Chapel and began to circle him, attempting to get ahead of him and block his passage into the trees where he would be much harder to stop.

Chapel opened his mouth, and that was a black hole, too, full of dark, timeless matter. As John watched, an eye rose, enucleated and pale, in the back of Chapel's throat.

John looked away, sickened, and saw Bix come running into the clearing from the direction of the cliffs. The dog skidded to a halt and snarled, tense and ready. John held out a hand, palm outwards.

"Wait, Bix," he said, but Chapel moved, twisting away from John and launched himself at the opening to the path from which Bix had just emerged. He tried to kick out at the dog, but Bix dodged Chapel's shoe and leaped at the man, teeth bared. Bix hit Chapel in the chest and sent him stumbling backwards. He tripped and fell, the jar spilling from his arms. Chapel screamed.

The jar hit the ground and broke, shattering against the rocky ground. Shards of thick, curved glass lay in the dirt, and the charred remains of the head broke apart, no more than cinders in the air.

Bix stood over Chapel, and John came across the clearing to stand at his side.

Chapel rolled over and raised himself to his knees. He opened his mouth and leaned over the remains of the jar. John reached into his pocket and withdrew the bradawl he still carried, the one he had used to kill the driver of the float in the grounds of the asylum. He stepped towards Chapel.

Something moved amongst the shards of glass. The ashes were stirring, lifting towards Chapel's face.

Before John could finish Chapel, the contents of the jar swarmed off the floor like flies. John staggered as the particles battered his face and he clamped his eyes and mouth shut. Bix barked and leaped out of the way of the swirling specks.

Chapel reached out and took hold of a long, curved shard of glass. He sprang to his feet, thick blood squeezing from his fist as the edges of the glass cut his flesh, and drove it into John's throat.

Chapel stepped away, blood dripping from his fingers. He opened his mouth as the swarming particles gathered at his face and he let them in. They pressed against his eyes and found a way in there, too, through the black membranes.

John fell to his knees, eyes wide, a hand clasped to his throat. Blood surged between his fingers. Bix howled.

Chapel no longer existed. What stood there now was a monster, the devil-in-dreams made flesh. It rippled with eyes, every inch of exposed flesh bugging with them. They peered from beneath the lank strands of hair on his skull, bulged from his nostrils, his cheeks, the flesh of his exposed throat. Chapel's body was now pure host and what it contained could sense the child.

Bix stood with John. He trembled with sorrow and fury.

John reached out a hand and moved his lips but made no sound. His pallor was ashen, his lips blue. Tears ran down his cheeks.

"Not here, John, please," Bix said. It was all he could think of now. He had to get John out of the Quay. No thoughts for the child now, no concern for the fate of the others. Just his John now. "Don't die here."

John Stainwright lifted his head. His pale eyes narrowed. He took his hand from his throat and the wound opened fully and blood jetted onto the forest floor. He pushed himself to his knees and with his remaining strength lunged towards the devil-in-dreams.

The Chapel-thing caught him and fell backwards. Bix leaped onto it and sank his teeth into the cold flesh of its wrist. He felt eyes burst like blisters in his mouth but clamped down as hard as he could.

John held the monster as tightly as his fading strength would allow and closed his eyes. They rolled in the dirt, and the devil-in-dreams shrieked.

"Take us home," John said to his dog.

Bix closed his eyes and they connected, for one last time, and a Gantry opened and they went home.

ANDY TOOK TREVENA'S sleeve and drew him close. His eyes were wide and full of candour.

"Even when I was trapped I could sense him, the other Chapel," Andy said. "My mother knew. She always hated him. He wasn't projecting me, it was the other way round. That thing would come and visit me in the darkness, the thing full of eyes, and try to corrupt me, but it couldn't be in two places. I weakened it and it chose to influence the other, the man I was growing into. Sometimes I could see through his eyes, and hear the things around him, but mostly

I was trapped in living darkness. I fought it, though, Phil. I really fought it."

"I know," said Trevena. "Bismuth wouldn't give up on you. He knew you were there and he never gave in."

"Yes, I could sense him, too. He was so close, so many times, but the devil-in-dreams would always know. It would pull itself away from Chapel and come rushing back, snatch me away. That's when Chapel would feel most desolate and unreal. Because he is."

Trevena continued to listen. Andy was becoming agitated, his cheeks flushed. The memory of his ordeal was raw and horrifying, and Trevena wanted to let the boy talk.

"I sent him to you, Phil."

Trevena was so intent on listening he missed what the boy had said. "What?"

"I had an opportunity to send him to you. Bismuth got *so* close, but that thing under the train did enough to distract him. He would have found me sooner but the devil-in-dreams was *there*. Bismuth saw it, inside the fridge, as it was taking me away. So I made Chapel try to kill himself while he was empty."

Trevena thought back to the first assessment.

"It was lucky he was found. He tried to hang himself. The police found him."

Andy was shaking his head.

"*He* phoned them. From a callbox at the park. The woods aren't deep. He could be seen from the street."

"But how could you know about me? How could you know he'd even be *seen* by me?"

"That's the point. That's what I need to tell you. You're my Paladin, Phil. We've always been destined to meet. If I hadn't been trapped in that fridge we might even have grown up together. Nothing could keep us apart."

Trevena stood up straight. White specks danced behind his eyes and he took a deep breath. He shut his eyes tightly to dispel the sensation of tiny bulbs flickering on and off inside his head. He had always wondered why *he* had been so integral to the story of these beings, and why the Autoscopes had gone after him with quite such vehemence. He had figured himself a small player, obviously, his involvement conditional on luck and proximity. He had been involved simply because, well, he'd been involved.

But here was the boy telling him he had a destiny, a preordained purpose that had been distorted, thwarted, but could somehow never be denied. He recalled Colin recounting something similar, how he had waited for John Stainwright to find him and Bix, the trust involved. The faith!

It would explain their affinity. The unexpected and robust affection he felt for the boy. He opened his mouth to say something, unsure as he did so what it would be, wanting to acknowledge Andy's honesty and courage, but he didn't get a chance, because Andy had turned away and was staring across the rails, his expression blank and his eyes as black as pits of tar.

Trevena grabbed him by the shoulders and turned him so that they were face-to-face. Andy was slack and did not resist.

"Andy!" Trevena said, and lightly shook the boy. "*Andy*!"

Andy blinked and his eyes were clear and blue again. His face was white, though, and his lips trembled.

"It's okay," Trevena said.

"No," Andy said and tears came then, "No it's not. I've killed John!" And he collapsed into Trevena's arms, howling with grief and horror.

INITIALLY INCONSOLABLE, EVENTUALLY they were able to calm and reassure him, and he settled although he remained drained. He had felt it, he said, the moment Chapel was taken entirely by the devil-in-dreams. He was gone now, no longer a part of Andy, no longer a part of anything. But Andy had felt the moment Chapel had stabbed John, had seen the man fall, had heard Bix howl, and heard John speak.

"They've gone home," Andy said. "What does that mean?"

Colin came forward. His face was drawn and white.

"I know where he'll go," he said, his old voice wavering, catching in his throat. "Please take me."

Index put a hand on Colin's shoulder.

"We don't have very long," he said. "We're scattered again but we have to use that to our advantage and take this to the devil-in-dreams on all fronts. Bismuth, take Colin with Andy and Phil and go to John. Save him if you can, but stop the devil-in-dreams. The rest of us will go to Chloe's Quay. Lesley, are you good with that?"

Lesley was standing with Steve and Claire. She was holding Anna's hand. Of them all, Index knew she would be the most torn. But without Bismuth, he needed her in the battle, and thinking clearly.

Lesley was biting her lip. Anna squeezed her hand, looked into her sister's face with nothing in her expression but love and encouragement. Whatever Lesley decided, Anna would understand.

Lesley nodded, her eyes bright with a mounting, but controlled, fury.

Bismuth took a lever from his belt. He walked to the edge of the platform and stepped onto the tracks. He found a patch of earth between the rails and used the edge of his boot to clear the pebbles and cinders from around it. He looked up, the lever poised just above the ground.

Daniel took Elizabeth's hands and looked into her sweet, patient face.

"I'll be fine here with Steve and Claire," she said. "You go and do what you have to do." She kissed his bearded cheek, then his lips, and they held each other.

Trevena and Andy helped Colin onto the rails. He felt frail and delicate and Trevena worried for him as he stood beside the old man, who had his head bowed and his hands clasped at his breast. He watched as a tear fell from Colin's averted cheek, caught the light and landed on the frayed plastic strap of his flip-flop.

Bismuth looked to each of them for assent. Colin sniffed, stood straight and held his chin up. He wiped his eyes with the back of his hand.

"I'm ready, big lad," he said, and Bismuth slid the end of the lever into the dirt and compressed the handle. A Gantry opened, the cool air in the train shed coming ajar in a brilliant white line, and then it broadened and they were able to step through.

CHLOE, ROBIN AND Doctor Mocking fell through the piling light, passing from the Compartment into the silent, racing corridor of the Gantry. Its mysterious gravity righted them at once and they were able to land on their feet without the sensation of any loss of balance. They were near the openings, despite the speed with which the Gantry cut through Dark Time, as it bent the space and fabric of the Firmament.

Chloe pointed to the opening behind Doctor Mocking.

"The Waking World," she said.

Doctor Mocking nodded and looked over her shoulder. The opening that led to her Quay was widening.

"Be quick," he said.

They stood for a moment, suspended between worlds and bathed in the flash and sparkle of the interior of the Gantry. And then they moved, Chloe and Robin towards the widening aperture, Doctor Mocking towards the narrowing doorway that would lead him back to the World, and the chance to be reborn. He stopped at the opening and looked back. Chloe and Robin were gone, and he wished them well. He turned and drew a long breath. He wondered if it would be worth the sacrifice. He wondered if he would see his girls again. With Robin, they might have a chance now.

Doctor Mocking stepped from the Gantry into gray daylight.

ALEX AND ELIOT had Railgrinder running hot and filling the roof of the train shed with a dense atmosphere of steam. Index, Daniel, Lesley and Anna got into the cab with them. It was tight, and hot, but they found space enough and waited for Alex to disengage the brake.

They pulled away watched by Elizabeth, Claire and Steve. Steve had his arm around his wife's waist. Claire was holding her still-flat belly, an unconscious, protective gesture. Elizabeth didn't wave.

Railgrinder gathered speed through the cutting and into the rolling fields of Quay-Fomalhaut. This was Alex's Quay, and *Railgrinder* was his Instrument. He stood at the controls and felt the firebox heat and smelt the coal dust, and exulted in it. He had been a boy the first time he had driven his engine, and learnt its purpose, and now he was nearly a man, hard and severe as the metal that carried him. He opened the throttle and peered through the porthole at a point in the distance.

As though somebody stood a mile distant shining a torch, the Gantry appeared. A circle of light that widened to a ring as the distance decreased. It grew, rippling, until it made an arch over the tracks, a blazing penumbra with a golden heart.

Alex fully opened the throttle and *Railgrinder* raced towards the Gantry. It shot over a set of points and its grinding wheels engaged with a jolt and scream.

They flew into the Gantry, a blistering iron comet.

TREVENA STEPPED OUT onto the tarmac of the car park outside the reception centre at the Reservoir End Caravan Site. He was disoriented for a moment at the sight of the gift shop and the bright, tacky souvenirs, and Colin's old Cortina parked in its slot in front of the building. It was all so unobtrusively mundane he felt a wave of nostalgia cramp his chest.

"Are you okay, Phil?" Andy asked.

Trevena nodded. "I just felt John for a moment. I felt how *he* feels about this place. What it means to him. He told me about his trips here as a child when it was a dogs' home, about meeting Colin and Bix. It's like nothing ever changed for him."

Colin was already heading away from the car park, towards the boulevard that led to the clubhouse. They followed, catching him up, and ran past the bright ranks of mobile homes that stood set back from the verges on their modest plots of land.

They heard a dog bark. It was not loud, nor was it happy. It was the enquiring, perplexed chuffing sound of a dog asking those around him, or the elements, or God, should no one be about to offer comfort, *why is this happening. I don't understand.*

"Bix!" said Colin, and doubled his speed, almost tripping as he stubbed the toe of his flip-flop and it folded beneath his foot. Trevena reached out and grabbed his arm. Colin caught his balance and hobbled on.

They reached the steps leading up into the clubhouse. Despite being breathless, Colin swore when he saw the open door and the tangled remains of the multicoloured fly blind lying on the floor.

They went up the steps and into the shaded interior of the clubhouse. Trevena noticed the string of dead fairy lights coiled around the legs of the overturned bar stools. Colin no longer seemed interested in the state of his bar. He cried out, and stumbled across the floor towards the back of the clubhouse.

John lay there. Bix lifted his head and whined. Colin knelt beside them and put his head in his hands. There was a lot of blood surrounding John's head and shoulders, but it was drying, and no more flowed from the wound in John's neck.

Colin embraced Bix and Bix sat, trembling, his forepaws dark red, soaked in his master's blood. There was blood on his muzzle, too, from where he had been nuzzling John's face. If they had been discovered by anyone else, Trevena thought, there might have been a very different interpretation of events.

Colin was rocking Bix. The dog's paws were sliding in the blood but he didn't appear to care. He just let the old man hold him and sob.

Trevena and Andy stood aside as Bismuth stepped past them.

"Colin," he said. "Colin."

Blinking, Colin looked up at the man who towered above him.

"Get a table cloth. We need to cover him."

Colin shook his head, more from shock than negation. Bismuth squatted beside him. Colin looked into his face with eyes glassy from exhaustion.

"Get John a cloth, Colin. For his dignity. For Bix."

"Yes," Colin said. "Yes. For Bix." Bismuth helped him stand and sent him over to the bar where Colin searched in his small store cupboard for a tablecloth.

Bismuth and Trevena shared a glance and Trevena could see the grief in the big man's face. Andy went to Bix and stroked the dog's head. Bix let the boy comfort him. Colin came back with an orange tablecloth decorated with small, silver stars.

"We put these out at Halloween," he said, handing the cloth to Bismuth. "We always have a do. John loves my fruit punch." He was crying again, and Trevena put an arm around him while Bismuth knelt and tenderly wrapped John's body in the cloth. Andy had led Bix away while Bismuth worked, and the dog had gone willingly enough. The boy found a couple of bar towels and wet them in the sink beneath the bar. He used them to wash the blood from Bix's muzzle and get the worst from his paws.

Bismuth stood and looked down at John's body. Trevena had taken Colin to a table and they sat together, Trevena watching Andy tend to Bix while Colin sat with his elbows on the table and his head in his hands.

Bismuth put a hand in his pocket and took out his compass. He flipped it open and peered at it. He tapped the glass with the tip of his index finger. He frowned, closed the compass and put it back in his pocket.

"What is it?" Trevena asked.

"Nothing yet," Bismuth said. He came over and sat with them, his bent knees higher than the top of the table. He appeared frustrated, and took the compass out again, opened it and put it on the table. The needle pointed southeast, unmoving.

They sat in silence, waiting for the needle to move.

Doctor Mocking stood alone in the orchard at the back of his house. He wondered whether Chloe had sent him here, or whether he had brought himself here by some default mechanism he did not fully understand. This time he was home and not in his Quay, and the sound of traffic on the road behind the house was louder than the sound of the stream that flowed between the two small bridges, and there was rain in the air. He looked up through the branches of the apple trees and saw the darkness of the sky. He shivered. What now? he thought. He had expected to feel weak, fragile, the terminal stage of his illness gripping him and bringing his end, and he had been happy to embrace it. But he felt strong, fitter than he had in the months since the onset of his heart failure. And this realisation brought fear, and a moment of light-headedness close to panic.

He knew, standing there in the shade of his apple trees, that he wasn't going to die.

He turned at the sound of a voice, his heart—no longer frail but powerful, too powerful—pounding in his chest.

Chapel stood smiling. There were eyes in his mouth. Eyes everywhere.

"How are you feeling?" he asked in a thick, clotted voice. "In fine fettle, I hope. It sounded like he'd said, *I' fie feddle.* Saliva mixed with some thicker humour ran from the corners of his mouth and dripped from his chin.

Doctor Mocking clenched his fists. Chapel laughed. "Come on then," he said.

There was nothing left of Chapel, Doctor Mocking realised. The creature was *embodied*, nothing more. He was looking at the devil-in-dreams, still contained, but for how much longer?

The devil-in-dreams walked Chapel's body towards him, and Doctor Mocking went to meet it.

The Autoscope army amassed at the edge of the meadow. Their machines idled, huge black metal engines made from the salvaged wrecks of sinking ships and the torn plates and turrets of battlefield tanks, blown up and mired in blood-soaked mud and the carnage of the trenches. Less than a hundred remained, drawn here by the call of their master. No generals to marshal them, their fallen stars quenched by the ferocity of the Firmament Surgeons. They waited, but could no longer hear the call. It had cut off moments before, sudden and unanticipated. There was confusion. They leaned their black, scaled bodies over the controls and out of cabs, waiting, irresolute. They moaned and growled. The tracks and wheels of their machines span and jolted as they revved, wanting to plunge on, across the meadow, and kill the thing that sat in the rocks. They could sense it, a child, and its grace and beauty filled them with revulsion. And they were afraid of the mountain. The mother's blood in the iron of the rocks; the terrible, unendurable love.

CHLOE AND ROBIN stepped from the Gantry onto soft forest earth. Robin carried his device in both arms. It was heavy, shaped like a triangular prism. It was covered in dials that twitched and fluttered, and luminescent bulbs, switches and a big brass lever set into a slot towards the right hand end of the control panel. It looked arcane and naïve, like everything Robin built, something knocked up in a shed that could never work, a child's science project, but Chloe knew different. She knew how powerful Robin's machines could be. He had salvaged this from the dashboard of the camper van and spent part of his time trapped in the Compartment making alterations.

Robin pointed in the direction of the mountains that lay behind them.

"You should go to your brother," he said. "Protect him."

Chloe nodded.

"Are they coming?" he asked. "Can you feel them?"

"Yes," Chloe said. "Six of them. Something's happened to John. You have to be quick."

Robin touched her brow, brushed a strand of hair from it.

"Take care," he said. "And thank you for coming."

Chloe smiled. She turned and followed a path that led through the trees towards the base of the mountains. Robin watched her for a moment, and then he took a different path, one that would lead him out onto the meadow. Already he could hear the sound of the

Autoscopes, the rumbles and oily piston-hisses of their machines, impatient yet momentarily indecisive. He broke into a run, ducking beneath branches and leaping over roots. The apparatus was light in his arms but cumbersome and he was careful not to let it slip or run it into the side of a tree.

He headed for a thinning of the trees, where daylight dappled through in weak, dusty shafts. He slowed, and stepped with great care onto the edge of the meadow. He kept low, the device held at waist height to prevent the setting sun catching the metal and sending an ill-timed semaphore giving away his position. He looked up and saw that the sky was storm-blue, and filled with clouds of an even darker shade. A chill wind blew and bent the grass, and rattled the branches and leaves at the edge of the forest. Robin smelt dust and hot sump-oil, and something sharper, like the savage stench from the pen of a great beast that had died in terrible heat and ferocious temper.

They were massed a quarter of a mile away, their engines steaming, smoking, sending up pillars of gas that hazed the air and made it tremble. Against the darkening sky it was difficult to tell where the silhouettes of the buildings at the top of the town ended and the piled clatter of black machinery began. Perspective made it look like the town was transforming into something industrial, extruding blocks and edges of metal, a morbid conversion with intent to shear the meadow and the forest to muck and splinters.

Robin clutched the apparatus to his chest and loped towards the middle of the meadow. When he had judged his position well enough, he stood up.

The sun, setting behind the dark rooftops of the town, caught the lenses of his glasses and reflected back in quick twin flashes.

The Autoscopes roared and gunned their machines. They poured onto the meadow, instantly churning it to a battlefield morass. Sheaves of grass flew into the air, blackened with oil. Mud sprayed, dense and bound with roots. Tracks and wheels bit, driving the black rigs towards where Robin stood. He was smiling. The sun set and the light went out of his face.

He looked down at the apparatus and put a hand on the brass lever. The metal hummed. He checked his dials, and waited.

CHLOE REACHED THE base of the mountain. She recalled the route well and emerged a few yards away from the ladder that led up to the cave. She went to the bottom of the ladder and started to climb. She didn't call out, just kept her chin up and made the thirty feet as fast as she could. She hoisted herself the last foot and climbed into the cave. It was as she remembered it, narrow and deep and warm, with a curving ceiling and a flat, worn and dusty floor. She went further, peering into the back of the cave. She had been here last with Bix, before her birth, and the dog had read to her and kept her safe. And now, here in the back, on her old pile of rugs… a child. A boy.

Her brother.

"Adam," she said.

The child was unmoving. He lay curled on his side, a thumb hooked loosely in his mouth. His eyes were closed and his face was white. Chloe knelt on the rugs beside him and put a hand on his cheek. The child was cold.

He moaned, and his eyes fluttered open, and then closed again. Chloe wrapped the rugs around him and sat in the back of the cave on the floor, her arms around the boy, and rocked him. She stared the length of the cave and watched the opening at the other end grow dark.

DOCTOR MOCKING FOUGHT the devil-in-dreams, and even as he did so, even as he rained punches and kicks, and grappled with Chapel's body, he felt his opponent grow. He had no plan, no hope of winning, and no strategy to delay the inevitable, but still he fought. He felt his strength, and it was good and fierce, his muscles responding, his heart pumping blood with thunder in his ears. He had gained something from his time in the Compartment, had drawn power from it. In his understanding of its immensity he had been charged, perhaps only briefly, but he used the supremacy it gave him to batter the devil-in-dreams across the orchard, between the apple trees, beneath the darkening sky.

The devil-in-dreams fought back, its thousand eyes rolling, blazing, and swelling shut beneath the Doctor's blows. It saw golden light flash behind the Doctor's own eyes, and *how* it wished to pluck them out and add them to its haul. It used Chapel's body to swipe at the Doctor's face but the old bastard was fast, and ducked beneath the lashing arm and brought a fist up into its ribs. It felt things mush there, against the bones, and another part of it went *dim*.

The devil-in-dreams enlarged within the casing of Chapel's flesh, the body too limited to contain it now. It knew the other was dead, the John Stainwright thing, but it knew also that they remained ten still, and it thought about the child in the cave and its dimness increased because it couldn't see its purpose. It was concealed. It spat scalding fury for its limitations and threw itself against the Doctor, grappling with Chapel's swelling, worthless flesh, feeling it split and peel. Its true form bulged from the lengthening gashes; imaginal, a horrible maturity of filth.

Doctor Mocking swung punches, took hold of an arm as it brought an inflamed fist around to club him, and bent it against the elbow. It snapped, but instead of rendering it useless, the flesh sloughed off leaving the black cancer of the devil-in-dreams pouring from the bone in a vile, expanding foam.

Doctor Mocking was weakening, but still he fought. He fought with a hope that he might die here, and be reborn as the child awaiting his spirit in the cave, and that would be acceptable, a victory. But as quickly as the thought formed he realised that the devil-in-dreams had out-thought *him,* or at least anticipated this, because there was a sick scarlet light blooming in the air behind the misshapen remains of Chapel's body. The devil-in-dreams was opening a Gantry to some hellish Quay, and he realised his adversary's intent.

* * *

Claire sat down on a chair in Johnny's café, her face drained of colour, suddenly afraid, and put a hand on her belly.

Steve knelt beside her. "What is it?"

Claire groaned and leaned forward, into her husband's arms. Her body tensed as a jagged pain twisted inside her.

"I'm bleeding," she said. She was crying. "I'm losing the baby."

Chloe held her brother and felt his life ebbing away. The sun had set and the cave was dark, the rock cold, and damp, lifeless. No ruddy glow throbbed within. It was a dead tunnel at the end of which, against a curving wall that lacked friction, it seemed, to bind them, they remained curled together. Chloe felt the mass of the mountain move above and behind her, a contraction throughout the rock, and with the quake came a thought, that in a moment the cave would tip, like a slide and send them tumbling through it to fall from its mouth onto the forest floor.

"Robin," Chloe said, "Hurry."

Robin waited.

The Autoscopes approached. Their machines lumbered, cutting through the grass. The twilight air filled with a lacy exultation of seeds and pollen, and petals from the wild flowers. They came on, flailing chains and shafts, clogged tracks and thudding fabric belts, a black and sterile wind across a dustbowl. Their distance closed.

Flying things rose at the rear of them, fanning out, three of them in formation, and flew low over the heads of the Autoscopes in their machines, and those that walked alongside. Heads twisted on black, corded necks and red eyes blazed.

Robin watched them come.

And then he pulled the lever.

Doctor Mocking felt himself lifted, held in a saturated embrace.

He moved his arms and pressed against the substance of the devil-in-dreams, but it had him fast. Chapel's misshapen head, a bulging dome of eyes, was at the level of Doctor Mocking's throat.

Doctor Mocking flexed against the devil-in-dreams. He pulled an arm free, brought his fist down on it, felt it sink into the viscous matter. He clenched his fist and pulled it free, bringing with it a handful of eyes. He squeezed, and the eyes burst, the leathery flesh splitting and spilling gelid muck. The devil-in-dreams bucked, loosening its hold, and Doctor Mocking kicked himself free. He stumbled away, and stood, breathing hard, watching the Gantry open.

It throbbed, a red slit widening, and limned the trunks of the apple trees a ghastly septic pink. It opened fully and the devil-in-dreams leaned forward and lashed itself around the Doctor again, and this time Doctor Mocking found he had little strength left to resist it. He was pulled against the devil-in-dreams, and felt the violation of absorption. It wanted to swallow him, and drag him into the Gantry. It wanted to draw him through into an Autoscopic Quay, a place of desolation and misery, and finish him there. So he could not be reborn.

The devil-in-dreams rolled backwards, taking the Doctor with it. The Gantry flushed, beckoning, and they slid into its trembling breach.

Doctor Mocking saw what lay beyond, and despaired.

THE FORCE OF the EMP lifted Robin off his feet. The apparatus flew out of his hands and disappeared into the long grass. He landed on his back and lay staring up at the sky. In the sudden silence he heard birdsong. A thrush, crepuscular and haunting, deliciously pure. He pushed himself to his feet.

The Autoscope horde had ground to a halt, their machines dead beneath them. Steam and greasy smoke rose into the air. Some of the machines had collapsed on buckled and powerless legs, others had collided, or drifted out of control and crushed those that marched alongside. The flying machines had dropped out of the sky. One had cut out above the army and had crashed onto something that looked like a customized plough. Tangled together, the blade of the plough was a distorted sneer of metal that had clearly torn one of the adjacent Autoscopes in half. Another flying machine had gone wheeling overhead into the canopy of trees somewhere in the heart of the forest. There were screams and roars, of agony and fury. Those that rode in cabs were dismounting, and pulling heavy weaponry from clasps and slots welded into the bodies of their contraptions. The march would continue, on foot now, to the cave in the mountain.

Robin watched them regroup, some carrying spears and clubs, others relying on the savagery of their own claws and brute strength. They crowded together and began again to cross the meadow.

A pinprick of light appeared behind them. Robin saw it. He forgot about the EMP device he had salvaged from Babur's camper van. Its job was done, the formidable modifications he had made to it during his time in the Compartment proving to be as effective as he had hoped. He left it lying in the long grass, turned, and ran back towards the forest.

The Autoscopes saw him and roared at his flight, mocking and contemptuous. They raised their weapons and shook them, jeering. They started to run, their victory assured, any dread of the mountain or what hid within it forgotten in the moment of conquest.

The Gantry at their backs opened fully as the rippling circle of light widened to the dimension of a tunnel mouth in less than a second. It lit up the meadow like a floodlight.

The Autoscopes choked on their cries, and stumbled, panicked, as they were picked out in the light. They froze, vermin on a country road caught in the headlights of a speeding vehicle.

Robin stopped and turned. He could hear the deep rumble coming from the Gantry. He squinted at both the sound and the light, his hair blowing back from his brow. Instead of retreating further he walked towards the Autoscopes again, and as he did so, he felt himself change. He threw back his head and opened his arms, welcoming the transformation.

Railgrinder thundered from the Gantry, its great bulk sheathed in smoke and embers, and bore through the mire of stalled machines. It cast them before it, tossing them in the air, sending them rolling and spinning into the horde of Autoscopes. *Railgrinder's* iron wheels bit into the earth and it slid, tilted to starboard, bellowing steam, through the machines and into the petrified creatures that stood huddled in the meadow. Those not crushed beneath it flew broken and screaming, landing in heaps, their weapons gone, their bodies smashed.

And as *Railgrinder* wrought its ruin, Robin yelled at the sky and soared across the ground to meet the others that were now coming down from *Railgrinder's* cab, glorifying into components of the Night Clock, and he fell on the remaining Autoscopes with the seething countenance of an enraged god.

THE BOOMING RED light of the Quay made Doctor Mocking's head pound. He could see the expanse, a desert of pitted stone, stretching boundless in all directions. Above, low plates of crimson clouds walked on surging tendrils, their composition unknowable. To Doctor Mocking, they could have been alive, and when an eye opened in the midst of one, mindless and vast, and stared with lidless hostility upon the plain, he felt he might scream.

This was the place where killers came to dream, and those who woke in the night, or at sunrise, with thoughts of violation roaring in their heads.

Doctor Mocking found his remaining strength and, despite the thoughts of death and despair that assailed his mind, the silent screams of those tossing in filthy beds who dreamed of desecration and unnatural flesh, he kicked himself free enough to reach into the pocket of his jacket in search of something—anything—to use as a weapon. And his hand closed on something.

He withdrew it and had a second to realise what it was before the devil-in-dreams could react, and he threw it back, over his shoulder, so that it sailed through the Gantry and landed on the grass in the orchard at the foot of an apple tree.

It landed open, and its needle began to move.

Bismuth jolted forwards on his chair. He picked up the Compass and peered at it. He stood up and marched to the door.

Trevena made to stand, too, but Bismuth stopped him, "Stay here. Look after Colin and the others."

Bismuth went outside and took a Lever from his belt. He placed it into the earth beside the wooden steps that led up into the clubhouse and compressed the handle. Instantly a line of light appeared, widening to the size of a doorway. Trevena watched from the window, his fingers making a gap in the blinds. Bismuth consulted the Compass once more and then entered the Gantry.

The devil-in-dreams threw Doctor Mocking to the pitted ground. It swelled against Chapel's remaining flesh, and the rags of clothes that still bound it. Doctor Mocking knew the true size of the thing. Once it had attained freedom from the containment, it would enlarge to fill this place. It would press against the base of those awful clouds and race, unstoppable, to the rims of the Quay. He would be absorbed and drift forever inside it, seeing nothing but the content of nightmares for eternity.

The Gantry was closing. He looked up, at the red sky and felt it pounding, pressing down onto him like the horrific weight of choking gasses on an alien planet. He shoved himself backwards and lunged for the Gantry.

The devil-in-dreams moved to intercept him, still pressing against Chapel's flesh. It uttered a vicious, implacable sound, a grunt of frustration and effort, and jolted on cumbersome legs towards the Doctor.

Doctor Mocking hurled himself at the Gantry but the devil-in-dreams battered into his back and he fell to his knees. He looked through the opening, reached out a hand trembling with pain and fatigue.

Bismuth was standing in the orchard, both Compasses held in one hand, his Gantry silver-white at his back.

His face ablaze in the light scorching out from the red Gantry, his hair and beard like wild fire, he leaped through and landed on the ground by Doctor Mocking's side. His boots lifted a cloud of crimson dust. Glaring at the devil-in-dreams, he reached down and helped Doctor Mocking to his feet.

The devil-in-dreams had reached a critical point in its transformation. Bands of rags and flesh now bound it and it bulged like black fat around the restraints.

Bismuth put the Compasses in his pocket. He clenched his huge fists.

And then he went for the devil-in-dreams, with thoughts of his father fuelling his wrath, and took it in his arms, hands clenched on flesh and tearing cloth. He lifted it, thrashing and bucking, a thing undermined by efforts of completion and distracted by its nearness, and twisted his body and carried it screaming from the Quay and into the wet, darkening air of the orchard.

Doctor Mocking gave the last of his energy to getting them out. He shoved them through, taking hold of the devil-in-dreams as they stumbled onto the grass.

The devil-in-dreams was raging, thrashing against them, but Bismuth was unrelenting, his strength growing with his wrath, and together they piled across the short distance between the Gantries and pitched through the opening of white light.

ELIZABETH BROUGHT CLAIRE a glass of water. The girl was so pale, she thought, from pain and fear. She didn't know what else to do but offer comfort. Steve was holding Claire's hands and peering into her face, trying to soothe her, but Elizabeth could see the dread writ large on his own face. Claire groaned and pressed both hands to her belly.

There was movement to Elizabeth's left and as she turned her head she saw a figure leaning over Claire. It was a man, one of the café's customers. He was wearing a smart gray suit set off by an almost luminescent pink tie. His face was kind and cultured.

He smiled, kneeling beside Steve and taking one of Claire's hands. "Ne pas avoir peur, chere fille," he said. "Je suis medecin."

CHLOE OPENED HER eyes. The quakes were more regular now, coming with greater frequency and intensity. Rock dust sifted down from the ceiling. She felt the floor begin to tip, as she had feared, and she scrabbled her feet on the surface to push them further into the back of the cave and against the wall.

Adam was still unresponsive. His body was cold and slack in her arms.

She listened. She could hear something.

The ladder. Something was on the ladder. She huddled as far back against the cave wall as she could, drawing her brother close to her side.

It was climbing up. There was the sound of scraping on the metal steps.

Chloe held her breath.

A silhouette rose against the entrance to the cave, large and distorted. It braced its arms on the floor and lifted its body into the cave. It stood on four sharp-looking crab-like legs. Its mouth clacked and its red eyes glistened like blood blisters. When it started towards them, Chloe saw that it seemed to limp, off-balance, as though injured. It put an arm out and steadied itself against the wall. It lowered its head and hissed. It clattered across the floor in a stagger, its intent clear. It raised serrated claws.

Chloe closed her eyes and held her brother's head to her chest.

And then something else was coming. Chloe heard it racing through the forest, and metal clashed against the wall of the mountain as it hit the ladder and was up it in one bound.

Chloe opened her eyes and saw the Autoscope a few feet from

her. It had stopped and was looking back towards the entrance to the cave and at what now stood there with huge chest heaving and mouth open in an uninhibited glee of fangs.

"Is all well?" asked Bronze John as he padded further into the cave, tail switching.

"My brother's dying," said Chloe.

Bronze John stopped grinning. He leaped for the Autoscope and smashed it into the ground. This time he didn't roar. It would have been too terrible a sound in this small cave and there were children present.

BISMUTH HELD CHAPEL in a bear hug. The devil-in-dreams was gone, the soiled-mattress bulk of it reduced in the giant's arms to the man again. Bismuth glared into Chapel's face, into the large, emotional brown eyes. Around them the walls of the Gantry rushed in soft coppery torrents. Doctor Mocking stood with Bismuth. He was breathless and pale. He had very little strength left.

"Thank you," said Chapel. "For never giving up on us."

Bismuth loosened his hold and let Chapel's feet touch the rippling floor of the Gantry. Chapel sighed, his shoulders slumping. He held out a hand.

Bismuth didn't take it.

He drew a lever from his belt and drove it into Chapel's right eye.

Chapel screamed as his face split from cheekbone to jawline and black filth spewed out. Bismuth twisted the Lever free and grabbed Chapel by the throat. He picked him up and held him against the wall of the Gantry. He forced Chapel's head through the curtain of particles concealing the golden Compartment beyond. Chapel's screams were cut off as the light poured into his remaining eye and gushed into his mouth. Bismuth felt heat. Chapel's body was burning, the black seeping muck of the devil-in-dreams was bubbling like tarmac. It was being seared, compressed to fusion point by the unimaginable forces within the Compartment. It was a place it could never exist, a matrix of pressure and radiance that would contain it forever.

"I never gave up on the *boy*," Bismuth said, and hurled the devil-in-dreams through the Gantry wall.

"It's gone," said Doctor Mocking.

"Yes." Bismuth carried his friend from the Gantry and into the cool drizzle of the orchard. They sat together beneath an apple tree. They could hear traffic. It was wonderfully commonplace. The Gantries were gone. Just cloudy early-evening moonlight.

Doctor Mocking was finding it harder to breathe. He wasn't in distress. He felt reassured. He would have liked to have seen his girls again but, he guessed, one day he would. He smiled.

"You'll wait with me?"

Bismuth looked dismayed. "What else would I do?" He settled back against the tree and flipped his long coat over his knees.

"Are you cold?" he asked Doctor Mocking.

"No. Are my lips blue?"

Bismuth studied the Doctor's face. "A bit."

Doctor Mocking nodded. "Not long now," he said.

Bismuth sighed, and patted the Doctor's hand.

"Lesley must have put the Compass in my pocket when she was helping Anna get me dressed." Doctor Mocking said.

"Clever girl," said Bismuth.

"You'll look after them, won't you? Lesley and Anna."

This time Bismuth didn't look at the Doctor.

"We all will," he said.

Bronze John dragged the remains of the Autoscope the length of the cave and nosed it out so that it dropped in tatters to the forest floor. He turned back and watched Chloe wrapping her brother in the rugs. When she was happy he was warm and comfortable, she joined the tiger at the mouth of the cave.

Bronze John went first, negotiating the ladder in two short leaps, and then waited at the bottom while Chloe picked her way down with more caution.

"Want a ride?" he said.

Chloe took a final look up towards the cave and then climbed onto the tiger's back.

They went through the forest, Chloe ducking beneath the lowest branches, and emerged onto the meadow. The tiger carried her with no effort, his head held high to see over the grass. Chloe pointed ahead.

"There they are," she said.

They reached the others. They stood amongst the carnage of ravaged black meat. No Autoscope remained intact. They had been decimated. *Railgrinder's* cooling iron ticked.

Anna went to Bronze John and stroked his face.

"You've got Autoscope in your whiskers," she said. She did as she had done before, and wiped pieces of shell and blood from the tiger's face with the hem of her shirt.

Daniel stood with Robin and Index. They all looked drained. Only Alex and Eliot seemed enlivened after the battle. They strode through the remains of the Autoscopes and their dead machines, still looking for survivors to dispatch. Eliot found something of interest, curled beneath an overturned chassis towards the rear of *Railgrinder*. He poked at it with one of the Autoscopes spears, and when it wailed he thrust forward with all his weight and impaled it.

"That's the last one," he called. He threw down the spear and came to join the others.

"Where's Lesley?" Alex said.

Index drew them together. "She's gone on ahead," he said. "Now we can join her."

He opened his hands and light raced from his palms. When it pinched out, leaving the Quay in darkness, the Firmament Surgeons were gone.

"Hi dad," said Lesley.

Doctor Mocking didn't open his eyes, but he smiled. "Darling," he said.

Lesley knelt and took him in her arms.

"Are you all right? Is Anna..?"

"We're fine, dad. Anna knows. She understands."

Doctor Mocking sighed.

"That's..." he said as Lesley kissed him, and her kiss was the last thing he felt.

BEHIND THE COUNTER in the Lacan-café, Johnny clapped his hands again.

"Nous parlons en Anglais!" he said. "The Autoscopes are dead! The devil-in-dreams is dead!"

A cheer went up. Newspapers were balled up and launched at the ceiling. Tables clattered as people stood and embraced.

Claire looked around, bleary-eyed but no longer in pain.

The doctor stood and smiled. He took Steve's hand and shook it firmly.

"Your wife is doing fine," he said. He had a Birmingham accent. "The baby is safe."

"Thank you," said Steve, but the doctor waved it off.

"I didn't do anything," he said. "Take care." He went back to his seat and picked up his coffee cup. He saluted them and took a sip.

Steve hugged Elizabeth and then held his wife, kissing her cheeks. Claire's colour was rising, Elizabeth noticed, her cheeks beginning to flush again.

"Now," said Steve. "How do we get out of here?"

Elizabeth laughed. "Don't worry about that, love. Daniel will come and get us."

TREVENA WAS STANDING outside the clubhouse, his hands in his pockets, looking up at the sky. He felt restless and detached. He tried to imagine what the others were doing, how the battle was being waged, but he found that he couldn't. He was too tired, and the loss of John had hurt him deeply. All he could think about was

Colin, and what was to become of the old chap. A Paladin without his charge was nothing. He thought about Andy, and what he had said in the train shed. Had his life been nothing up until now? Of course not. A journey. It had been a journey. Colin had been getting on a bit when he finally found John, and it had been the fulfilment of his life's purpose, a joy. Maybe now he and Andy might embark on a similar adventure. Trevena wondered if the boy liked fishing.

"Phil!"

Trevena wheeled around at the sound of Andy's voice. The boy was standing at the top of the steps. He beckoned for Trevena to come back up.

"What is it?"

"They've gone, Phil. John, Colin and Bix. They've all gone!"

Trevena followed Andy into the clubhouse.

He looked at the orange tablecloth, the one with silver stars John and Colin had put out at Halloween for parties that had become John's shroud. It lay flat against the floor, nothing of John remaining but dried blood.

"I was fussing Bix," Andy said. "And then he looked up at me, really saw me for the first time, I think. He looked happy. I could see it in his eyes. And then he was gone. I turned round and Colin and John were gone, too."

Trevena poked at the shroud with the toe of his shoe.

"Do you have a good feeling about this?" he asked Andy.

"Yes," the boy said. "Yes, I do. I think they've gone somewhere together. They would have been miserable apart. I know how that feels."

Trevena appraised the boy again, as he had found himself doing repeatedly ever since they had met. Andy's expression was open, solemn without the slightest hint of guile.

"So do I," said Trevena. "We might as well get out of here. We need to find the others."

"Do you know where they are?"

Trevena shrugged. "Well, when I say, 'We'll have to find them,' what I mean is, they'll probably find us first, but I reckon we should head back to Doctor Mocking's house and see what happens."

"It's a plan," said Andy.

"Yes, it is. Come on, let's take Colin's car."

"Have you got the keys?"

"No, but I had a misspent youth before I did my training. That Cortina is ancient. I reckon I can still remember how to hotwire."

Andy beamed. "Great!"

They left the clubhouse. Trevena pulled the door shut but couldn't lock it. He stood for a moment looking up at the old wooden building, and then he reached out and patted the side of it, where the old boards were painted a faded shade of Carolina blue. He knew the history of the place, from stories John had recounted, and hoped her ghosts would be good-natured ones for whoever took her on again.

They walked together along the boulevard towards the car park. Lights were on in the caravans that lined the road, and Trevena could smell burgers cooking. He experienced a moment of flashback, an olfactory jolt that took him back to a pub garden in his youth, and a man called Lenny who he hadn't thought about since. Maybe it was a fragment of a dream, he thought, but the moment passed as he was distracted by a sensation to his left.

As they walked together, Andy had taken his hand.

WHEN TREVENA AND Andy reached Doctor Mocking's house, lights were on and the front door was open. Trevena pulled into the drive and parked the Cortina next to John's Minx.

"Told you," Trevena said. They got out and went up to the porch.

On the way down, they had talked. There had been much to discuss but the conversation had centred on Andy's future. He had been missing for the best part of four decades and although he had been able to ascertain the passing of time to some degree, and had been aware of the world around Chapel the man in flashes and patches, he was still ignorant of most of it. He knew his mother was dead. He had felt the separation through Chapel, and had done his grieving in the dark. And most importantly, he knew what he was and had an appreciation of its importance and its comfort for him. Trevena wasn't concerned for Andy's mental state or well being, but there were practicalities.

Namely, where Andy would live and under what name.

Not only could he hotwire a car, Trevena had a few contacts, from back in the day and from the forensic work he often got involved in. A bit of paperwork and a computerised paper trail and Andy could very well be his distant relative. Andy liked this idea. He also liked Trevena's subsequent idea.

An orphan now, Andy would have to live with Trevena.

They went inside.

THEY HAD TAKEN Doctor Mocking to his bedroom. Elizabeth and Claire had washed and dressed him. Now Lesley and Anna sat with him and watched over their father until other doctors came. His death was to be treated as natural causes, which in the end, it was.

Bismuth and Index were in the study sorting out paperwork for the girls. Robin was sitting at Doctor Mocking's desk scrolling through his computer. They all appeared distracted but acknowledged Trevena and Andy with a nod or a gesture.

Daniel and Elizabeth had their coats on. They embraced both Trevena and Andy.

"It's been good to see you again, Phil," Daniel said. "Keep in touch."

"For sure," said Trevena. "Where are you going? Need a lift?"

"No, we're fine. We're going to take the bus."

"Seriously?"

Elizabeth took Daniel's arm and kissed his cheek. "Normality is what this man needs," she said.

Steve and Claire were in the lounge with Chloe.

"Hey, Phil! Andy!" Steve said and stood to greet them. Chloe smiled and remained seated on the rug, the toy tiger in her hand, trotting it through the patterns. Claire looked well, a little flushed, but content.

"Don't get up," said Trevena, and bent to kiss her. Andy sat on the rug with Chloe. She let him take the tiger and prowl it around a bit.

I'm going to have to buy him games, Trevena thought. *Fantastic!*

"What now?" asked Steve.

"For me?" Trevena said. "I'm going to take retirement." The fact was suddenly without doubt in his mind. "Andy's coming to live with me, so I'll have plenty of time to make up with him."

"That's awesome," said Steve. "Nice one. I'll be going part time now we've got another on the way."

"What do you do?"

Steve glanced at Claire, who was listening, her expression patient but well versed.

"This and that," Steve said. "You know."

Trevena laughed. "I'm sure you'll be well looked after," he said.

Alex and Eliot came into the hallway from the kitchen.

"Curry's ready," said Eliot. "Come and help yourselves."

Trevena looked down at Andy, who screwed up his face.

"Don't like curry?" asked Steve.

"What is it?" said Andy.

Trevena laughed, "Something else for you to find out, son. Come on, we should go home."

THEY WALKED OUT with Daniel and Elizabeth and paused by the cars.

"Thanks again, Phil," Daniel said. They shook hands.

"Is it really all over?" Trevena asked.

Daniel shrugged beneath his heavy coat. "For the most part," he said. "What we do, though, when we are permitted, that will continue." He looked at Andy. "We'll show you."

Andy looked up at Trevena. Trevena nodded. "I'll make sure of it," he said.

"People will continue to suffer until the re-creation," Daniel said. "That's without doubt. We'll have more freedom now to help them, if they allow us. Easier access to their dreams. It's what we were created to do. And there might be more of us, too. Maybe trapped like you were, or just lost. We might be able to find them. We're still learning."

They stood for a moment in silence, all contemplating Daniel's words. Trevena knew Andy needed rest, and acclimatisation, but he also knew the others wouldn't push him, not until he was ready.

He was about to open the door to the Cortina but stopped when his phone rang. He took it out of his pocket and looked at the display. He sighed.

"I should take this," he said. He stepped away from the group and walked over to where a bright oblong of yellow light shone onto the drive through the drawing room window.

"Hello, Rob."

"Phil, it's Rob!"

"Yes, I know. What's up, mate?"

"I missed our appointment. I'm sorry. I met up with a couple of fellas and lost track of time."

"It's ok. Pop in tomorrow and we'll sort you out."

"I had another *very* strange dream."

"Yeah, we'll talk about it tomorrow."

"See you tomorrow."

"'Bye, Rob." Trevena disconnected and as he did so, he felt someone's eyes on him. He looked up.

Chloe was sitting on the window seat. She smiled and raised a hand, placing it palm-outwards against the glass.

Trevena smiled back, and waved. He held up his phone, made a quizzical face.

Chloe nodded.

Trevena put the phone back in his pocket and went to join the others, thinking, *When I retire, Rob, I'm going to discharge you into Peter Foreman's care. You deserve each other.*

Daniel was smiling.

Trevena looked at the old, weary Ford parked next to John's vintage Minx, and felt the completeness of it, and with that came a small surge of pleasure, despite the poignancy of it.

"We ought to leave these for the kids," he said. He could hear Eliot and Alex shouting and horsing about inside the house. "It's what Colin and John would want."

Daniel nodded.

"That's nice, dear," Elizabeth said.

"Let's *all* take the bus," Trevena said.

"Excellent," said Andy. "Can we sit downstairs? I don't like the top deck. Too smoky."

Trevena put an arm around the boy's shoulders.

"Such things I have to teach you, son," he said.

The four of them walked away from the house together.

IN A FIELD on a hillside overlooking a wide and beautiful bay, where overgrown lanes of wild roses and honeysuckle hid tiny wooden shacks, two men stood and watched a young dog not long out of puppyhood chase cornflower butterflies.

"I love it here," said Colin. He was younger, stronger. He was the man John had first met as a child, working behind the counter at the Reservoir End Dog's Home. His moustache was dark, with only a few gray hairs beginning to show.

"Me too," said John Stainwright. He breathed deeply of the cool sea air.

They remained standing on the edge of the Plotlands looking out over Quay-Endula, watching Bix prance and leap, making no attempt to catch the butterflies but enjoying their flirting dance above the dog daisies.

"Will you have to go again?" Colin asked, still staring out to sea. "Will you be reborn?"

John thought for a while.

"I really don't know," he said. "I don't think we know much at all, really."

Colin turned to look at his friend. As he did so, Bix barked and stumbled and rolled head-over heels in the grass. He came up with grass in his mouth, tail wagging.

"Come on," John said. He turned and started walking back to their shack. They had painted it Carolina blue and had begun gluing shells and driftwood to its slats. "That punch will be about ready now."

Bix perked up at John's voice.

He ran to join them, skipping at their heels, his soft ears blowing in the wind, eyes shut with delight.

Printed in Poland
by Amazon Fulfillment
Poland Sp. z o.o., Wrocław